A KING OF INFINITE SPACE
TYLER DILTS

PUBLISHED BY

Published by AmazonEncore
P.O. Box 400818
Las Vegas, NV 89140

ISBN-13: 9781935597094
ISBN-10: 1935597094

For my mother

PROLOGUE

Awake in the darkness, long after midnight, I imagine it like this. He waits patiently in the restroom, the early November sun fading in the small patch of sky visible through the row of windows along the top of the back wall. Standing near the door, he reads the first bits of graffiti on the freshly painted wall above the urinals:

"Mr. Jackson Sucks Dick," "Fight the Power," "I Luv Sweet Pussy."

The sound of a squeaking wheel in the hall catches his attention. It's almost time. He pulls the door open quietly, just enough to peek out. Carl Peters, the custodian, stops his janitorial cart in front of the open classroom door across the hall.

"Hello, Elizabeth," Carl says into the room.

"Hi, Carl," she answers.

"Another late night, huh?"

"Seems like they all are."

He can hear the smile in her voice.

"Getting dark. You give a shout if you want me to walk you out."

"Thanks, Carl. I will."

He eases the door back into the jamb as Carl's cart begins squeaking down the hall toward the far side of the building. He waits expectantly. There's plenty of time. Carl always starts upstairs at the distant end of the building and works his way back. It'll be at least ninety minutes before Carl will be close enough to hear anything at all.

As he waits, he feels the butterflies tingling in the pit of his stomach, a feeling much like the nervous anticipation he used to feel driving his father's car to a girl's door for a first date. But this…this is something more…something so much more. His pulse quickens, and his breaths grow deeper and faster. The tightening in his crotch comes as no surprise.

Inching the door open, he slips into the hallway. Like a child crossing the street, he looks first to the right, then to the left. After a deep breath, glancing around the edge of the wall of student lockers and into the open classroom door, he sees Elizabeth.

She is sitting at her desk at the front of the classroom, focused intently on the student paper she is grading. Her long chestnut hair is pulled into a tight ponytail, and she holds a pen in her mouth as she pushes her glasses back up her nose. A loose strand of hair falls across her face, and she brushes it back, tucking it behind her ear.

He likes to watch her like this. Seeing her after a long day in the classroom, after the students have gone, the sleeves of her faded blue chambray blouse pushed up above her elbows, the tails untucked, one more button open at the collar, show-ing just the barest hint of her cleavage. But he knows the time for watching is now over.

He steps into the doorway. His eyes take her in, and the beginnings of a smile form at the corners of his mouth. He stands there for a moment before she senses his presence. Just as she starts to turn toward him, he speaks.

"Hi, Beth."

"What are...? Hi," she says, surprised, but not afraid. Good.

"I'm sorry to just stop by like this," he says, smiling charmingly. "I was driving by and I saw the school, and of course, I thought of you."

"That's nice." She smiles tentatively. "But you really shouldn't be here. School policy."

"I know. I just wanted to say hi." His eyes sparkle. "Want to take a break? Walk me out?"

She hesitates, and he gives her his sweetest "aw, shucks" smile. As she walks toward him, he slips the blade from under his coat.

ONE

Longing to kill my dreams, I poured half a glass of orange juice. I was just taking the bottle of Grey Goose from the freezer when I heard the chirp of the pager. Ignoring it, I unscrewed the cap and topped off the drink. Lifting the glass to my lips, I smelled the citrus tang of the orange juice, imagined the cool, sweet taste flowing through my mouth and the sensation that would spread outward from my stomach in a warm wave, and for the briefest moment, I paused.

It was the pause that got me.

I looked down at the pager as I emptied the glass into the sink. Work, I knew, would do more than vodka to quiet my sorrow and regret. I picked up the cordless phone, and just as I was about to dial, it rang in my hand.

"Hello?" I said.

"He call you yet?"

"Hey, Jen. I just heard the page. What do we got?"

"Dead teacher," she said, a trace of exasperation in her voice. "Hacked up right in her classroom."

"Where?"

"Warren High."

"That's right by—"

"I know. I'll pick you up."

I took just enough time to change out of my suit and into a pair of khakis and a polo shirt before slipping my arms through the harness of my shoulder holster, draping my navy blue LBPD HOMICIDE Windbreaker over my shoulder, and walking out into the middle of the street in front of my duplex. From there, looking to the north, in the distance, you can see the corner of the bleachers facing the Warren High School football field. That's where I was standing and what I was looking at when a pair of headlights illuminated me from behind and stretched my shadow onto the street in front of me. I stepped out of the way and watched Detective Second Grade Jennifer Tanaka's Explorer slow to a stop.

"Long time no see," she said as I climbed into the passenger seat. It had been barely an hour since we had turned in our daily reports and told each other to have a good weekend. She wore the same tan coat, dark pants, and white blouse she'd had on all day. You wouldn't know it to look at her, though. The clothes looked as though they'd been freshly plucked from a dry cleaner's bag, and she had an eager gleam in her brown eyes that belied the fact she'd already put in a ten-hour workday.

"So much for the weekend," I said.

"You had big plans, huh?" She rolled her eyes.

"Maybe I did."

"Don't worry." She turned on the blinker to signal a left turn. "Vodka doesn't spoil."

"Maybe not, but my Blockbuster coupon expires on Monday."

Another turn, and the front of the campus was in sight. The main building of the high school had been built not long after the turn of the last century. It had arching doors and windows, columns flanking the entrance, and wrought-iron handrails along the front steps. A tower, in which a bell would not have seemed at all out of place, rose from the roof of the second floor and overlooked the neighborhood. The rest of the school, though, was not so lucky. The other buildings had been added, decade by decade, in a ramshackle fashion, and they bore the stamp of the uninspired, boxy, and utilitarian Southern California high school architecture that had seemed the height of modernity during the sixties and early seventies.

We drove past a row of patrol cars and parked in front of an unmarked Chevy Caprice. Eyeing herself in the rearview mirror, Jen ran a hand through her short black hair and gave herself a nod of approval. We got out, put on our matching Windbreakers, stuffed a few pairs of latex gloves into our pockets, and followed the trail of uniforms to the front of the building.

A young cop stood near the door, visibly shaken, but trying not to let it show. His partner, a vet who was only a few months shy of his twenty, nodded to me as he watched us approach.

"Hey, Stan," I said, returning the nod. "What do we have?"

"Dead woman, carved up. Janitor called it in. He's in the office."

I looked at the younger man. His polished brass name tag read G. Adams. "What's the G stand for?"

"Greg," he said.

"First homicide?" I asked.

"Yeah," he said. "I was the first one in."

"Don't worry." Stan put his arm on the rookie's shoulder. "You'll get used to it."

"That's what I'm afraid of." Greg looked away and shook his head back and forth as if the motion might somehow erase the images burned into his memory.

We walked through the glass doors and turned left, following the trail of lights and hushed voices. As we passed the main office, we saw David Zepeda, another member of the Homicide Squad, through the window. He was interviewing a smallish man who looked to be in his midsixties and was wearing gray coveralls with the name Carl embroidered over the left chest pocket. Carl seemed unable to raise his eyes from the floor.

"Janitor?" Jen asked.

"Must be."

We turned as a uniform approached. "Scene's right up there," he said, motioning backward with a hooked thumb, "and around the corner." He went down the hallway and out the door.

Jen and I turned away from the office. On our right was a large glass wall, behind which were housed three-quarters of a century's worth of sports trophies, mementos, and photographs. I fought the urge to wallow in the history and followed her down the hall.

Around the corner, half a dozen cops stood in a small huddle and spoke in soft voices. I searched the faces, and although I knew most of them, we passed each other with wordless nods. The light spilled out of the classroom and into the relative dimness of the hall. On the floor, a single red-black rivulet had found its way past the threshold. At the door I took a deep breath, held it for a moment, and slowly let it out.

Looking through the door, the first thing we saw was the blood. The thickening liquid pooled on the floor, and spatters covered everything in the front quarter of the room—desks, walls, chalkboards, bookcases, file cabinets were spotted with scattered drops of blood.

Marty Locklin, Dave's partner, squatted on his haunches and bent over the victim, with his back to the door, blocking our view of the dead woman's upper body. He wore a charcoal gray suit that strained across the backs of his shoulders. With his salt-and-pepper hair, which was almost the same color as his suit, and his massive bulk, he reminded me of a silverback gorilla I'd seen on the Discovery Channel the week before. I almost expected him to bang his fists against his chest and roar at the carnage in front of him.

"Hey, Marty," Jen said, carefully circling around the pool of blood on the floor.

He looked over his shoulder and stood up, flipping his notepad closed and tucking a small pencil behind his ear. "Hi, kids."

He turned around and stepped toward us, giving me my first clear look at the dead woman. Her khaki slacks and chambray blouse were soaked a deep crimson, and only a few small, unstained patches near her ankles and shoulders allowed me to identify their original colors. She had been stabbed in the torso repeatedly. The wounds were so numerous that her midsection had been rendered a bloody pulp of tissue and shredded fabric. Her vaginal area had also been mutilated. Her attacker had apparently penetrated her with the blade. Most troubling of all, at least from the investigative standpoint, was the fact that her left hand was gone, severed just above the wrist. Her blood had soaked into her wavy chestnut hair, which was now matted and tangled under her head. The color had disappeared from her face, and her dead green eyes stared at the ceiling.

"Danny?" Jen said. Although she stood two feet from me, her voice sounded far away.

"Yeah?"

"You alright?"

"Sure," I said. "Why?"

"You know her?" Marty asked.

"No," I said, looking back down at the woman's face. Something was familiar, though. Something I couldn't quite place. The eyes? The hair? Had I seen her somewhere before? "I don't think so."

Jen studied my eyes a moment and then turned her attention back to the victim. "Where's the hand?" she asked.

"That's the sixty-four-thousand-dollar question," Marty said, lifting his shoulders toward his ears.

I squatted next to her body and noticed something in the slowly drying blood. "Marty, you see this?"

"Yeah. Looks like a partial footprint."

A half-inch-wide pattern curved through the outside edge of the pool, but none of the blood had seeped back into the area. I slipped my hands into a pair of latex gloves and delicately dabbed the tip of my index finger into the edge of the puddle near the print. The blood was tacky, like freshly applied glue.

"Hang on," I said as I stood up and went back out into the hall, walking past the swelling number of our city's finest. I turned the corner and looked in on Dave and the janitor. Dave wiped a handkerchief across his forehead as I watched him. Even though I couldn't hear a word he said, I knew Dave was asking Carl to take him through it one more time. Carl shook his head slowly and looked down at his feet as he began to speak. He wore heavy black work shoes that had a waffle sole.

I went outside and took a look around. I spotted the man I was looking for sitting on the edge of a brick planter a few yards away from the entry steps.

"Greg," I said as I approached him. He looked up at me. "Got a second?"

"Sure thing, Detective." He started to rise.

"No, that's okay." I motioned with my hand for him to stay seated. "How you doing?"

"I'm alright. What can I do for you?"

"You can lift up your left foot."

"What?"

"Lift up your left foot." Kneeling in front of him like a shoe salesman, I took his foot in my hand. I shined my Mini Maglite on the sole of his shoe and saw specks of blood coagulating in the treads. Stan had found us and was standing a few feet to my right with his arms crossed and a stern look on his face.

"What's wrong?" Greg asked.

I pulled the shoe off his foot.

"You stepped in evidence. I've gotta bag and catalog this shoe."

"Shit, I'm sorry...I didn't mean..."

"You have another pair in the unit?"

"No. Should I?" The nauseated expression on his face had turned to one of distress.

I shook my head as I walked past Stan, who tried not to crack a smile. Carrying the shoe with my index finger curled under the laces, I went back inside. Marty and Jen were both hunched over the body.

"You see this?" Marty asked, shaking his head. He was pointing at the stained and ragged crotch of the victim's pants with the eraser on his pencil.

"Not enough bleeding," Jen said. "Probably postmortem." She made a few more notes in her notebook.

"Footprint's a dead end," I said, "unless the doer's that rookie outside who's still fighting to hold onto his dinner." I held up the shoe.

"You took his shoe?" Jen asked.

"Of course."

"Why?"

"So that maybe next time he'll think twice before queering evidence."

"What are you going to do with it?" she asked.

"Might as well bag it."

Marty was grinning. "Danny Beckett," he said with pretended awe, "Detective Supreme."

"Detective Supreme, huh?" Jen said with a snicker.

"Yeah," I said, "just like a regular detective, but with tomatoes and sour cream."

The crime scene techs arrived a few minutes later. Jen and Marty were at the front of the room studying the spatter patterns on the chalkboard. They cleared out of the way and moved into the hall as the flashes began going off. Crime photographers snapped photos of the corpse and the room from every conceivable angle. The electric white light of the strobes threw the crimson stains into stark relief.

I stood in the back, behind the wood-grained Formica desktops, and tried to imagine the room as it had been only a few hours before. Along the front wall, just below the clock and above the top edge of the blackboard, a row of pen-and-ink portraits of famous authors spanned the width of the room. Some I recognized—Shakespeare, Twain, Hemingway. Others I guessed at. Faulkner? Eliot? Ellison? I strained to remember my college English classes. I wasn't sure if the black woman at the end of the line was Toni Morrison or Maya Angelou. It had to be one of the two. The dead teacher had known.

My eyes wandered. Her desk faced the students. On it were the stack of papers she had been grading, a red ceramic apple, an At-A-Glance desk calendar, and a smiley-face coffee mug filled with pens and pencils. To the left of the desk stood two scratched, ancient gunmetal gray file cabinets. The one nearest the windows was topped with a philodendron whose leaves cascaded down the cabinet's side. On the wall opposite the windows, another chalkboard was flanked by two bulletin boards covered with short poems, pithy quotes, and snapshots of her students.

As one of the techs opened his latent fingerprint kit, I wondered how many people came through this room every day. One hundred? One hundred fifty? The tech sighed at the futility of the task before him. I slipped along the wall and out of the room to join Marty and Jen.

"Have any blinding flashes of insight in there?" Jen asked.

"No," I said. "That was just the photographers."

All the cops in the hallway turned their heads in unison as Lieutenant Ruiz rounded the corner and headed toward us. He was tall and lean, with slick black hair and a leathery, sandblasted face. His eyes held a degree of hardness that I'd rarely seen and that I associated more with jail-wise cons and career button men. A lot of cops try to cultivate that look, but few succeed as well as Ruiz had. According to rumor, which he would neither confirm nor deny, he'd grown up on the South Texas border and started his law enforcement career in his hometown department. He worked his way through college and moved to the West Coast when the Texas Rangers informed him that they'd reached their quota for Mexican Americans. Ruiz had ridden a squad car for a decade in the East LA barrios, been among the first of the CRASH anti-gang officers, and received half a dozen commendations. Still, he had to come to Long Beach to make lieutenant and run his own homicide squad.

Dave Zepeda followed close behind Ruiz as we formed a loose circle a few yards away from the uniforms.

"Hey, Boss. Welcome to the party," Marty said.

"Looks like we got our hands full here, folks." Ruiz had tried hard to lose the accent, but a bit of Texas twang still lingered in his voice. "Run it down for me," he said.

"Six o'clock, six fifteen," Dave began. Every trace of the geniality he'd shown to Carl only minutes before had vanished. "Janitor's starting to make his rounds of the classrooms." He checked his notepad as he spoke. "He comes to this one here, sees the pretty teacher parked behind her desk, grading papers. Nothing unusual about that, he says. Hard worker, that one. He gives her a heigh-ho and goes on about his business. An hour or so later, working his way back toward the front, he finds her. Doesn't touch anything, except to check she's dead. Runs right to the office there and calls nine-one-one."

"Call came in at seven forty-eight," Marty said. The lieutenant looked at him as he continued.

"She's standing, maybe moving toward the door. She sees the doer, doesn't look like she starts panicking. Maybe she knows him, maybe she's fronting him. He meets her halfway

to the door and starts hacking. With something big, too."
Marty inhaled deeply through his nose and continued. "Maybe a machete, something like that, or a cleaver. Big and heavy anyway, and except for the crotch, he chops at her, doesn't stab."

"Danny? Jen?" Ruiz looked at each of us.

We nodded in agreement.

"Any thoughts on the suspect?"

"Definite wack job," Marty said. "It's ugly. Thrill kill. Trophy hunter."

"Trophy?" The lieutenant's face darkened.

"The left hand," Jen said. "It's missing."

"Fuck." In the five years I'd worked with Ruiz, this was only the third time I'd heard him use that word.

Stan approached with another uniform and a civilian who wore sweatpants, Velcro-fastened running shoes, and an ice blue Members Only jacket over a green-plaid sport shirt. The long hair on the right side of his head had been awkwardly brushed over the top, leaving lines of pink scalp visible between the strands of brown.

"Excuse me, Lieutenant," Stan said. "This is the vice-principal."

"Mr. Everett?" Ruiz asked, shifting into civilian-contact mode, his voice concerned, his slight smile overtaken by sadness.

"Yes," the man said. He seemed to be trying hard to focus his attention on us rather than giving in to his own morbid curiosity by looking over his shoulder.

"We'll need to see her personnel file. Emergency contact, that sort of thing." Ruiz held the man's gaze, trying to keep him focused.

"Yes, of course. We'll just need to go back to the office."

"You go ahead." Ruiz nodded to Stan. "We'll be right behind you."

Stan took the man by his elbow. He turned him around so that Everett would be closer to the door as they walked down the hall. "How long have you worked here?" Stan asked.

"Been in the district nearly thirty years."

"You must have some fascinating stories to tell."

Everett, surprised, looked at Stan and nodded just as they passed the classroom door.

As soon as the two men rounded the corner, Ruiz was all business again.

"Marty, I want you back in the room. Make sure the techs don't miss anything and get squared with the ME as soon as he shows." He turned to Dave. "Organize a canvas. Find somebody who saw something." Dave nodded. "You two," he said, facing Jen and me, "you're with Everett and me in the office." He turned and strode down the hall.

"I just love it when he gets all butch like that," I said.

Marty piped in too. "I wanna be just like him when I grow up."

Jen shook her head and started after the lieutenant.

"Hey," I said, "wait up."

Ruiz, Jen, and I stood as Everett dug through a file cabinet drawer. "Here it is," he said, placing a manila file folder on his desk. "I just can't believe this, it's so...so..." His voice trailed off, and he looked down at his hands. The venetian blinds behind his desk were open, and I looked out at the street.

"Boss," I said. When Ruiz looked at me, I inclined my head toward the window. Outside, a blue Ford Econoline van with an encircled yellow 7 emblazoned on its side had parked across from the school. The satellite antenna mounted on its roof unfolded and telescoped toward the sky.

"Wonderful," the lieutenant said, eyeing the news van. "You two got this?"

"Sure," Jen said. "Mr. Everett," she said as Ruiz left the room, "can we ask you a few questions?"

"Of course." He clasped his hands nervously on the desk as we sat in the two chairs across from him.

"What can you tell us about her?"

"Elizabeth? She's a fine teacher. A fine teacher. The students really love her." He was still talking about her in the present tense. I wondered how long that would last.

"She was very good at her job, then?" Jen asked.

"Oh yes." He looked down at his desk calendar. The tense shift hadn't eluded him. Maybe he'd been an English teacher too. "One of our best."

"How about the other faculty, the staff? How did they feel about her?" He looked up at Jen. I reached across the desk and slid the personnel file toward me.

"Well," he said, "no real problems there."

"No?" Jen asked, trying to open him up.

"No." Everett began to rub his hands together. The motion was slight, but Jen caught it too. We both looked at him silently.

"Well," he said after a moment, "there was a bit of friction with some of the other teachers. Nothing serious."

"What kind of friction?" Jen asked innocently, her brown eyes sparkling.

He looked back at her, a slight smile playing across his lips. "Well, competition, you might say," he said as he inched forward.

"Really?" Jen leaned into the desk, her eyes widening and locking onto his.

"Oh yes."

I might as well have left the room at that point. She'd set the hook and was beginning to reel him in.

"You see, Elizabeth—Beth, her friends called her—she was very committed. Very driven. She'd put in hours and hours, after school, weekends, seemed like she never stopped."

"And that was a problem?"

"Well, for some of the faculty," he said, catching himself, "just some, mind you. That's not always looked so kindly upon."

"Really?" Jen asked, feigning surprise. "Why?"

"You see, not all of the teachers are that dedicated." His comfort level was rising, and as he imparted his hard-won wisdom, he began to exhibit more confidence. "Some of them actually believe Beth's work ethic reflects poorly on them."

"In what way?" Jen smiled, feigning a fascination with his perceptiveness.

"They view it as a challenge to their own dedication and commitment. If she's working so hard and getting such good results, well then, darn it, why aren't they?" He slid his palm across his scalp, smoothing his comb-over.

Jen continued questioning him, asking about specific people who might be holding grudges, anyone who might have harbored ill will—each of the old homicide interview standards—all the while maintaining her doe-eyed innocent shtick. While she was reading him like a book, I flipped open the folder and started reading it like a file.

Elizabeth Anne Williams. Born February 12, 1979. Received her BA in English literature from UC San Diego in 1991 and her MA and teaching credentials from Cal State

Long Beach two and a half years later. Began teaching at Warren High in 1995 after a brief stint at a high school in LA.

Her address caught my eye. She lived on Newport, a few blocks from the beach, not more than a mile and a half from me. Was that why she looked familiar? Maybe I'd seen her in the 7-Eleven. Or in Blockbuster. Or Ralph's. Maybe.

I thumbed through the rest of the pages. I found what I was looking for on the back of the last page of her Long Beach Unified District application: "In case of emergency please notify: Rachel Williams." Listed were her address, phone number, and relationship. The way things were playing out, odds were that shortly Jen and I would be telling Rachel that her sister had been found dead.

"Thank you so much," Jen said, reaching across the desk to shake Everett's hand.

"It was my pleasure, Detective." He held onto her hand and stared into her eyes. "If there's anything else I can do, please don't hesitate—"

"Oh, don't worry," I said, closing the file and tucking it under my arm, "we won't."

When we were outside his door Jen whispered, "Looks like I've got a date for the prom."

While Jen went to find Ruiz, I walked back down the hall to the crime scene. The medical examiner had arrived. A gurney, on top of which was a neatly folded black vinyl body bag, had been parked outside the classroom door. Inside, the ME, a squat black man whom I'd never met, was checking the body for rigor and lividity. Marty stood next to him, his arms folded across his chest.

"Anything interesting?" Marty asked.

"Nope," the ME said.

I looked down at the teacher's face again and tried to place her in my memory. I tried to imagine her walking through my neighborhood, renting a video, or checking bananas for ripeness. Nothing clicked.

Feeling an uncharacteristic pang in my gut, I looked into her dead green eyes. The last thing you want to do while standing over a victim's body is to imagine them alive. It may sound cold, but they need to be objectified, viewed as a thing, simply a piece of meat, nothing more than an object to be studied for evidence: a strand of hair, a cotton fiber, a fleck of skin under the nail, a latent print on the smoothness of the watchband, a drop of semen soaked into the panties. Once you begin to imagine glowing green eyes and chestnut hair flowing in the wind, your objectivity and detachment turn to shit and you start missing the little things—and it's the little things that make the story.

"Danny?" Marty asked.

"Yeah?"

"What is it?"

"Nothing. Just thinking."

"We're about ready to bag her," he said, eyeing me curiously.

I found Jen just inside the school's main entrance. Two more news vans were setting up across the street. A few feet away, Ruiz was consulting with a captain from Public Affairs who'd soon be forced to make an official statement.

"What's up?" I asked her.

"He wants us to make the notification, feel out the sister. If she doesn't turn us on to anything, we check out the vic's place."

"Work up the victimology?"

"Yeah."

Most homicides, if they are solved at all, are solved in the first forty-eight hours after the crime. Ruiz was putting his money on Marty and Dave, hoping they would turn up some hard physical evidence or a reliable witness. If they came up dry, the best shot at finding our doer would be combing through Beth's life, turning her past inside out, hoping, probably in vain, that we would be able to find someone with a motive, someone who wanted her dead. Someone unhinged and twisted enough to do what had been done to her.

I found myself hoping that Dave and Marty would come through. I knew, even then, that this case was different.

TWO

We drove west on Seventh Street in Jen's Explorer, listening to the radio for news of the murder. Fortunately, a man in West LA had taken an assault rifle into the office that afternoon and killed three people before turning the .308 on himself. With any luck, that story would lead and take some of the media attention off Beth's murder. So far, there had been no mention of dead teachers, but we'd already seen the first news van, so it wouldn't be long before others picked up the scent.

Jen took out her cell phone and speed-dialed a number. "Tom," she said, "it's Jen. It's a little after nine on Friday night. I'm not going to be able to make class tomorrow. Just keep them going on what we worked on last week, okay? Especially the *ukemi*—none of the newbies can roll for shit. And let me know if Rudy shows up. I'm really starting to worry about him. Just give me a call on my cell, all right?" She hung up and slipped the phone back into her bag.

Jen earned her first black belt in tae kwon do before she learned how to drive. Since then, she'd studied half a dozen other martial arts before finally committing herself to aikido.

Last spring I joined her parents and brother to watch her take the test for her third-degree black belt. Our eyes widened as we watched her *randori*. Five men, most twice her weight, attacked her simultaneously, and in a spinning and twisting whirlwind of motion, she sent each of them flying in a different direction. They rolled back onto their feet and repeated their attacks over and over again, but not one of them landed a single blow.

When Jen first made detective and could count on having a reasonable number of weekends off, she began teaching Saturday afternoon martial arts workshops in a city program for at-risk youths. After seeing her belt test, I was intrigued enough to visit the first session of one of her classes, for a particularly tough crew of juvenile repeat offenders. As Jen walked to the front of the gym, she was met with snickers, snide comments, sexual innuendoes, and shaking heads. She held up a hundred-dollar bill in one hand and a police baton in the other. She told the class that the first person who could hit her with the nightstick got the bill. After she repeatedly assured them that there was no trick and that the offer was legit, one cocky teen volunteered to give it a try. She handed him the weapon. He attacked her with force, but she effortlessly slipped to the side and, in one continuous spinning motion, disarmed him and pinned him to the floor. Four more brave souls tried the attack, and they all wound up face down on the mat, unable to move. She broke the hundred when she bought me lunch after class.

"Still teaching kung fu to the miscreants, huh?" I asked.

She said the same thing she always did when I asked that question. "It's not kung fu, and they're not miscreants."

"Who's Rudy?"

"Rudy Nguyen. Just one of the kids. Getting ready for his brown belt test." She was quiet a moment and then went on. "His brother was a small-time banger, ran with one of the Little Saigon crews. Helped take care of the family. He got popped a few months ago as an accessory to that drive-by in Westminster. The one that killed the ten-year-old girl? He stood up, so he's doing five to seven. The family's struggling to keep on. Father's long gone, so it's just the mom, Rudy, and two little sisters. The mom does laundry at one of the downtown hotels."

What she didn't say, of course, was how worried she was that Rudy would follow in his brother's footsteps. Single mothers working for poverty-level wages don't make it far without help. It wouldn't be the first time we'd seen a kid take a wrong turn while trying to take care of his own. The cops, the politicians, and the media don't like to admit it, but it's not always about the bling.

I opened a red and white tin of mints. "When you can snatch the Altoid from my hand," I said, in my best Master Po imitation, "it will be time for you to go."

Her right hand snapped away from the wheel, and as quickly as I could, I closed my hand on the mint. I didn't realize that she wasn't going for it until I felt her knuckles strike my biceps "Ouch," I yelped.

"Pussy."

Jen turned left onto Pine Avenue. The Friday night crowd was lining the street full of trendy restaurants and nightspots. Thanks to the city's massive urban renewal effort, people who wouldn't have been caught dead downtown after dark only a few years ago now flocked there every weekend.

She turned left again on Broadway and parked in a red zone near the Blue Cafe, a club that featured live blues seven nights a week. The crowd was just starting to thicken on the patio outside as people lined up for the bigger names who played later in the evening. She took the laminated LBPD placard from the slot on the sun visor and dropped it onto the dash so we wouldn't be towed by an overzealous parking enforcement officer.

"You ready for this?" she asked.

"No."

"Well, that makes two of us."

We walked along the pedestrian-only concourse that joined Broadway and Third. Passing the cafe patio, which was enveloped in a cloud of tobacco smoke, we heard the pulsating rhythms that seeped out into the still night air. I followed Jen around the corner and into the alley behind the old brick building, which housed the club and several other establishments. Halfway along the alley, we came to a glass door set back into the brick wall. Through the doors we saw a flight of dimly lit stairs, which led up to the apartments above. I reached out and pulled on the door handle. It didn't open.

"Should we buzz?" Jen asked.

"Rather not." On the off chance that something was hinky with the sister, I didn't want to give her a heads-up. "She's probably not even home," I said. "Friday night and all."

"So what's the plan?"

I looked at the door. It had seen better days. The glass was scratched and dirty. The metal frame showed signs of corrosion and rust around the edges, but there was still a steel plate over the latch to prevent unsavory types from loiding the lock with a credit card.

I grabbed the handle again and rattled the door back and forth. There was a lot of play in the hinges and locking mechanism. I wrapped both hands around the handle and braced my right foot against the door frame. Pulling gently at first, I slowly increased the force. After a few seconds, the latch slipped and the door popped open. I lost my grip on the handle and fell back, landing hard on my ass. Jen grabbed the open door before the hydraulic mechanism could ease it closed.

I expected a snide comment from her, but none came. We were too close to Beth's sister now. She extended her free hand and helped me up. We climbed the stairs in silence. On the upper landing, a short hallway formed a T shape with the flight of stairs. Facing the door to unit B, we flipped open our badge holders so that both our shields and IDs would be clearly visible.

If you ask most homicide cops to describe the worst part of their job, they won't mention the grisly finds at crime scenes that haunt their dreams, or the violent offenders who would just as soon slip a blade between their ribs as speak to them, or the hours spent waiting on courthouse benches for a defense attorney who questions not only their honesty but their humanity, or the toll the job takes on their family, or even the inordinately high rates of alcoholism, drug addiction, and suicide among members of their profession. What they'll most likely tell you is that the worst part of their job is notifying the next of kin. It has to do with pain. When we come upon a fresh crime scene, the pain is just an abstraction, existing only in our own imaginations. The reality for us is that, no matter how horrible a crime, the pain is no longer present. It died with the victim. We only witness it after the fact. But when we look in someone's face and tell them that their spouse or child or parent or sibling has been murdered, the pain is immediate and palpable—and it cuts deep.

As Jen knocked softly on the door with the back of her hand, I remembered the two CHP officers who had knocked on my door two years before. Somewhere down deep in my gut, I felt a churning sensation, and I found myself hoping that Beth and her sister were not close. Estranged, perhaps. Indifferent. We watched the dim dot of light that shone through the peephole. As it disappeared, a muffled voice spoke from behind the locked door. "Who is it?"

"Long Beach Police Department," Jen said, holding her badge next to her face so the person on the other side of the door could see both clearly. Two dead bolts clicked open, one after the other, and the door cracked open a few inches, still secured by a safety chain. A woman's left eye peered around the edge of the door. "Yes?"

"Rachel Williams?" Jen asked, her voice soft.

"No."

I stood silently behind her, trying to feel detached. My gut was still churning, so I must not have been doing very well.

"Is Rachel at home?"

"What is this about?" the woman behind the door asked. She was slowly coming to the realization that police never come to your door with good news.

"We need to speak to her," Jen said. "Is she at home?"

"Just a minute."

The door closed, and we heard the snick of the safety chain being unfastened. The woman opened the door. She was Jen's height, maybe five-six, late thirties, with her red hair in spikes and no makeup or jewelry. She wore a black T-shirt and faded Levi's over her Doc Martens.

"I'm Detective Tanaka, and this is Detective Beckett," Jen said. She looked expectantly at the woman, an unspoken invitation for an introduction.

"I'm Susan." She didn't extend her hand. "This is bad, isn't it?"

We didn't need to answer. I looked at her, judging her reaction. "Can we come in?" Jen asked.

The main room of the loft apartment was long, stretching the length of the building, perhaps thirty feet. To our right, artificial light trickled in through a row of windows that lined the wall facing the alley, adding to the isolated pools of illumination from strategically placed floor lamps. Above us was a high ceiling with exposed beams and ventilation ducts.

The large room was divided by groupings of furniture. A sofa and two chairs arranged around a coffee table formed the living area near the windows. Along the wall from the windows to the front door were a variety of painting supplies: easels, a worktable, dozens of canvases in varying sizes—some painted, some not. To our left was a kitchen with old appliances and a dining area with new furniture. Directly in front of us, a wall, apparently a fairly recent addition, hung with dark and brooding portraits, was divided by a short hallway, which, I assumed, led to the bedroom and bathroom. The odor of stale cigarette smoke hung in the air, and the dull pulse of amplified blues filtered in through the brick walls.

"I'll get Rachel," the woman said. As she walked toward the hallway, I glanced at a painting that was leaning against the wall. In it stood a woman, rendered in harsh, sharp lines of deep grays, blacks, browns, and greens. She seemed isolated, stoically holding forth against a swirling background of deep reds and purples.

"Danny," Jen whispered.

I turned to see Rachel coming into the room. Although she was taller than Susan by an inch or two, she seemed much smaller. The loose denim overalls she wore over a white tank top accentuated the slightness of her frame. Her fine blonde hair was pulled back into a ponytail. As her bare feet brushed across the floor, I could see the fear and trepidation in her green eyes. Beth's green eyes.

"Rachel?" Jen asked.

She nodded.

"I'm afraid we have some bad news."

Rachel reached out to her right, and Susan took her hand. "It's your sister, Elizabeth," Jen said softly. "She was murdered tonight."

I'd once recorded a TV documentary that showed the growth of a sunflower in time-lapse photography. In the span of a minute, the flower sprouted, grew to maturity, and bloomed brightly. I had been so captivated by the process that I rewound the tape to watch it again. As I stared at the image, the flower closed in upon itself, the bud tightened into a green knob, and the stalk shrunk into nothingness, disappearing beneath the soil. As the realization grew in her, Rachel seemed more and more like that sunflower. A question began to take shape in her expression, and she looked at Jen, who nodded silently. Susan's hand tightened around Rachel's.

Jen spoke before the shock could fully take hold. "Do you know of anyone who might have wanted to harm your sister?"

Rachel looked blankly back at her, barely managing to shake her head.

"Had she mentioned anything to you? Was there anyone she might have had reason to be afraid of?" Jen waited a moment for a reply, but none came. "Anyone at all. An ex-boyfriend? Someone who may have been watching her? Or following her?" Jen asked. "Someone suspicious?"

"Do you have to do this now?" Susan asked.

"Yes," I said, as gently as I could.

"Was there anyone she seemed concerned about?" Jen tried to hold Rachel's gaze, but she was drifting away. "Rachel?" She looked back at Jen.

"Anyone at all?"

"No," Rachel said, her voice barely a whisper. "No one." She turned to Susan, who took her in her arms and pulled her head into her shoulder. Jen and I looked at the floor.

Susan led Rachel to the dining table and gently sat her down, kneeling beside her. "I'm right here, baby," she whispered. She looked over her shoulder at Jen and me. I wanted, more than anything, to walk out the door and leave them alone.

Jen moved slowly toward the table and put her hand on Rachel's shoulder. She looked into Susan's eyes and then inclined her head slightly toward me.

Susan rose, whispering again, "I'm right here," and started in my direction. Rachel didn't let go of Susan's hand. "I'm not going far. I'll be right over there, and I'll be back in just a minute, okay?" Susan pulled her hand away from Rachel's and crossed the room.

"This won't take long," I said softly. We moved away from Jen and Rachel and stood near the windows.

"Did you know her sister well?" I asked.

"Very well." Susan looked back at the table.

"Were she and Elizabeth close?"

"Yes."

"How long have you and Rachel been together?"

"Three years, next month."

"Any other family in the area?"

"Their parents live in Arizona."

"We'll need their number and address."

Susan watched Rachel, who was now holding Jen's hand tightly. Jen kneeled down, placed her free hand on Rachel's shoulder, and spoke softly to her. I couldn't make out the words.

"Susan?" I asked. She looked at me. "Can you think of anyone who might have had cause to harm Elizabeth?"

"No." She turned back toward the other end of the room.

She answered half a dozen more of my questions, her body growing more tense and rigid, without taking her eyes off of Rachel and Jen for more than a second or two. I slipped a business card out of my pocket and handed it to her.

"We'll need someone to make a positive identification of the body. Tomorrow, possibly Sunday. If you think of anything that might be helpful, anything at all, you can call me anytime, okay?"

"All right." Susan looked at me once to be sure we were through and then hurried back to Rachel. I followed. Susan shot Jen a suspicious look as she slipped in between her and Rachel.

"One other thing," I said. "Did Elizabeth have a spare set of keys?"

Susan hesitated a moment. Then she turned, went into the kitchen area, and took a ring of keys off a peg next to the refrigerator. She walked past Jen and handed them to me. "Anything else?"

"No," I said. "Thanks for your help."

"I'm just going to show them out and lock up," Susan said to Rachel, placing a hand on her shoulder. "I'll be right back." She eyed the business card Jen had left on the table before leading us to the door. As I went out, she spoke to Jen. "Those shoes look comfortable," she said. Was that a twinge of jealousy in her voice?

I stopped, turned around, and looked down at Jen's black Rockports. "Trust me," Jen said, her eyes meeting Susan's glare, "they're not." Susan studied her for a moment before closing the door.

In the alley, on the way back to the car, I said, "Well, that was interesting." Jen nodded just as a plaintive blues guitar riff escaped into the night.

Jen took the LBPD placard off the dash, tucked it back into its slot on the visor, and looked at her reflection in the rearview mirror.

"Do I look gay?" she asked.

"What?"

"Do I look gay?"

"That's the thing with Susan and the comfortable shoes, right?"

"Is it the hair?"

"You don't look gay."

"Really?"

"Yes, really." I looked at her and smiled. I wasn't used to seeing Jen exhibit this kind of insecurity—or any kind for that matter. "Those pants don't make you look fat, either."

She looked at herself again and ran a hand through her short hair. "Maybe I should let it grow out." She hadn't had a date in months, but it wasn't for lack of opportunity. Everett, the vice-principal, was only one of many who had eyed my partner and imagined the possibilities. Jen slipped the transmission into drive and pulled out into the street.

Beth had lived in a one-bedroom box of a guesthouse situated behind a 1930s vintage Craftsman-style two-story with a broad porch fronting Newport Avenue. A sign on a metal rod, plunged into the front lawn, announced that the main house was for rent. Well, I thought, I guess that makes two of them now. Jen looked at the sign. "Maybe that number's for the landlord. Think we ought to call?"

"We've got the key."

Jen and I walked up the long driveway. The back unit sat next to a two-car garage behind the truncated backyard of the front house. I took a good look at the outside of Beth's place. The porch was clean and recently swept, the bushes were trimmed away from the windows, and a white steel security screen covered the front door. A 100-watt bulb, screwed into a sensor socket that activated the light at dusk, glowed brightly.

I took the key ring out of my pocket and began trying the keys in the screen door's dead bolt. On the third try, the bolt slid open. The same key unlocked the knob, and the locks on the front door were keyed alike too. As I pushed the door open, I noticed a steel strip that ran down the jamb, providing secure points for the dead bolt and latch to lock into, adding reinforcement against a forced entry.

I showed it to Jen. "Glad we didn't have to kick it."

"What do you think," she asked, "paranoid landlord?"

"Somebody was interested in security."

I ran my hand along the wall inside the door and found the light switch. I flipped it on and stepped inside. We stood silently and looked at the room.

The house seemed bigger than it had from the outside. A fairly large room was divided into living and dining areas by a sofa placed in its center. The sofa faced a coffee table and a large oak entertainment center that held a TV, a VCR, a small stereo, and an array of knickknacks and framed photos. On the opposite end of the room, behind the sofa, was a small round dining table. Beyond the table, two tall bookcases stood against the wall, flanking a doorway.

"Where do you want to start?" Jen asked.

"Let's give it a walk-through and see what we see."

A few steps to our left, a door led into the kitchen. An empty coffee cup sat unwashed in the sink. We walked through the kitchen and into a small laundry room, which had a side entry, and then continued straight into the bathroom. A door on our right led us into the bedroom.

Jen crossed the room to turn on the light. A queen-sized bed took up the bulk of the floor space. There was a dresser, a chair, two more bookcases, a small desk with a computer on top, and an oak-veneer file cabinet that served double duty as a printer stand. Jen ran her finger along the top edge of one of the bookcases and held it up to look at it. "No dust." The bed had been hastily made, and a few articles of clothing—apparently, dirty laundry—sat on the floor in front of the closet, next to another door that opened into the dining area.

I stepped back into the bathroom. In the sink I saw a few stray hairs and a bit of dried white crust caked on the porcelain. I scraped up a bit of the white stuff with my fingernail.

Toothpaste. One toothbrush, a blue-tinted Oral B with a blue stripe in the bristles, stood alone in a holder next to the faucet. A few disintegrating bits of unflushed blue tissue floated in the toilet. The peach-colored towel that was draped over the shower curtain rod was dry to the touch.

I used the end of my pen to dig through the dirty clothes in the hamper in the laundry room. Nothing much there. A T-shirt, two bras—one white and one black with a bit of lacey frill around the edges—cotton underwear, panty hose, and a pair of socks. Nothing unusual.

When I arrived back in the bedroom, Jen asked, "Any thoughts?"

"She was neat," I said. "No recent overnight company Maybe left in a hurry this morning."

"That and three fifty will get you a decaf grande latte."

"Let's start digging," I said.

"Dibs on the bedroom." As Jen started searching, I went out into the living room—and found myself looking into the blue-steel barrel of a Smith & Wesson .357 Magnum.

THREE

"Stop!" The voice was harsh and sharp. My pulse thumped in my ears, and I froze, fighting the urge to go for my gun and dive for cover. He stood on the other side of the room, but my tunnel vision made the muzzle of the revolver seem only inches away.

The man pointing the gun at me was tall and lean with a fringe of white hair around his gleaming bald head, steel gray eyes, and a surprising steadiness in his liver-spotted hands. He stood in a textbook two-handed isosceles combat firing stance. I moved my arms out, away from my body, and held them there. Speaking as calmly as I could, I said, "Easy there, partner," as I watched his eyes for any slight motions. "I'm a cop."

Something gave in the hardness of his face. His nostrils flared as he released a breath of air, and his shoulders released some of their tension.

"I'm just going to lift open my coat, nice and slow so you can see," I said, "and take out my badge, okay?"

He nodded. Very slowly and deliberately, I opened my coat with my left hand and reached into my inside pocket with my right thumb and forefinger, maintaining eye contact with him all the while. I let the leather holder fall open so he could see both the ID and the shield.

"Step toward me slowly," he said.

I did as I was told. A few steps closer and he was able to get a good enough look at my credentials to lower his gun. I took a deep breath and tried to center myself.

"Jen?" I said, without looking behind me.

"Yeah?" she answered. From the direction of her voice, I could tell she was in a low crouch position in the bedroom door. From the surprised expression on my new friend's face, I could tell she hadn't yet reholstered her Glock.

"Danny Beckett," I said, extending my right hand. "LBPD Homicide."

The guy switched the revolver from his right hand to his left in order to shake. "Harlan Gibbs," he said. His grip was firm. "My apologies, Detective."

"This is my partner, Jennifer Tanaka." She nodded. The three of us stood for a moment in an awkward silence and tried to compose ourselves.

"You on the job?" I asked.

"Used to be. LA County sheriff. Pulled my thirty and got out."

"Now you manage a few rental properties?"

"Own 'em," Harlan said, tilting his head slightly to the right. "How'd you figure that?"

"Locks. Light timers. Hedges trimmed away from the windows. Steel strip in the doorjamb. Somebody knew what they were doing."

The corner of his mouth turned up a bit as if it was attempting to smile but was long out of practice. It only lasted a second, though. "Elizabeth's dead, isn't she?"

Jen raised her eyebrows at his use of her first name.

"Yes," I said. "She is. Murdered."

"Son of a bitch." His shoulders slumped, and his ramrod posture relaxed, as if his strength and will were leaking out of his body, leaving him old and weary. "You know who did it yet?"

"No. That's why we're here. Did you know her well?"

"I suppose so. I just live across the street there." He gestured vaguely with his arm. "Saw the lights on and no car in the driveway. That's why I came over."

"You don't know of anyone who might have meant her harm, do you, Mr. Gibbs?" I asked.

"Harlan." He thought for a moment. "Can't say as I do."

"Boyfriends, ex-husbands, anything like that?"

"Nope."

"She have much company?"

"Well, not that I kept tabs or anything, but no. Not much." He looked over at Jen. "Can't say as I ever noticed her with a man here. Not like a date, I mean."

"Notice anyone at all?" I asked.

"Just that friend of hers, Angela, I think her name is. And her sister." Jen scribbled a note on her pad.

"Do you have a last name on the friend?" I asked.

He shook his head, and a glint of light reflected off his scalp. I walked back toward the front door and pointed at the steel strip in the jamb. "Any problems in the neighborhood?"

"Just the usual," Harlan said. "I believe in being cautious."

"Thanks, Harlan," I said. "One more thing, though. It was pretty ugly. There's going to be a lot of media. Probably will get a news van or two out here."

"Fucking vultures."

"Just wanted to give you a heads-up."

"Appreciate it, Detective. Give me a shout if there's anything I can do. She was a good kid." Harlan nodded at Jen and went out the door, the Magnum dangling at his side. Through the screen, I watched as he paused, rubbed the back of his hand across his eyes, and stepped off the porch. We listened to his footsteps growing fainter as he walked down the driveway.

I went to the door and locked the dead bolt on the security screen.

"Wish you'd done that before," Jen said.

Thumbing through Beth's address book in the kitchen, I scanned the first names that were penciled in, looking for Angelas. There were two. One lived in Arizona. The second was Angela Markowitz, in Huntington Beach. I peeled a blue Post-it note off the pad next to the phone to mark the place and then added her name and address to my notes.

Jen was sitting on the floor, rummaging through the garbage.

"Think I got the friend." I looked down at her. "Anything?"

"She ate a lot of frozen dinners." Jen held up an empty carton of 1 percent milk and looked at the expiration date. "And she kept her milk too long." She held the carton to her nose and squinted at the odor. "Expired two weeks ago."

In the other room, I started with the bookshelves. They were tall and made of satin-lacquered pine. I scanned the titles. The shelf on the left seemed to be devoted to academic volumes. *A Rhetoric for Writing Teachers*, *Actual Minds, Possible Worlds*, and *Teaching Shakespeare into the Twenty-First*

Century filled the top shelves. Below these books was an array of British and American literature, the titles of which I had heard often. I knew I had read many of them at some point in my life but, for whatever reason, couldn't remember much about them. *A Tale of Two Cities, Heart of Darkness, Moby Dick, Huckleberry Finn, For Whom the Bell Tolls.* The bottom shelf had been reserved for the really thick books—five Norton anthologies and two different editions of *The Complete Works of William Shakespeare*. I found myself wondering what all morons wonder when they look at a collection of books like that and ask, "Have you read all these?" Too late for an answer to that question.

The shelf on the right was more my speed. That one was filled with popular fiction, with a few biographies and memoirs sprinkled here and there and even a science book or two— the kind of stuff you find at the front of the store in Barnes & Noble. I scanned the novels. Beth obviously had a soft spot for mysteries. I followed the alphabet through the Sue Grafton titles from *A Is for Alibi* all the way to *Q Is for Quarry*. She also had series written by Patricia Cornwell, Sara Paretsky, James Lee Burke, Lawrence Block, and Dennis Lehane. I'd read more than a few of them myself, and these I actually remembered.

There was a stack of mail on the dining room table. Nothing terribly interesting. Two credit card bills, four mail-order catalogs, and half a dozen ads and solicitations. I opened the bills. Between the two cards, she owed a bit less than eighteen hundred dollars. She'd only made two charges in the last month, one for gas, and the other at Mum's, a downtown restaurant.

I walked around the room. On the coffee table in front of the sofa were copies of last week's *Time, Newsweek,* and

Entertainment Weekly. A week's worth of the *Los Angeles Times* was stacked neatly under one end of the table. How did she manage to read so much?

I turned around to face the entertainment unit. Framed pictures were scattered among the other items on the shelf. There were two pictures of Beth with her sister, one with a woman I assumed was her mother, two graduation photos of her in different-colored gowns, and one of her standing alone at the beach, with the golden light of a setting sun illuminating her face.

I picked up the last photo and stared at it for a moment. There was a brightness in her smile, a glow in her expression, that made it hard to look away. I tried again to place her face. Seeing her in the picture made me wonder if I actually had seen her before. I couldn't imagine that I wouldn't remember her.

On the shelf below the VCR were a number of videotapes. Without bending for a closer look, I counted three versions of *Hamlet,* two each of *Macbeth, Richard III,* and *Romeo and Juliet,* and single copies of *Much Ado About Nothing, A Midsummer Night's Dream, Julius Caesar, King Lear,* and *Twelfth Night.* Beth was serious about her Shakespeare.

I pushed the power button on the small bookshelf stereo. The display lit up, indicating there was a CD inside. Expecting Mozart or Bach or some other classical composer I'd never be able to identify, I pushed the play button.

As I recognized the opening notes, I felt as if I was losing my balance. I reached out to the shelf to steady myself. The CD was Springsteen's *Born to Run,* and I closed my eyes as I listened to the first lines of the first track. I jabbed the stop button and rubbed my face with both hands.

"Danny?" I looked up to see Jen staring at me, her eyes searching my face. "You all right?"

I nodded, but apparently not very convincingly. Jen kneeled down and looked me squarely in the eyes. "C'mon, partner," she said, "you're getting a little weird on me here. What's wrong?"

FOUR

A little less than a hour later—most of which time we'd spent digging through Beth's file cabinet and desk drawers—Jen and I were just completing the list of all the items we'd be back to catalog and collect as evidence when Jen's cell phone rang.

"Tanaka," she said, placing it to her ear. I watched her nod her head as she listened. "We'll be heading out soon." A few more nods. "Sure thing, Boss." She folded the phone and slipped it back into the pocket of her jacket.

"We've got to head back to the squad and get with Marty and Dave," she said. "See if anything adds up yet."

"Ruiz gonna be there?"

"Yep."

"I smell a task force coming on."

"Well, we've got to do our part if the chief's ever gonna make mayor."

I sat back down in front of Beth's notebook computer and saved the file I'd been looking at—a three-and-a-half-year-old letter to her mother about how she was enjoying the new teaching job. She had liked the conditions, she wrote, and the administration seemed supportive. There were more letters, lesson plans, old term papers, lecture notes, and even a few short stories. It seemed as if Beth had saved on the hard drive just about everything she'd written in the last few years. There were dozens and dozens of files that stretched back as far as 1993. I wanted to take a look at the rest of them. If we weren't able to come up with any other solid leads off the physical evidence and interviews, there would be a lot here to sort through.

I also wanted to get into her e-mail account. Technically, we'd need a court order for the company to release her password and allow us access. Maybe we'd get lucky and someone from the Computer Crimes Squad would be able to bypass the red tape. I shut down the ThinkPad and folded it closed.

"Ready?" Jen asked.

"You go ahead. I'll be out in just in a minute." I got up from the desk chair and stood for a minute next to Beth's bed as Jen walked into the other room. I took another look around and studied the furnishings: the bed with its off-white comforter, the windows with their frilly white curtains edging the matching miniblinds, the light gray carpeting just beginning to show signs of wear in front of the closet and bathroom, the oak desk and bookcases piled with papers and books. Taking a deep breath through my nose, I tried to identify the slightly sweet scent in the room. Was it a faint hint of perfume or just a bit of leftover air freshener? I wasn't really sure what I was hoping for, but whatever it was—a hunch, a sign, an epiphany, anything—it never came.

As I walked through the kitchen and living room, shutting off the lights as I went, I heard the distinctive sound of strips of crime scene tape being ripped from a roll. I locked the door behind me, and Jen made a yellow and black X across the security door with the tape, the bold block letters proclaiming, "Long Beach Police Department Crime Scene—Do Not Enter."

Outside, the air was clean and crisp. The late fall nights were just beginning to grow colder. Standing on the porch, we peeled off our latex gloves and slipped them into our pockets. "What do you think?" I said.

"I think we need to find some fucking clues."

As we walked down the driveway, I noticed a dark figure sitting on the porch of a house across the street. When he lifted his hand and nodded his head, I realized it was Harlan Gibbs. I pulled the passenger door of Jen's Explorer closed behind me, and as she settled into the driver's seat, I asked, "Does that count?"

At the station, Marty, Dave, Jen, and I sat around the small table in the coffee room that was adjacent to the three larger rooms that housed the Homicide Squad. I sat with my back to the worn avocado green sofa and faced the refrigerator, both of which must have been nearly as old as me. I read the note that was taped to the Frigidaire's door: "To whoever stole my lunch on Tuesday be warned. I will not rest until I find you. And when I do, I will kill you. Sincerely, Bob." A box of Dunkin' Donuts and five fresh cups of coffee sat on the tabletop in front of us. I was eyeing a chocolate-iced buttermilk when Lieutenant Ruiz came in. His eyes were tired, and the crags in his face seemed deeper, adding a hard decade to his appearance.

"Long night, huh, Boss?" Dave asked, biting into a maple bar.

"Yeah," Ruiz said. He sat down and took a glazed doughnut out of the box and dropped it onto a napkin on the table in front of him. "Just left the school. Media all over the place." His voice was rough and gravelly. He had already been talking for hours. "The brass decided not to issue a statement until eleven forty-five."

"What went out on the air?" I asked.

"You didn't watch?" Ruiz asked.

"Nope," Jen said.

"Didn't miss anything," he said, looking down at his doughnut. "All the local stations led with the West LA shooting. We made the second slot. Unconfirmed reports of a murder, sketchy details at present—the usual."

"Why'd they hold off?" Marty asked. He took a swig of coffee, wincing at the taste.

"The chief's hoping we'll find the doer before the morning news." He paused and looked at our faces, one by one. Apparently, he didn't see what he'd been looking for. "We're not going to, are we?" No one replied. "Well, what do we have?" he asked.

"Canvas came up dry, no wits. Nobody noticed anything unusual," Dave said. "We'll have some uniforms go around the neighborhood again tomorrow, but I wouldn't count on anything."

"Big surprise there." The lieutenant seemed disappointed, but not surprised. He turned to Marty. "Anything?"

"Not yet." Marty sipped on his coffee again. "Classroom's a high-traffic area, though. A hundred fifty to a hundred seventy-five people through there every day. The techs are gonna be at the scene all night picking up latents and trace evidence. Doubt they'll come up with anything useful."

Ruiz turned to Jen and me. "I don't suppose that by any chance you two found a psychotic ex-husband," he said, without a trace of irony in his voice.

"Nope," Jen said. "Sorry."

"Running a few people, though," I added.

The lieutenant's eyes opened wider—that was the closest he came to looking hopeful.

"The sister's girlfriend," I said, "and an ex-deputy sheriff neighbor who popped in on us."

Dave looked up, licked some maple from the edge of his mouth, and said, "Girlfriend?"

"Yeah," Jen said, "they were all naked and oiled up, rolling around on the living room floor when we showed. Wanted me and Danny to join in."

Marty and I couldn't help but smile.

"You like either one of them?" Ruiz asked, refusing to acknowledge the joke.

Jen kicked me under the table, suspecting I'd make some lame crack about liking one of the lesbians. She was right, I was tempted, but she didn't need to kick me. The lieutenant clearly wasn't in the mood.

"Too soon to tell," I said. "Might be something with the cop. Got kind of a weird vibe off him." I thought about old Harlan for a moment. "Don't see him with a blade, though."

"Who ran the MO? Any matches?"

"No similar murders locally in the last five years," Dave said. "We'll see what we get from the state and the feds. You know how they are on weekends, though. Might have to wait a while."

"I'll get on it in the morning, start sweet-talking people. Maybe get 'em to move their asses on this," Ruiz said. He took the doughnut in his fingers and lifted it an inch or so off the table before placing it back down on the napkin. "Chief wants a task force."

None of us was thrilled with the prospect. Sure, the extra manpower would be helpful, but everyone from the chief and the DA to the mayor would be jockeying for control, trying to take credit for any successes we had and pass the buck on any failures. Task forces, in my experience, are always more about politics than solving crimes.

"Who's running it?" Marty asked.

"So far," Ruiz said, "it's me. But we gotta come up with something quick, or he'll hand it off. Kick it upstairs."

"Oh joy." Dave stuffed another bite of his maple bar into his mouth. "Nobody runs a murder investigation like a douche-o-crat." Ruiz walked out, leaving his glazed doughnut uneaten.

It was after one o'clock in the morning Marty and I volunteered to stay to start on the paperwork while Dave and Jen went home to get some sleep. We sat alone in the squad room. The bare cinder block walls were lined with bulletin boards, file cabinets, bookcases, and long tables. At the far end of the room were a door and window that led into the lieutenant's office. Three clusters, with two desks each, took up the bulk of the floor space. There was an unusual stillness to the place. We shared the floor with several of the other detective squads—Violent Crimes, Missing Persons, Burglary, Fraud, and Computer Crimes—but as far as we could tell, we were the only ones pulling an all-nighter.

While Marty typed with his index fingers in one corner of the room, I three-hole-punched photocopies of the initial reports and inserted them into the thick three-ring binder that would become the murder book. Everything would go in there—copies of the crime scene and ME's reports, notes on interviews, witness statements, evidence logs, anything and everything pertaining to the case. With any luck, the last pages would be arrest reports.

"Who pulled the autopsy?" I asked.

Marty swiveled around in his desk chair. "Paula," he said.

Paula Henderson was a round, fiftyish woman with white hair and a pleasant smile. She always wore her bifocals on a chain around her neck. She was also the city's chief pathologist and the best ME in southern Los Angeles County.

"Ruiz call in a favor?" I asked Marty.

He shook his head. "Somebody upstairs. She was pissed off about it too. Friday night and all. Least until I told her about the vic. Then she was all business. You know how she gets."

"You tell her we'd be here?"

"She's gonna give us a call soon as she has the preliminaries."

"You wanna call it a night?" I asked. "I don't mind waiting."

"Naw. I'll just wind up staring at the ceiling again. Empty house still weirds me out." Marty's fourth wife, Joan, had moved out only a few weeks earlier. He seemed to be taking it well. Maybe he was used to it by now.

"I'll go make some more coffee," I said.

When the phone rang at three fifteen, Marty was "resting his eyes" on the couch in the coffee room. I caught it on the second ring. "Homicide, this is Beckett." I expected to hear Paula's voice on the other end. I didn't.

"Daniel?" Geoffrey Hatcher was the only person besides my mother who ever called me by my full first name. He covered the crime beat for the *Press-Telegram* and was the only reporter whom I wouldn't have hung up on simply as a matter of principle. I'd dealt with him on a few cases since I'd joined the Homicide Squad, and he'd always been straight with me. He never complained about holding back on details that might interfere with our investigations, and when he said "off the record," he meant it. Once he'd even helped us plant a misleading story that fingered the wrong suspect so the real perp would come out of hiding. For a reporter, Geoff was a pretty stand-up guy, but that didn't mean that I had anything to tell him.

"Hi, Geoff," I said. "Somehow, I doubt you're calling to shoot the breeze."

"Can you give me anything at all about the teacher?"

"No."

"Off the record?"

"What have you heard?" I asked.

"Elizabeth Williams, English teacher, thirty years old, unmarried," he paused for a breath. "Brutally stabbed to death."

"Sounds like you've got about as much as we do."

"Was it as bad as they say?"

"Worse," I said, although I had no idea who "they" were or what "they" were saying.

"Suspects?"

"None."

"Links to any other murders?"

"Not yet." I winced as soon as I spoke, wondering if I should have given him the "yet." I'd tipped my hand. Geoff let it go, although I knew it didn't escape him.

"Are the task force rumors true?" he asked.

"Of course," I said. "Election's next year."

"Never too early to start a campaign, is it?"

"Apparently not." I gave him a minute for another question. He didn't ask one. "Check in with me tomorrow. I might be able to give you something."

"Will do. You should get some sleep."

"So should you," I said, and I hung up the phone.

I went into the coffee room and poured myself cup number four. Marty was still snoring. His head was propped on one arm of the couch, and his feet hung over the other.

As I dumped a packet of sugar into my mug, I thought about what I'd said to Geoff. None of us had openly acknowledged what we had been thinking all night. It was not likely that this was a case of acquaintance murder. Jilted lovers or greedy siblings rarely have a taste for the kind of brutality we'd seen. From the state of Beth's body, the violence inflicted upon her, the sheer number of wounds, and the postmortem vaginal penetration, we knew one thing—in all likelihood, our perpetrator had killed before. And unless we found him, he would kill again.

FIVE

"Wake up, Marty," I said.

"Five more minutes, Mom," he said without opening his eyes.

He sat up and rubbed his eyes as I poured two cups of water into the top of the Mr. Coffee.

"What time is it?" he asked.

"Six thirty."

"Anything new?"

"Paula called," I said. "No surprises in the initial workup." The coffeemaker gurgled and spurted behind me as I took a seat at the table. "Fucker chopped her more than a hundred times. Her abdomen was hacked into too much of a mess to get an exact count."

"Lovely." Marty lifted his arms above his head and yawned as he stretched. "Trace evidence?"

"Bunches. Hairs, fibers, all kinds of stuff."

"But?"

"Most of it was posterior. Probably picked it up off the floor." I glanced over my shoulder. The coffeepot was just about full. "And since our pal, Carl the custodian, hadn't cleaned the room yet, we got maybe two hundred high school students tracking shit in and out of there all day long." I got up and poured us each a cup. A few drops fell onto the heating surface of the machine and sizzled into nothingness. "Gonna take a month just to coordinate with the Crime Scene Unit and catalog it all."

"Even then," Marty said, "we'll probably just be pissing in the wind." He tore open a packet of Sweet'N Low and emptied it into his cup. "Semen? Prints?"

"Negative on the semen. She's gonna keep trying for prints, but probably not."

I could see him tossing the ideas around in his head as he stirred his coffee. "So our perp's either very lucky or very careful."

"Or both," I said.

At ten to seven, armed with two-dozen copies of the pre-liminary case reports, Marty and I headed upstairs and knocked on the door of the chief's conference room.

"Come," he said.

We opened the door and found Ruiz arguing with Deputy Chief Baxter. The DC was a round little man with transplanted hair plugs that he'd had done gradually over the course of several months, as if no one would remember that he used to be bald. A community relations officer, whose name I couldn't remember, sat next to Baxter, looking a bit lost and studying the pale blue wall.

"You can't release that," the lieutenant said. His voice was calm, but the knuckles on his right hand went white as he clenched it into a fist around a pencil.

"I don't see why not," Baxter replied, puffing up his chest and straightening in his chair. "We need to reassure the community of our commitment to—"

Ruiz turned to us, dropping the pencil on the desk before Baxter could finish his sentence. "What have we got?" he asked.

"Prelims," Marty said, sliding one of the copies across the table to him. "Nothing solid yet."

Ruiz rubbed his temples. "Save the rundown," he said. "No point in going through it twice."

"There's fresh coffee," the CRO said after a moment of silence. He smiled at us unassumingly and gestured toward the door at the end of the conference room. He took the photocopied packets from us and distributed them around the conference table, placing one in front of each chair, with the packets' bottom edges perfectly parallel to the edge of the table.

"First task force?" Marty asked him.

"Is it that obvious?"

"Only to a seasoned and experienced detective such as myself," Marty said.

I wandered into the kitchenette and saw a large chrome urn that had a bright red light glowing next to the spigot. Thinking back over the night, I tried to remember how many cups of coffee I'd had. I lost count somewhere after five. I opted instead for a small bottle of Arrowhead spring water, which I took from the fridge.

As I looked through the doorway into the conference room, I saw Jen come in with Bob Kincaid from the DA's office on her heels. His blond hair was freshly moussed, and he had a charm-oozing smile carved into his pretty-boy face. He said something to Jen that I couldn't hear. Whatever it was made her grin.

"Morning," I said to her as I crossed back to the table.

"Hi, Danny," she said, looking at my face. "You look like shit."

"It amazes me," I said, "the way you always know exactly the right thing to say."

"I'm serious," she said softly, looking into my eyes. "Are you all right?"

"Yeah. Just too much caffeine and not enough sleep."

We sat down. Kincaid, Ruiz, and Baxter conferred on the other side of the table as the rest of the task force trickled in. In addition to the four of us from Homicide, who were already working the case, the task force was assigned two detectives each from Violent Crimes, Burglary, and Missing Persons and one from Computer Crimes, another from the Organized Crime Detail, and a watch commander from Patrol to coordinate uniform support. None of them was happy to be there. They knew that unless we caught a break in the case, they'd be spending the foreseeable future running criminal record checks, interviewing high school students, and knocking on neighborhood doors.

"Is this everyone?" Baxter asked when we were all seated.

Ruiz looked us over. "Still waiting on one—"

Dave Zepeda opened the door and came in. "Sorry," he said. He was carrying a brown McDonald's bag and a coffee cup. Dave took a seat next to Marty, and the smell of warm Egg McMuffin drifted down the length of the table.

"Very well, then," Baxter said, sitting up straight in his chair in an unsuccessful attempt to seem authoritative. "I'm sure you all know why you're here. This is, of course, a very serious case. I spoke with the chief last night, and he—"

"Where's the chief?" asked Patrick Glenn from Computer Crimes. "Doesn't he usually head up task forces?"

Baxter looked flustered for a moment, the rhythm of his well-rehearsed speech broken. "He's in Seattle on personal business. He's given me full authority to—"

"I was just wondering," Glenn said, grinning affably.

"Yes, well, he's given me full authority to—"

"Sorry," Glenn interrupted, "I didn't mean to interrupt."

The DC nodded decisively. "Well. All right, then," he said. We watched, trying not to let our amusement show as he ran through his speech in his head and located the point at which he'd been distracted. He apparently had no idea that his already-tenuous authority had just been undermined further.

"As I was saying," Baxter continued, "I spoke with the chief last night, and he wants a speedy resolution to this matter. As you might imagine, with the recent citywide reductions in violent crime—homicide, in particular—he's very concerned about this incident. We need to reassure the community of its safety. To that end, we've organized this task force to fully and completely address the..."

Through the conference room window, I watched a jet in the distance angling through the blue morning sky on its descent toward Long Beach Airport. I first noticed it in the upper-right corner of the window. As the jet made a diagonal line toward the lower left, it flew directly behind Baxter's head, disappeared for a moment, and then seemed to emerge from his ear. It continued its downward path just as he was saying something about "violence in our schools." When he finished, he paused, as if we might feel the need to clap.

"With that," he said, "I'll turn it over to Lieutenant Ruiz."

"Okay," Ruiz said, "let's get down to business."

Marty and I ran everyone through the preliminary reports, explaining the little we actually knew and attempting to expand upon on the facts with educated guesses. When we were through, Efram Kennedy, the guy from the Organized Crime Detail, said, "So, basically, we don't have anything to go on." His annoyance covered his pointy face like a ferret mask.

Marty and I exchanged a glance. "Basically," I said. "No."

Within five minutes, Ruiz had us organized. Most of the new detectives were going to work with Dave recanvassing the neighborhood, running background checks, and interviewing Beth's students. Marty had two detectives to help him with cataloging and processing the crime scene evidence, and Jen and I got Pat Glenn to help do background on our victimology workup.

Within another twenty minutes, I was in the passenger seat of Jen's Explorer, and she was driving east on Seventh Street. The traffic was light, which was not unusual on a Saturday morning, and I caught Jen stealing glances in my direction.

"Want to get some breakfast?" I asked.

"No. You need a break," she said. "I'm taking you home."

"So I finally get to go up and see your etchings?"

She wasn't amused. "Not to my home. Yours."

"Probably a good idea. I need to get cleaned up."

"You need to get some sleep."

I didn't want to admit it, but she was right. The caffeine and adrenaline rushes of the night before were fading quickly. I'd crash before long, whether I wanted to or not.

"Okay," I said. "I'll meet you back at the squad at, what, noon?"

"Nope. I'll pick you up at one. We'll go down to Huntington and talk to the friend." She turned right onto Roycroft and
double-parked in front of my duplex.

"What about the ID?"

"I'll take care of it. I'm going to pick up the sister in
about an hour." I nodded my appreciation of the fact that she
was leaving me out of the victim ID. I'd been dreading it all
morning.

"Don't go solving anything without me," I said.

"Go to sleep."

She waited for me to unlock my front door before she
pulled away.

Inside, I peeled off my coat and holster and hung each
over the back of its own dining room chair. In the kitchen,
the morning sun was glowing off the bright yellow, blue, and
red walls. A graphic designer with a lively flair for color had
rented the place before me, and I hadn't repainted, imagining
that the vivid colors might occasionally perk me up. Usually,
though, they just made me want to squint.

I noticed that the message light on my answering machine was blinking, but I ignored it and opened the freezer.
My bottle of Grey Goose was just where I had left it. I poured
a shot into a paper cup, topped it off with orange juice, and
drank it down.

I set the alarm clock on the nightstand in the bedroom for
12:15 and took off my shoes and belt. Lying down, I closed my
eyes and hoped I wouldn't dream.

The alarm went off, and at first I thought I must have
made a mistake when I set it, but a double check of the time
on my watch confirmed that three hours had passed. I hadn't

even noticed falling asleep, and there I was—already awake. I felt like I'd missed out on something.

I looked in the bathroom mirror. Jen's comment in the conference room had been accurate. I did look like shit. Three hours of sleep hadn't helped. Maybe a hot shower and a shave would. Maybe.

They made a dent. The puffy bags under my eyes were less pronounced, and losing the stubble shaved a bit of the weariness off my face. I wondered if salt-and-pepper whiskers on a thirty-four-year-old qualified as premature graying. I ran a comb through my hair and got dressed just in time to hear the doorbell ring.

I opened the door expecting to see my partner, but was surprised to see instead an LBPD uniform officer standing on my porch. He was small, not more than five-seven, but sturdily built, with red hair. He held his hat under his left arm. His blues were crisply pressed, and his Sam Browne belt and holster had a fresh-from-the-quartermaster sheen to them. The polished brass name tag on his chest identified him as Officer Roberts. I didn't recognize him, and apparently, he didn't recognize me either.

"Good afternoon, sir." His voice was filled with an earnest eagerness.

"Hello, Officer," I said, trying my best to sound like a concerned citizen.

"I'd like to ask you a few questions, sir."

"Is this about the murder at the high school?"

"Yes sir, it is."

"Please come in." I pushed open the screen door for him. Rather than attempting to squeeze past me, he held the door and waited for me to step back inside.

"Thank you," he said.

I gestured for him to have a seat on the couch in my living room. "Can I get you something to drink? Coffee?"

"No thank you, sir." He sat on the end of the sofa while I lowered myself into the chair facing him. From there, looking past me, he had a clear view into the dining room.

"How can I help, Officer?"

"We're canvassing the neighborhood, looking for anyone who might have seen anything unusual or out of the ordinary yesterday between five and eight p.m. Were you at home during those hours, sir?"

"Yes," I said. "Yes, I was."

"Did you happen to see or hear anything," he said, pausing briefly as he spotted the shoulder holster and Glock .40 hanging over the chair at the dining table, "that struck you as unusual?" His posture stiffened, and he rested his right hand on his thigh near his sidearm. If I hadn't been looking for his reaction, I wouldn't have noticed it. Not bad.

"It's all right," I said. "I'm—"

"Danny!" Jen's voice shot at me from the porch as she opened the screen door.

Roberts's eyes widened, and his muscles tightened. Instinctively he placed his hand on the grip of his pistol. He relaxed almost immediately as he recognized her. Everybody knew Jen.

"Detective Tanaka?"

"Hi," she said.

"Careful, ma'am. He may be armed," Roberts said.

"I know," she said. "He's my partner."

Roberts looked confused. I watched the wheels turning in his head.

"Danny Beckett," I said, extending my hand.

"I'm sorry, sir…I should have recognized you." He shook my hand and looked down at the floor.

"Don't mind him," Jen said to the rookie. "He's an asshole."

Roberts smiled awkwardly. He stood there for a moment trying to decide what to do. "I guess I should get back to the canvass." He walked past us and out the door.

"Hey," I called after him, stopping him on the porch. "You're doing a good job. Keep it up." He didn't have the slightest idea what to do with that.

As I climbed into the passenger seat and buckled the safety belt, Jen reached down between her legs and lifted up a cardboard tray that held two large Styrofoam cups emblazoned with Juice Stop logos on their sides. She handed one to me.

"What's this?"

"A strawberry-banana smoothie with ginseng. It's good for you," she said.

I popped off the plastic lid and looked down into the cup. It was filled with a thick pinkish liquid with dark red flecks. Lifting it to my mouth, I took a tentative sip. It wasn't bad.

"Yuck," I said, exaggerating a wince.

"Stop whining or I'll make you drink my wheatgrass juice."

I stopped. "How'd the ID go?"

"Well enough," Jen said as she checked the traffic and turned east onto Seventh Street. "Rachel's coming apart, though. She was too zoned out on tranqs and booze to handle it. Susan, the girlfriend, identified the body." I watched the clear plastic straw in her cup turn a pale green as she sucked up a mouthful of juice. "The parents are flying into John Wayne in a couple of hours. No one seems too happy about it."

"We got anything on them?"

"The parents? Only what we heard last night. Retired in Arizona. Ruiz said he'd handle them."

I slurped some more of my smoothie, glad for small favors.

SIX

Angela Markowitz lived in a quiet Huntington Beach neighborhood just off Brookhurst. She and her husband owned a white-on-beige three-bedroom ranch house at the end of a short cul-de-sac. The front yard looked professionally landscaped and maintained, like the yards of the neighboring houses, with a deep green lawn bordered by planters that were filled with wildflowers and small succulents. I drank the last of my smoothie just as Jen parked the Caprice at the curb.

Angela had been waiting for us. Just as we stepped up onto the porch, the door opened.

"Ms. Markowitz?" Jen asked.

"Yes," she said, her voice weak.

"I'm Detective Tanaka. We spoke on the phone earlier? This is Detective Beckett."

"Come in." She stood back from the door to let us pass. Her dark hair was pulled back loosely into a ponytail, and a few individual strands fell down her cheeks. She was dressed in old sweatpants and an oversized T-shirt with a UCI Anteater logo across the chest. Her eyes were bloodshot and puffy, and her nose was red. The lines on her face were deep and pronounced, but they didn't look like they belonged there. She led us into the living room and gestured for us to sit on the sofa. She took a seat on a chair, the sunlight from the sliding glass door behind silhouetting her and leaving her face in shadows. A box of Kleenex sat on the corner of the coffee table in front of her.

"May I?" I asked, taking my notepad from my pocket and pointing to a floor lamp next to the couch. She nodded, and I turned on the lamp.

"I know this is a difficult time for you," I said, "but we're hoping you might be able to answer a few questions about Beth."

She shook her head slowly. "Who could do something like this?"

"We don't know," Jen said, "yet."

"The two of you were close?" I asked her.

Angela nodded and pulled a tissue out of the box. She wrapped it loosely around her fingers and dropped her hands into her lap.

"How long have you known her?" Jen asked.

"Since high school. She was going to be a writer, and I was going to be an actress. We had bigger plans in those days." A warm glow lit her face and then disappeared just as quickly. Her lower lip began to quiver. She closed her mouth tightly for a moment. "We drifted apart for a while, then reconnected when she came to Warren." She was quiet a moment. "We both wound up as teachers," she said.

"How did you meet her?" Jen asked.

Angela closed her eyes, and when she opened them again, a slight, sad smile played across her face. She told us how, in their sophomore year at Marina High, she and Beth had both tried out for the cheerleading squad. They bonded through whispered sarcasm directed at the airheaded blond bimbettes whose entire being seemed to revolve around the auditions. Neither of them made the cut, but they became friends. Jen nodded at the story and gently prodded Angela into talking more about the women's shared history.

Jen was taking the long road with the interview, letting Angela open up gradually and tell us her story on her own terms. She was trying to get beneath the simple facts of their lives and find the genuine core of their friendship. Most detectives have neither the patience nor the empathy to work that approach. My partner did.

We listened to Angela speak for almost an hour. She told us how she and Beth had decided to go to the same college, how they'd taken different paths but both finally settled on English education majors, how they'd experimented, rebelled, and matured. She told us what she knew of Beth's strained relationship with her former fighter-pilot father, her doting relationship with her housewife mother, and her overprotective tenderness toward her little sister. She told us that Beth had introduced her to her husband and been her maid of honor. What she didn't tell us was anything about Beth's own love life.

"Had Beth ever been seriously involved with anyone?" I asked.

"Not that I know of. There might have been someone while we were out of touch." She told us how they'd drifted apart after their graduation from college and how, when they'd run into each other again at Warren, it was like no time had passed at all.

"Beth always had trouble trusting men," Angela said. She pulled a fresh Kleenex from the box and dabbed at the corner of her eye. "Because of her father. He wasn't—" she caught herself, as if she were about to say something she might later regret. There was a quiet anger in her eyes. "She never really would talk about him, but I know he wasn't the best father while Beth and Rachel were growing up."

"Had she been involved with anyone recently?" I asked.

"Not seriously."

"Anyone at all?"

"A few months ago. She went out with a guy she met on the Internet. But she only saw him a few times."

"What happened?" I asked.

"She broke it off. His wife died a year or two ago. She said he still had too many unresolved issues."

Jen and I exchanged a glance.

"How many times did she see him?"

"Oh, maybe four or five times."

"Did you ever meet him?" Jen asked.

"No."

Jen leaned forward. "Had they been intimate?"

"No."

"And she would have told you about that?" I asked. Jen shot me a stern look.

"Yes," Angela answered, "she would have."

I shut my mouth and let Jen handle the next few questions. "How did he take it?" she asked.

"I don't know," Angela said. "She didn't say anything about that. I assumed he was all right with it."

"What was his name?"

"Daryl. She never told me his last name."

I scribbled the name in my notepad.

"Had she mentioned anything unusual lately?" Jen asked. "Maybe something at work, a student or a teacher?"

"No."

"Maybe she mentioned seeing someone odd, phone calls, someone approaching her or following her?" Jen looked into Angela's eyes. "Anything like that at all?"

"No. Nothing at all. I've been thinking about that all night." Angela's voice trailed off, and she raised the tissue to her nose.

Jen gave her a moment. "Is there anyone who might have wanted to hurt her?"

Angela shook her head and reached for a fresh Kleenex, but the box was empty.

An hour later, Jen, Marty, and I stood in a cold room with tiled walls, staring down at Beth's naked body on a stainless-steel table. She'd been cleaned up, and we could clearly see the extent of her wounds. Most of her body was a pale white blue, but the back of her torso and the underside of her legs were a purplish hue, as the blood that had remained in her body pooled there while she was lying on her classroom floor. A single gash bisected her left breast and penetrated deep into the chest cavity. Below the rib cage, most of the skin was gone. It looked as if some large animal had chewed through her abdomen, leaving behind only a tangled mass of organ tissue, muscle, and flesh. The sight was similar, on a smaller scale, between her legs. I swallowed hard, glad that I had nothing more substantial in my stomach than blended strawberries and bananas, and looked at her face. The bright overhead lights shone dully in her open green eyes.

The door at the end of the room swung open, and Paula came in. She was wearing blue surgical scrubs under her white coat, and her bifocals hung on a librarian's chain around her neck. Her short, white hair was mussed, as if she'd been running her hands through it.

"Well, the gang's all here," she said. We said our hellos as she approached the side of the table opposite us.

"The good news," Paula said, pulling a pen out of her pocket, "is that she died quickly." She pointed to the gash in Beth's chest. "This was wound number one, while she was still standing. Cut through her aorta and deep into the right lung. She couldn't have lasted more than a few seconds after she fell." She moved the pen down. "Next came the groin. Full penetration, ten to twelve times."

Jen shifted her weight and exhaled through her nose.

"Finally," Paula went on, "he went to work on the abdomen." She looked at us. "What do you see?"

The three of us looked at the wounds. Marty saw it first. "No stray cuts."

"That's right," she said. "Except for the first cut, everything stayed between the rib cage and pelvis. He took his time and aimed each slash."

"Why?" Jen asked.

"I don't know," Paula said. "I just do the how. The why is your job."

"The hand?" I asked. "Postmortem?"

Paula came around the table, and we stepped back to give her room. She raised Beth's left arm and bent it at the elbow. The rigor was beginning to let go, and Paula held the arm in place. She made a few slight adjustments in the positioning and said, "Danny, stand up on your toes and look down at this."

I did as she said, and I saw it at once. The angle of the wound to the wrist matched almost exactly the angle of the gash in her chest.

"What?" Jen asked.

"It was a defensive wound," I said. "She raised her arm like this." I held my left hand up as if I were trying to shield myself from a blow. "And the blade came down through her wrist," I said, demonstrating the arc of the attack with my right, "and went straight into her chest."

"Jesus," Marty said. "What was the bastard using? A broadsword?"

"No," Paula said, "not a sword."

"What then?" he asked.

"I can't tell you that," Paula said, "but it was a heavy blade, a quarter-inch thick, twelve to thirteen inches long, with a downward curve to the cutting edge."

"Like a sickle or scythe?" I asked.

"Like that," Paula said, "but I doubt that you'd find one of those with a blade that thick and heavy. Or one made of 440C stainless steel." She smiled. "I found a flake on her pelvis."

"Holy shit," Marty said. "A bona fide clue."

When Jen and I entered the squad room, we saw a man and a woman in Ruiz's office, staring at him across his desk while he spoke. The man sat flagpole straight in the chair, his lean face expressionless, his white buzz-cut hair tinged a slight yellow by the fluorescent overhead light. Under the navy blue golf shirt and khakis, he looked as if he might have been carved from blond oak. Every now and again, he'd incline his head slightly, just enough to make you wonder if he was nodding. Otherwise, he sat completely motionless.

The woman, I thought at first, seemed his opposite. She sat in a loose pile, her wool sweater hanging from her slumping shoulders, with a handkerchief, with which she'd frequently rub her eyes or nose, twined in her fingers. If everything about him was hard, then everything about her was soft. Even the lines etched around her eyes and mouth seemed as if they'd been formed with the edge of a dull spoon. But to suggest that the two were opposites would be to suggest that there was something complementary about them, that they fit together in some yin-and-yang kind of way. They didn't. They might just as well have come from different worlds.

When the lieutenant saw us, he motioned us into his office with a wave. "Detectives Tanaka and Beckett," Ruiz said, raising his hand toward us, "this is Colonel and Mrs. Williams." The colonel stood a shade under six feet, but if he hadn't been less than a yard away, I would have guessed his height a solid two inches taller due to his bearing and posture. There was a hard-set arrogance in his eyes, the dull glint of superiority I've often seen in the faces of those who've held the power of life and death over others and enjoyed it too much. He extended his hand, and I shook it. When he let go, I tried not to be too obvious about checking my hand for broken bones or swelling.

"Detectives," the colonel said, "it's a shame we have to meet under these circumstances. The lieutenant here says you're two of the best. I'm sure we can expect solid results." His hands found each other behind his back, and his feet drifted into a wider stance. If he was aware he was standing in parade rest, he didn't show it.

"I'm sorry for your loss, sir."

"You're going to catch the man who did this," he said. It wasn't a question. It couldn't have been further from one, actually. He spoke directly to me, completely ignoring Jen. He must have assumed that she handled the typing and filing and such.

"Detective Tanaka and I will do everything we can, sir." That was two "sirs" in a row. I wasn't sure where they came from. Something about that military bearing. Maybe it was his unwavering confidence. Or maybe just the way he left no tone unsterned.

"You're talking to the other one," he said. Another statement.

"The other one?" I caught myself before I said "sir" again.

"Her sister," he answered.

"Rachel," Mrs. Williams said, a brief spark firing and extinguishing in her eyes.

"Why should we be talking to her?" I asked the colonel.

"That one," he paused, as if trying to find a euphemism strong enough to convey his disgust without offending anyone, "that woman she's involved with." He looked as if the words tasted sour as they passed through his mouth.

"Which one is that?" I asked. As a homicide detective, you see a wide variety of reactions to loss. As I listened to him, I had to make a concerted effort to keep my voice friendly and remind myself that I was talking to a grieving father. At least that's what he should have been. Maybe he was grieving on the inside.

"Just pay attention," Colonel Williams said, "and I'm sure you'll do fine."

"Pay attention," Jen said, as if the thought had never before occurred to her. "We'll be sure to do that."

The colonel looked at Jen, for the first time since we had entered the room, and gave her a slight nod. I began to wonder if his neck were capable of a full range of motion—or if the stick in his ass extended all the way up into his skull.

"Especially," I added, "to the other one."

Ruiz cut us off before it went any farther. "Danny, Jen. Why don't you two check in with Dave. See what he came up with."

"We already—"

Jen interrupted me. "Will do, Lieutenant."

"You two catch the man who did this," the colonel said.

"We'll do our best, Mr. Williams," I said. His lip twitched at the "mister."

Jen reached in front of the colonel and placed her hand on Mrs. Williams's arm. "I am sorry," she said. The woman looked up into Jen's eyes, seemingly surprised that someone had acknowledged her presence. She tried to smile, but it was a halfhearted attempt, and the expression didn't rise above her cheeks.

For just an instant, the contrast between the woman's smiling lips and her devastated eyes gave her the pained and confused look of someone who is just realizing that everything they had ever believed is a lie. In a sense, that was exactly the case—no one wants to believe that those they love, particularly their children, are actually mortal, that their deaths can come as swiftly and as easily as a phone call in the middle of the night. I wondered, in that moment, how much I really was learning about Mrs. Williams and if anyone else would ever see what I had just seen. I certainly didn't have much faith in the colonel's chances of understanding the depth of his wife's pain.

"Asshole," Jen said as I closed Ruiz's door behind us. The couple spent another ten minutes in Ruiz's office. When they left, Jen and I were sitting at our desks. Colonel Ronald P. Williams, USAF, Retired, gave us another semi-nod as he passed. His wife paused at the edge of Jen's desk.

"He's—" she caught herself in midsentence and looked down at her hands for a moment. When she looked up again, she simply said, "Thank you," and walked out the door with her husband.

"Semper Fi," I said.

"That's the Marines," Jen said.

"Same difference."

After we finished our reports and squared away our plans for the next day, I loaded my notes and copies of the day's paperwork in the leather postal-carrier bag I use for a briefcase.

"Want to grab some dinner?" I asked Jen.

"I've got plans."

"Plans?" I asked. "Family thing?" Jen was one of the few people I knew who actually came from a functional family. It was an unusual week if she didn't see her parents and brother at least once.

"No. Bob Kincaid and I are going to grab something."

"You've got a date with Dimple Boy?"

"It's not a date," she said. "He's looking for some martial arts classes for his son. I told him I'd help him out. And don't call him Dimple Boy. He's a nice guy."

"He's a lawyer."

"You want to come? I'm sure he wouldn't mind. We can go over the case."

"Thanks. I'll take a rain check," I said.

"Okay. See you tomorrow."

"Night," I said, looking at her clothes and wondering if she'd be wearing the same outfit in the morning.

At home I unloaded three supreme steak chalupas and a side of pintos 'n cheese from my Taco Bell drive-through bag, grabbed a Sam Adams from the refrigerator, and parked myself on the couch. I ate while I watched a rerun of *Jeopardy!*

"What is the Magna Carta?" I said, wiping sour cream from my chin. Slurping down the last of the refried beans, I finished just in time to turn off Pat Sajak before he and Vanna began their nightly repartee.

I threw my dinner trash in the can under the sink in the kitchen. On the counter were the week's dishes—six coffee cups, six teaspoons, and the one tall glass that usually only needed a rinse. I thought about washing them but decided against it. There were still two more of each in the cupboard. I opened the freezer and took out my Grey Goose and the shot glass I kept in there with the bottle.

Two drinks later, I was at the dining table, The Chieftains' *Long Black Veil* playing softly in the background, reading through my case notes, looking for anything that might stand out. I went through everything we'd done, everyone we'd talked to, every place we'd been, looking for a pattern that we hadn't seen yet, some connection we hadn't made. If there was anything there, it was beyond me, but still, I read through the notes two more times. You never know when something will click into place and the tumblers will begin to fall. I looked through the copy of the case file again too. Nothing new there, either. I went through everything again—and again, and again.

I tried to imagine the crime. Beth, sitting at her desk, grading papers, looking up startled to see—who? That was the question. I couldn't picture Harlan Gibbs on the other end of a blade like that. Maybe the last man she dated? He was still a cipher, though, just a name in her address book. Daryl Waxler. I couldn't imagine him at all. Not yet. I was still searching for the story.

Three insight-free hours later, I'd practically memorized my notes, and the exhaustion was taking hold. I knew I couldn't put off sleep any longer. I took another shot of vodka, brushed my teeth, and went to bed.

Once in a great while, in a small bar a block or two from a police station, an hour or so after last call, with empty beer bottles and shot glasses in front of him, a cop will speak in a quiet voice, almost as if embarrassed, of his dreams. Invariably, they are dreams of death. Images of those we find or of those we kill—or worst of all, of those who were our own. We don't speak of these dreams out of any particular need for understanding or to vent our emotions. We do it simply so that when those long nights come, and we lie awake in the darkness, we'll know that we're not alone, that for cops the nightmares are par for the course.

SEVEN

The first time I killed a man, I was still a rookie in uniform, responding to a 911, armed robbery in progress. In a North Long Beach 7-Eleven, a fifteen-year-old gangbanger named Walter Jackson opened up on a pregnant Vietnamese teenager with a pump-action twelve gauge, which he then turned on the clerk. When the time-controlled safe took too long to spit out another twenty bucks, Walter put the clerk down too. I arrived just as he was coming out the front door, trying to manage both the shotgun and a case of malt liquor. When he saw me, he dropped the bottles and turned the sawed-off barrel of the Remington toward me. I tapped four 9mm rounds into his chest, and he died in a puddle of blood and Colt 45.

That was ten years ago, and Walter doesn't visit often anymore. On this night, as on countless others, I dreamt of a Toyota Corolla northbound on I-5, not far past Valencia. The blue compact is following a tractor-trailer up a long incline. As they crest the hill, the truck brakes hard. The Toyota has left plenty of room to stop. The second eighteen-wheeler behind the Toyota, though, doesn't. It slams into the back of the Corolla and rams it forward into the rear end of the trailer. The compact car is crushed like a beer can between the two rigs. Gas begins to leak onto the ground and is ignited by a stray spark. The drivers of the trucks are unhurt. As they scramble onto the highway, they approach the Toyota, but the flames begin to spread. The two men move in closer and see a red-haired young woman with freckled cheeks and shining green eyes pinned in the driver's seat, bleeding profusely from her forehead, but the increasing heat drives them back.

I walk unseen past the two men, through the growing fire. The flames engulf me, but I feel no heat, only the cold wind blowing across the highway. The flames dance beside me as I approach the window of the Toyota, which has shattered. I move in very close, placing my hand on the roof and leaning over to look inside. The weather stripping and dashboard are already beginning to melt. The sheet metal pings. In quick succession the tires pop like gunshots.

From the driver's seat, Megan looks at me, her eyes wet, and says, "Save the baby, Danny, the baby."

"What baby?" I try to say, but no words come out of my mouth.

"Help us, Danny." She looks at me, pleading.

I want to ask, "How?" but still I say nothing.

The flames are engulfing the car. I can smell her hair beginning to burn. "Danny, please!" Megan screams. "The baby! Danny, the baby!" Her voice trails off into whimpering cries as I watch her skin redden and begin to burn. Her green eyes beg me to help. They are the most beautiful eyes I've ever seen, but I do nothing. Seconds later, the life drains out of them, and they pop, oozing fluid down her blistering cheeks, like thickened, boiling tears. I stand unhurt in a world of flames and watch my wife burn.

A psychologist once told me that my dreams were likely not any more vivid than most people's. The reason, she said, that I remembered them in such detail was that I was a light sleeper. Most people only remember the dreams they have shortly before waking, and because I wake frequently during the night, I remember more, she said. As for the disturbing images within the dreams and the fact that I place myself at the scene of Megan's death, the doctor simply added that it is not at all uncommon to dream of the dead and even involve ourselves in events in which we had no part, especially when we feel culpable in the death. I nodded as if I understood, as if I were cataloging the information for future reference. But ultimately, she was of little help.

It was after four a.m. when I woke. My head was resting on a cold, sweat-soaked pillow. Sitting up, I whispered Megan's name. Then I got out of bed, put on a hooded pullover sweatshirt, and went into the kitchen. I ran the tap until the water got as hot as it was going to get, filled a mug, and scooped in four teaspoons of instant coffee.

I stood in the living room for a minute, staring at the blank, black TV screen, thinking about turning it on. But I'd been here often enough to know that nothing that was on at four in the morning would come close to occupying my thoughts.

Behind the duplex in which I live is a small backyard I share with my upstairs neighbors. They keep a set of green, plastic Adirondack chairs on the well-tended lawn. I sat in one of them and sipped my bad coffee, staring at the sky and waiting for the first light of dawn.

EIGHT

The morning light came not in shafts of golden sunlight spill-ing over the horizon, but in the almost imperceptibly bright-ening grayness of the overcast sky. In a different season, we'd call it June gloom, but the Southern California weathermen hadn't yet come up with a catchy name for the phenomenon when it occurred in November. When the streetlights shut themselves off, an idea occurred to me. I went back inside and pulled a pair of Nikes onto my sockless feet, slipped my gun into the waistband of my shorts at the small of my back, and locked the front door behind me.

Half a block north, toward Seventh Street, Warren High came into view. I stood for a moment, eyeing the backs of the football bleachers. A freshly repainted six-foot-tall cartoon badger leered out at me from the wall behind the visitors' gate. He stood upright on his hind legs and flexed his biceps like a roidhead bodybuilder. His eyebrows were raised and his teeth bared in an expression that I assumed was meant to be a smile, but the fangs and the gleeful sparkle in the eyes came off as borderline psychotic.

Passing him, I began to walk along the fence around the school's perimeter, stopping here and there to peer through the chain links at, around, and between the assortment of buildings. I wondered what the neighbors might think if they saw me—a disheveled man, unshaven and unshowered, gazing intently through the high school fence, trying to catch a glimpse of what exactly? After I completed the first lap of the campus and saw the psycho badger again, I turned around and retraced my steps. Not once, from anywhere around the entire perimeter of the school, was I able to see the windows of Beth's classroom. Son of a bitch, I thought. Just might be on to something.

"News?" Ruiz asked. Marty, Jen, Dave, and I were crowded around the desk in the lieutenant's office.

"One lead worth checking out," I said. "Guy she met on the Internet and went out with a few times."

"Grieving boyfriend?" Dave looked hopeful. A smear of powdered doughnut sugar clung to the corner of his mouth. "What are we waiting for?"

"Ex," Jen said. "She cut him loose a while back. No priors."

"Still…" Marty said.

"I know. We're looking at him today." Jen sucked smoothie through a straw. I couldn't tell what kind it was, something with an orangey tint—at least it wasn't the green weed juice. She'd brought me another strawberry banana.

"How are we working it?" Ruiz asked.

"Got through about half the faculty and staff yesterday," Dave said. "Do the rest today. Nothing much yet. Nobody with a bloody knife in their back pocket."

"ViCAP, NCIC?" Ruiz asked. The Violent Criminals Apprehension Program and the National Crime Information Center were both federally funded through the Department of Justice and ran databases through which local law enforcement agencies could run criminal MOs to compare them nationwide for possible matches.

"Still waiting." Dave slurped out of a bright yellow mug. "They keep giving me some kind of weekend-backlog crap. Should know about any hits soon."

"Marty?" Ruiz asked.

"Nothing new on forensics." Marty rubbed his temples with the thumb and middle finger of his left hand and then slid his palm down his face, as if it were a wrinkled shirt that he was trying to smooth. "You know what we're looking at here, Boss?" His eyes turned to Ruiz.

"No," Ruiz said.

"It's got all the signs of a disorganized serial," Marty said.

"News flash, partner," Dave said, the fluorescent light glinting on his scalp, "one murder ain't a serial."

"Still," Jen said, "Marty's right. That's exactly what it looks like. Serial or no, this is a textbook disorganized sexual predator."

"So?" Ruiz asked, as if he didn't follow. He'd always been big on the whole leading-question, Socratic-method thing.

No one said anything. I was staring out the window at the unbroken gray sky when Jen turned her head toward me. "What?" she asked.

"I didn't say anything," I said.

"What?" Ruiz was rolling with the monosyllables.

"It's not that simple," I said.

"Why not?" Marty asked.

"Think about it. What are the signs of a disorganized predator?" I asked.

"Extreme violence," Jen said. "Trophy taking."

"No attempt to dispose of the body," Marty added.

"Makes a fucking mess," Dave said.

"Random victim." Ruiz was beginning to see it.

"Leaves physical evidence." Jen picked it up too.

Marty shook his head slowly. "I don't know…"

"Somebody wanna fill me in here?" Dave asked.

"Danny thinks we've got us a criminal mastermind on our hands," Marty said.

"I'm not sure I'd go that far," I said, "but think about it. Number one—and I checked this out this morning—there's no way the doer could have seen Beth alone in her classroom from outside the school. Makes it unlikely that she's a random victim. Two, there's no trace of physical evidence. Means he's either very careful or very lucky. So, we know he's done his homework picking the vic. It follows he's going to be careful with the evidence, right? Then why such a mess?"

"Okay," Dave said. "I'm with you so far."

"We've got to wonder," I went on, "is it just a set of contradictory facts, which I'm not ruling out, or was the whole thing planned to look exactly the way it does?"

"You're asking how sharp is the doer?" Dave asked.

Marty spread his hands. "Come on," he said. "You know what you're suggesting? He plans this whole thing out, every detail, in advance, just to make it look like he didn't plan it out? Why?"

"I don't know," I said. "Maybe to throw us off."

"Are you serious?" Marty shook his head. "What? The killer's some kind of evil genius? Come on." He snorted a laugh. "How often we bust one of those?"

"Oh, evil geniuses," Dave chimed in. "They're right up there with the crack whores and gangbangers."

"I'm just saying we have to be open to the possibility that he may be smarter than we want to admit," I said. "What's the alternative?"

"The alternative?" Marty thought for a moment. "The doer is a planner, okay? Takes his time, plans it out, all the details. But it's his first time, right? So he doesn't know what's going to happen to him when he actually starts. Once he's in there, hacking away, he loses it—can't keep control, shoots his wad, whatever. He gets so excited the plan goes out the window. The organization goes to shit, and we wind up with the mess he left us with." Marty sat back in his chair

"Maybe," I said. "Maybe. Either way, though, we're looking for someone who planned the crime. That means access to Beth of one kind or another before the murder. And it means we have to go at him like an organized, no matter how the scene ended up."

"Touché," Marty said.

"Still," Ruiz said, "don't rule anything out."

"Especially evil geniuses," Jen said.

Upstairs, Pat Glenn sat in the blue glow of three computer monitors, his fingers working the keys in front of him with short and sudden bursts of speed that sounded like suppressed automatic weapon fire.

"Hey, Danny," he said, without looking up. "Check this out." He swiveled the monitor toward me, and I saw a screen-ful of knives. On display was an online cutlery catalog for a company called The Cutting Edge. "Right here," Pat said, pointing to a large blade at the bottom of the screen.

"Can you make that bigger?"

He slid the little arrow onto the blade and double-clicked. A full-color photo of what the catalog copy called a Gurkha kukri filled the screen. The knife looked something like a lopsided boomerang, with the cutting edge curving downward and widening before tapering into a point. According to the specs, the stainless-steel blade was eleven inches long, and the handle was made of a black plastic called Micarta. A small inset photo showed a burly man chopping though a piece of lumber, and the caption proclaimed, "Our kukri cuts through a 1x3 in a single stroke!"

"Look like a murder weapon to you, Danny?" Pat asked.

"Maybe so," I said. "How soon can we get one?"

"Already ordered two." He leaned back in his ergonomic chair and grinned. "Be here tomorrow. Rush order."

"Good work."

Pat opened the small refrigerator at his feet and pulled out a can of Coke. It popped and fizzed as he opened it. "So," he said, "what brings you upstairs?"

"E-mail," I said. "Can we get into Beth's account?"

"Legally or practically?"

"Both."

"Well, mostly it depends on her ISP." He took a long drink from his Coke and swallowed. "See, if she had an account through the school district—or any employer, really—we'd just need their permission because, technically speaking, it's their property. But she has AOL. That's a private account, so it's hers, and that gives her a reasonable expectation of privacy."

"So we need a court order?"

"Legally, yes."

"Practically?"

He wrote his answer on a Post-it note. Jen and I had some work to do before I'd have a chance to pry into Beth's e-mail.

NINE

Daryl Waxler lived in Palos Verdes, an exclusive community on the peninsula that jutted from the LA County shoreline and divided the South Bay from its less well-heeled neighbors, Wilmington and San Pedro. We were riding in Jen's Explorer as she drove out of Long Beach and across the Vincent Thomas Bridge over Los Angeles Harbor. Along the deepwater canals on both sides of us, cranes towered above worn docks, surrounded by thousands of multicolored containers that looked like huge rusted LEGOs, waiting to be snapped onto the flatbeds of trucks and trains. The unmistakable smell of the harbor—a mixture of engine oil, smog, and dead fish, carried on a fresh ocean breeze—blew in through the vents. At the other end of the bridge, we spent thirty seconds southbound on the Harbor Freeway and then headed up the hill into some of the priciest real estate in Southern California.

"Find out anything interesting about our pal Daryl?" I asked.

"Not much," she said. "Forty-six. Widowed three years ago. One son, Daryl Jr., eighteen, with a sealed juvie record. A little bad fathering, maybe?"

"Might be," I said. "What else?"

"Works as some kind of real estate development exec. Minimalls and such. Made close to five hundred thou last year and lives on two acres."

"Two acres in Palos Verdes? That's worth what? Five or six million?"

"Not even close. He's got an unobstructed view of the bay. Try eleven or twelve."

"Shit. Where'd the rest of the money come from?"

"Apparently, Daryl's an astute investor. Bought Microsoft and Cisco back in the trickle-down years."

"Anything hinky about him?"

"Had his Range Rover towed from a no-parking zone last year, but apparently the kid was driving, so I don't know if that counts."

"How'd the wife die?"

"Complications from breast cancer."

"Probably safe to assume he didn't kill her then, huh?"

Jen gave me a courtesy smile and turned onto Malaga Cove Road. The blue-gray expanse of the Pacific came into view. It was a nice view, but not one I'd pay ten million for. Maybe it was better on sunny days.

We drove through an open gate that split a long brick wall into two massive halves. "Daryl must not be too big on security," I said.

"It's Sunday. Maybe he put his faith in God."

Expansive lawns planted with huge oak trees flanked the long, curving driveway. Beyond the trees, the edges of the property faded away into well-tended greenness. The inside of the wall was hidden completely by lush plant growth. This was the kind of neighborhood in which the residents didn't want to be reminded that seven-foot brick walls were the only things separating them from the rest of the world.

Jen slowed to a stop in the circular parking area in front of a surprisingly unassuming two-story, Spanish Colonial–style home. But the landscaped gardens, the fresh tan stucco, the leafless red-tile roof, and the five-car garage matched the price tag of the address. We got out and followed a walkway that had been tiled to match the roof, inset with polished blue and brown squares, until we reached the expansive porch. I pushed the doorbell button next to the double oak doors and looked at Jen.

"Eat the rich," she said.

I rang the bell again. Thirty seconds later, a shadow moved across the frosted-glass inset in the door.

"Who's there?" the dark shape asked.

"Police." Jen and I held up our badges.

The door opened three inches, and a nervous blue eye peeked out over the safety chain.

"We're looking for Daryl Waxler," Jen said.

The door closed enough to allow the person inside to unfasten the chain and then opened again. "That's me. I'm Daryl. Everybody calls me D.J., though." D.J. was tall with shaggy blond hair. A blue, pigment-dyed tank top and baggy, knee-length shorts hung on his lanky frame. He shuffled his bare feet on an expensive-looking rug. "Is this about the accident the other night?" His eyes darted back and forth from Jen to me.

"What accident?" I asked.

His mouth hung open for a moment as he realized that he had spoken too soon. Jen let him off the hook. "What's the D.J. stand for? Daryl Jr.?"

"Yeah," he said, shifting his weight back and forth.

"It's okay, D.J.," Jen said. "We're not interested in the accident. Can we come in?" He exhaled audibly, and his posture unraveled into a comfortable slouch. Taking a step back, he ushered us into the foyer. Twelve feet behind him, on the far wall, a full-length mirror reflected our images. To the right, a short hallway led into the kitchen. Straight ahead was the sunken and very large living room. He leaned on the edge of the open door.

"Actually," I said, "we're looking for your father. We need to ask him a few questions. Is he home?"

D.J. looked down at the rug on the polished hardwood floor. "No, he's not here."

"Do you know when he'll be back?" Jen asked.

"Tuesday."

"Not until then?" Jen looked at me in the mirror.

"No," he said, "Dad's at some conference in San Diego. One of his consulting things."

"When did he leave?" she asked.

"Thursday morning."

"Did you know a woman named Elizabeth Williams?" I asked.

"Elizabeth? No, I don't...wait, you mean Beth? My dad's girlfriend?"

Jen raised an eyebrow at me. "Is he still seeing her?" she asked him.

"Well, no," he said. "I guess it's more like she's his ex-girlfriend." He looked at Jen, then at me, then back at Jen. "Is she all right?"

"That's what we need to talk to your dad about," I said. "Do you have a bathroom I could use?"

"Sure," he said. "You can use mine. Just go through the kitchen and into the hall. It's the first door on the left."

As I walked through the kitchen, I heard Jen speaking behind me. "So," she said, "do you go to Palos Verdes High?"

"I graduated last spring," D.J. said, deepening his voice. That'll impress her, I thought. The Waxler kitchen, on the other hand, was impressive even to me. The space was at least twenty by twenty, with three walls taken up by vast expanses of stainless steel, oak, and polished granite. The fourth wall, except for a freestanding island equipped with stools on three sides, was open to a coastline view that stretched all the way to the north end of Santa Monica Bay.

I walked through the kitchen and, following D.J.'s directions, found myself in a similarly oversized bathroom. Tiled all around, with double sinks and separate tub and shower stalls, it was nearly as big as my bedroom. The only things that made the room even moderately tolerable was the crust of dried toothpaste in one sink and the overflowing dirty-clothes hamper next to a second open door.

Instead of relieving myself, I poked my head into D.J.'s room. Furnished in late modern-teenage-boy, the mess was at least consistent—dirty clothes draped over anything drapable, a skateboard upside down and three feet from the nearest wall, a helmet another two feet away from that, a single dirty sock in the middle of a king-sized pillow. Hanging over the unmade bed, two posters shared the wall. In the first, Samuel L. Jackson glared out at me in full SWAT gear, looking at once exponentially cooler and more menacing than Steve Forrest ever could have imagined. The second poster was from the LA County Coroner's Office gift shop—a white victim outline on a black background over the words "Got Death?" The logo had been a huge hit for the coroner—especially among homicide crews—until the milk people sent a cease-and-desist letter to the county supervisor's office last year.

In the corner of the room was a large, L-shaped computer desk, on which was perched what I assumed to be the latest big-screen titanium Apple notebook computer. The power was on, and a cartoon Japanese swordsman spun in choppy circles across the screen, in front of the name "Samurai Jack," which was displayed in a font designed to mimic the brushstrokes of Japanese calligraphy.

But the bookshelf next to the desk was what really caught my attention. A familiar-looking spine jumped out at me from the top shelf. I moved in closer and saw a textbook I remembered from both my college and academy days. *Criminal Investigation*. I scanned the rest of the titles. The top shelf was full of academic texts on criminal justice, recognizable to just about anyone who'd majored in the subject and probably to just about anyone who'd ever been through a major city's police academy: *Practical Homicide Investigation*, *Criminalistics: An Introduction to Forensic Science*, *Techniques of Crime Scene Investigation*, *The Forensic Casebook*. D.J. had more cop books than most cops I knew. On the lower shelves, he had a section devoted to true crime, and below that crime fiction. He seemed particularly fond of James Ellroy, Elmore Leonard, and Richard Stark. D.J. was into the cops and robbers.

I didn't want to take too long, so I went back into the bathroom, relieved myself, washed my hands, and headed back out to join Jen and D.J. The foyer was empty. They had retired to the living room, where they were sharing the leather sofa.

"Hey, Danny," Jen said as I took the two steps down into the room. "D.J.'s going to major in criminal justice at Long Beach State next semester."

He smiled sheepishly at me, as if he was used to people frowning upon his chosen career path. "My alma mater," I said.

"That's what I told him."

I looked at D.J. "It's a top-notch program. I made detective less than four years after I graduated."

"Really?" he asked.

"You want to be a detective?" I asked.

"Yes sir, I do."

"I think that's great. Don't get too many kids from Palos Verdes signing up for police work." Law school, maybe, I thought, and for the very civic-minded, maybe a three-year stint in the district attorney's office before moving into the private sector. Not many of the locals even enroll at Long Beach State, for that matter. The ones who don't make it to the Ivy League or to the University of California usually have their parents buy them a nice private-college education. That's how USC earned its nickname, University of Spoiled Children.

Jen stood up, and D.J. rose in response. "We should get moving," she said. He walked us to the door and out onto the porch.

"Thanks, D.J.," Jen said, handing him a business card. "Ask your dad to give us a call when he comes home, okay?" She shook his hand and held it just a second or two longer than she should have.

"Sure," he said.

I nodded at him. "Have a nice day."

After a moment's pause, in which his gaze drifted from me to Jen and back again, he smiled at us and replied, "You too."

Walking back down the tiled path, I waited for the heavy sound of the closing door but didn't hear it. When we were a safe distance away, I whispered, "He's watching us." I turned my head just enough to see Jen nod. As we drove toward the gate, Jen said, "What do you make of that?"

"Him watching?"

"Yeah."

"Nothing," I said. "But I think you've got yourself another groupie. Seems like a nice kid."

Jen caught my eyes in the rearview mirror. "So," she said, a bit of hardness in her voice, "I guess Waxler's alibied for Friday night."

"Won't hurt to check it out," I said.

"What is that?" she asked. "Strike three?"

"Couldn't say. I'm not big on baseball metaphors."

On our way back, we stopped for lunch at Ruby's, a retro-themed restaurant franchise on the ground floor of The Shops at Palos Verdes. Several years before, I'd worked a murder on a joint task force with the LA County Sheriff's Department. Then, The Shops had been simply an upscale suburban shopping mall. Since then, though, someone with a lot of money decided that traditional enclosed malls weren't the rage any-more and ripped the top off the place. They covered the walls in beige-pink stucco, planted a few trees and little patches of grass, and—presto change-o—the mall was now a trendy open-air shopping plaza. But the ivy-covered hillside behind the four-level parking structure remained unchanged, and the memory of a thirteen-year-old boy named Jesus Rojas, whose body had been found there, still seemed to hang in the air. I wondered if anyone else noticed it.

Jen needed a restroom, so while I waited, I killed time by wandering along and looking in the shop windows. I paused in front of a jewelry store's display of men's watches. The Seiko on my wrist had seen better days—the crystal was scratched, the bezel nicked and dinged, the stainless-and-gold finish of the band worn to a dull sheen, and the batteries seemed to wear out quicker and quicker. After nearly eleven years of almost constant wear, it was probably due for retirement. But it had been a gift. Megan had given it to me to celebrate my college graduation.

"Finally buying a new watch?" Jen asked. I'd never told her where I'd gotten the old one.

"Nah, just looking."

Ruby's was on the ground floor, next to an ice-skating rink, and both had survived the mall's scalping relatively intact. Jen and I sat down among the Sunday afternoon crowd of angst-ridden teens and trophy wives, who gazed out at their daughters on the ice with Olympic ambition in their eyes. I ordered a cheeseburger and a vanilla malt. Jen had a chicken sandwich and iced tea.

"How's your brother?" I asked between french fries.

"Got his MCAT scores back."

"Yeah? How'd he do?"

"Better than he expected. Ninety-eighth percentile."

"That as good as it sounds?"

"Yeah," she said. "With those scores and his grades, he can go to med school pretty much anywhere he wants."

"Your folks must be proud."

"They are." She was watching a dark-haired girl of about twelve spinning in place on the ice.

"What about you?" I asked.

"I'm proud too."

"Johnny's a good kid," I said. "He's worked hard. He deserves this."

The girl on the ice jumped and spun in the air. "I used to skate," Jen said.

"I didn't know that."

She looked back at me and took a drink of her tea. "Danny," she said, "there's a lot you don't know." I wasn't sure how to take that.

Back in the car, Jen dialed a number on her cell. "Hello. Can I speak to Rudy, please?" She didn't get the answer she was hoping for. "He's not? Is this Michelle? Hi, this is Sensei Jen. Do you remember me? We met when Rudy took the test for his green belt." She gave the girl on the other end a moment to process the information. "Yes, that's right." She smiled at something she heard. "I'm fine. How are you? That's good. Would you ask Rudy to call me as soon as he can?" Jen asked the girl to write down her phone number and then made sure the girl repeated it back to her correctly. Then she thanked her and hung up.

"He still hasn't been to class, huh?"

"Nope."

"He's how old?"

"Seventeen."

"Doesn't mean he's doing bad," I said, more out of blind hope than confidence. I didn't want to see Jen hurt again.

She started the car and backed out of the parking spot without answering.

"Damn it," Ruiz said. "Where's Dave?" Marty hunched his shoulders. Jen and I looked down at our laps. The plan had been for the four of us to meet in the lieutenant's office and fill him in before we all headed upstairs to sit down with the rest of the task force. Dave was nowhere to be found.

"Marty?" Ruiz asked, his black copstache curling with his lip.

"Don't look at me," Marty said, raising his hands from his lap with his palms held outward. "I'm his partner, not his mother." He was trying to stay calm, but I could see the tension in the clench of his jaw.

"I've had it," Ruiz said. "If he doesn't get his shit together, I'm going to take—"

The door opened, and Dave came in with a broad grin on his face and a thick file folder in his hands.

"Where the hell you been?" Ruiz stood behind his desk.

"What?" Dave stopped just inside the door. He looked confused.

"You're fifteen minutes late, Dave." The Texas inflections were creeping back into the lieutenant's voice.

"Sorry, Boss." Dave began to lift the folder as if he wanted Ruiz to look at it. "But you've got to—"

"I don't want to hear any of your excuses."

"Look, if you'll just—"

"I'm sick and tired of this. You're a disgrace. You disrespect me. You disrespect the squad. You should be ashamed of yourself, you—"

Dave threw the file folder like a Frisbee into Ruiz's chest. It bounced off, and papers scattered all over the desk and floor.

"ViCAP came back with a hit," Dave said. "A matching MO. I was running it down with Organized Crimes. It's all in the file." He slammed the door behind him on his way out.

Ruiz grunted and looked down at the mess of papers. He shook his head and stood there, ignoring us. After half a dozen deep breaths, he put his hand in his pocket, jingled some change, and walked out without a word.

The rest of us sat there in silence. I watched the brass hands on the clock behind Ruiz's desk circle the faux-marble dial. A small engraved plaque on the base read "Compliments of Ocean Crest Credit Union." After a minute and seventeen seconds, Jen spoke.

"They say it might rain tonight," she said.

"Yeah?" Marty said.

"I think it was a thirty percent chance."

"Really?"

"Yeah."

Twenty-four seconds of silence.

"I like the rain," Marty said.

"Me too," she said.

Thirty-eight seconds.

"How long do we wait?" I asked.

"Supposed to be upstairs in ten minutes," Jen said. "Should we pick up the papers?"

"It's not our file," Marty said.

"Well," I said, "since procedure already seems to be deteriorating…"

Jen went for the papers on the floor around the far end of the desk, I took the near end, and Marty started gathering the pages that had landed on top of the desk. When we'd put together three neat piles and were sorting through them, the door opened, and Dave poked his head in.

"The lieutenant wants us all upstairs." He looked at us trying to make sense out of the mess of papers in our hands. Ruiz had managed to turn the heat down, but the anger still burned behind his eyes. "What are you doing with my file?"

Ten minutes later, the task force was assembled in the conference room. Deputy Chief Baxter was the only absentee. None of us was knocking ourselves out to track him down. The lieutenant and Dave were all pleasant smiles, buddy-buddy, but if you looked close, you could see the residual anger in the tightness of Dave's neck, the tension in Ruiz's jaw, the way they refused to make eye contact.

"We may have a break," Ruiz said. Immediately the table quieted. "Dave came up with a hit through ViCAP. I'll let him fill you in."

"Just got this a few minutes ago," Dave said, "so no copies on any of this yet. Here's what we got. Guy named—shit, how do you say this?" He paused and looked down at his notes. "Yev...uh...Yevgeny Tropov? Something like that. Two years ago, Seattle police find a woman hacked up, just like our teacher. They get lucky, though. A witness spots a car, traces to this Tropov.

"Further investigation yields some matching fiber evidence. They think they got a case, right? Turns out this guy's a big-time button man for the Russian mob. The dead woman's the wife of some petty bureaucrat, a city commissioner or something, who's been on the take with the Russians and wants out. Now, the city guy and his wife have been trying for years to have a baby, and she's finally managed to get herself knocked up. They're all happy and shit, right? So this is why the guy wants out—so he can make a clean start with the new family and live happily ever after. The Russians, though, they have other ideas. They send Tropov to make an object lesson out of the wife. He takes a machete and goes to town. Chops out her womb, baby and all."

One of the guys from Missing Persons whispered, "Jesus," looking down at the table.

"That's not all," Dave went on. "The clincher is Tropov's a local now. Been working out of Long Beach Harbor. Organized Crime spotted him two months ago working with a smuggling crew they're trying to nail."

"If Seattle had a case," Jen asked, "why didn't they put him away?"

"The Russians play hardball," Ruiz said. "First the witness disappeared, then one of the jurors. Wound up in a mistrial, and without the witness, the DA didn't have enough to refile the case."

Everyone at the table turned toward Kincaid. Cops always blame the lawyers. We can't seem to help it.

"So what's our next move?" Marty asked.

"Pick him up," Ruiz said.

TEN

I once read that when children suffer an emotional trauma, their minds can wipe themselves clean of not only the memories of the event itself, but also of much or all of what happened before. Sometimes, late at night, I'll close my eyes and try to remember something or other that occurred in my first six years, something I'd seen in an old photo album or on one of the old Super Eight home movies stored in the back of my mother's closet. There's only one event I'm ever able to recall.

It's a warm late fall day, not long before I'll begin the first grade. I'm riding my Big Wheel around the driveway, into the empty garage, and out again, circling around my father's sky blue metallic Plymouth Fury. The sunlight gleams off the fresh wax job as if the entire car were plated in translucent silver. He's inside the car, crunched down onto the floorboard and working on something under the dash. As I loop around the car's rear end, plastic wheels rattling across rough asphalt, I turn wide to swerve around my father's feet, protruding from the passenger door. I don't know how many laps I did, but it seemed as if I were riding a perpetual motion machine made of red and yellow plastic, as if I'd been going forever and might never stop. But I do stop.

As I make a tight left turn at the rear of the garage and the Plymouth comes back into view, my father sits up in the driver's seat. He calls to me.

"Hey, Danny." He's grinning broadly as I ride up and stop the Big Wheel next to the open driver's door. When I put my feet down and stand up, I can feel the hot asphalt through the thin soles of my Keds.

"Come here, champ," he says as he lifts me across his lap and plops me down on the blue vinyl seat next to him. He smells like sweat and Aqua Velva. "Look at this," he says. There is a new metal-and-plastic box about the size of my Snoopy lunch pail attached to the bottom of the matte-finished-steel dashboard. It has a rectangular opening and half a dozen buttons on its front. "You know what that is?" Dad asks me. I shake my head and look up at him. Drops of perspiration trickle from his crew cut and down the sides of his tanned face. "It's a tape player," he says, smiling. "It's for music. What do you say we give it a try?" He turns and reaches for something on the backseat. He pushes a red plastic cartridge into the slot, and I wait. Nothing happens.

"What's wrong?" I ask.

"Not a thing," he says. "You just need to push right there." He points.

I reach out and touch the button. "Here?"

"That's it. Just push."

I do. After a few seconds of fuzzy static, the music begins—Johnny Cash singing "Folsom Prison Blues." I look up at my father, and he smiles down at me and puts his hand on my shoulder. "It doesn't get any better than this, Danny boy." I smile up at him.

Four days before Christmas that year, my father pulled his LA County Sheriff's cruiser to a stop outside a small tract home in Carson. He was riding alone that day because his partner had called in sick. He was answering a call about a domestic disturbance, a neighbor complaining about the noise made by an arguing couple next door. He got out of the cruiser, pulled on his hat, and slipped his baton into the O-ring on his belt.

Yells and shouts were audible from the curb in front of the house. My father crossed the lawn. The neighbor who phoned in the report later said he heard a man inside scream "goddamn bitch" and the sound of breaking glass. My father rapped on the door with his knuckles. No one answered. He pounded harder, with the bottom of his fist, and announced loudly, "Sheriff's Department, open up!"

The man who unlocked the door wavered, grasping the frame for balance. "You got no business here," said the man, slurring the *s* sounds in his words.

"We've had complaints about the noise," my father said.

"This is private."

"I need to see your wife, sir."

"No, you don't," he said. "It's none of your fucking business!" He shoved my father back and followed him onto the porch. The drunk lunged and missed, his momentum carrying him onto the lawn. He spun and threw a wild punch. My father ducked it, stepped behind the drunk, and raked his baton down hard across the man's hamstring, collapsing him into a groaning pile. Pulling the drunk's right arm behind his back, my father kneeled on the man's spine and snapped a cuff around his wrist.

He was pulling the man's left arm around when the wife stepped onto the porch with a double-barreled twelve-gauge

coach gun and pulled both triggers. The blast caught my father just above his left hip and nearly cut him in two. Less
than twenty minutes later, he was pronounced dead on arrival
at Harbor General Hospital.

I have copies of all the police reports and witness statements—even a full transcript of the trial that sent the woman
to prison for life. The man did twenty on a conspiracy-to-
commit charge. Once a year or so, usually around Christmas,
I dig the documents out of the closet and read through them
again. I'm not sure why I feel compelled to do this. Maybe just
to be sure he's really gone.

It had been dark for half an hour when we got the go order. Marty, Jen, and I had been in the back of an unmarked
Ford Econoline van with another detective who had been assigned to the task force, a woman from Violent Crimes named
Hoskins. We were parked a block up the street from the house
in which Tropov was known to be residing. He'd been seen
returning home around dinnertime and hadn't left. We were
waiting for Ruiz to call and let us know if Kincaid had been
able to rush an arrest warrant. Marty's phone chirped.

He said "Yeah?" into it and listened. "It's a go," he said to
us. He clicked the mic on his radio headset. "Dave, you get
that?"

"Yep." Dave's voice spilled out of each of our earphones.

"We've got a green light." Dave was in the alley behind
Tropov's house with another of the task force detectives. "Let
us know when everybody's set, Butler," Marty said to the narc
watching the front of the house. "You with us?"

"Roger," we heard in our earpieces. "Ready whenever
you are."

Marty moved to the front of the van and slipped into the seat behind the steering wheel. He left the headlights off and pulled up to the curb in front of the house next to Tropov's. As we moved, Hoskins, Jen, and I made a last check of our weapons and tightened the straps on our Kevlar vests. Butler, a lanky black man, met Marty at the driver's door. Marty turned to Jen and me. "You two go," he said. "Let me know as soon as you're in position."

Jen and I got out of the van and approached the house. It was a fifty-year-old two-bedroom with peeling off-white paint and wood eaten by termites and dry rot. Yellowing weeds grew in every exposed bit of dirt. There were three doors. Marty's crew would take the front, Dave's the back, and Jen and I the side.

As we made our way along the side of the house, Jen held her Glock .40 in her right hand and a Maglite in her left. I had a pump-action Remington 870 riot gun in the low ready position, butt against my shoulder, muzzle to the ground.

We took positions on either side of the door. Beyond the frame, Jen crouched under what looked like a kitchen window. "We're set," I whispered into the mic attached to my ear.

"Dave?" Marty asked.

"Set."

"Stand by." Marty's voice was calm, but the adrenaline was pumping, and I knew that I wasn't the only one listening to the sound of my own heartbeat. Jen and I made eye contact, and we each gave a nod. She held my gaze while we waited for Marty's command. Her hand touched the knob and gave it a gentle twist. She nodded. Unlocked. At least we wouldn't have to kick it.

"Ready." Marty's voice crackled in our ears.

In my head I began counting. One one thousand, two one thousand...

"Go!" Almost simultaneously we heard the crack of the forced front door and the shattering of the rear sliding glass.

Jen opened the door and braced her gun against the Maglite in her left hand. I switched on the light attached to the magazine tube of the Remington. From the cover of the door frame, we swept the circles of light across the walls of the kitchen.

"Clear," I said.

"Clear," she echoed.

I was facing the only door in the room. "Door on the right."

"Covering," she said.

I stepped into the kitchen and moved past Jen. She stood, and both of our lights illuminated a faded and stained green door. Circling around an old Formica-topped table, I checked the hinges—the door opened into the kitchen. From the front of the house, I heard the sound of wood splintering, then quiet. I moved toward the door.

Tropov was smart. As soon as I began to turn the knob, the door burst open and knocked me sideways into the refrigerator. Before Jen could get a clear look, Tropov was across the room, crashing into her, and the two of them tumbled out the exterior door. I scrambled across the kitchen, knocking the table into the stove with my thigh as I passed.

Through the door I saw them struggling. He was on top of her, pinning her with one hand and raising the other above his head, holding what appeared to be an ice pick. Everything slowed down, and the color seemed to fade from my field of vision, as if someone were turning a knob on an old TV. I felt a burning sensation behind my eyes.

With Jen beneath him, I didn't have a clear shot. I charged them, raising the Remington above my head. I cleared ten feet in three steps and rammed the butt into the side of his neck. He screamed—more, it seemed, in rage than pain.

The blow threw Tropov off balance, and Jen attempted an escape. My second stroke raked upward, and the sharp edge of the butt caught him in the jaw. The force of the blow lifted him enough so that Jen, with a deft twist, could slip out from beneath him. As he stood up, I threw my weight into the next blow and caught him with the stock in the rib cage. His wind burst out of him, and I shoved him hard against the wall of the house. I slammed the shotgun's stock into his abdomen. Before he could recover, I did it again and then again. From somewhere far away, I thought I heard someone call my name.

I pointed the muzzle of the Remington at Tropov's chest and flicked off the safety. As my finger slipped into the trigger guard, I saw the cold emptiness in his eyes and knew, with a certainty I've only rarely glimpsed, that I would kill him.

"Danny!" I felt Jen's hands on my shoulders, tugging me back. "Danny," she said, her voice soft in my ears, "I'm okay."

I heard Marty's voice behind me and heard the others coming through the kitchen. Tropov leaned against the wall, barely able to prop himself up. His eyes stayed locked on mine until Dave and two other cops shoved him face-first into the weeds, patted him down, and cuffed his hands behind his back.

Dave picked up a Phillips-head screwdriver and held it up to the light. "Check it out," he said. "This look like a deadly weapon to you, Marty?"

"Yes, it does." Marty knelt down next to Tropov, took a good look at his face to make sure it matched the black-and-white mug shot we'd all memorized that afternoon, and told him he was under arrest.

"You okay, partner?" Jen pulled me a few feet away and took the Remington out of my hands. I didn't want to let go.

"Yeah." I looked at her. "You?"

"Son of a bitch ripped my Windbreaker."

"Nice work, kids." Marty clapped me on the shoulder. "You want to hang out and wait for the Crime Scene Unit or go with us to take him back to the house?"

I stuck my hands in my jacket pockets and clenched them into fists so I wouldn't have to feel them shaking. From far off in the distance, I heard a lone train whistle crying in the night.

ELEVEN

Tropov didn't make it back to the station, at least not right away. He lost consciousness as Marty and Dave were dragging him to their car, so they took him to Long Beach Memorial instead. That left Jen and me to fill Ruiz in on the arrest. When we finished, I looked down at the paperwork on the table in front of me and pretended to read. But I could feel the lieutenant's eyes drilling into my forehead.

"How bad was he hurt?" Ruiz asked.

I looked up at him and shrugged my shoulders. He turned to Jen and raised his eyebrows.

"Bad," she said. When she saw his expression, she added, "Probably nothing permanent."

"Probably?" Ruiz said, snorting and shaking his head. He turned to me again. "Well, he's mobbed up, so at least we don't have to worry about a lawsuit."

"No," Jen said. "Just about him popping out of an alley somewhere and firing a twenty-two into the back of Danny's head." Ruiz parted his lips, but then closed his mouth, clenched his jaw, and left the room without saying anything else.

A few minutes later, Marty called to let us know they were bringing in Tropov. The docs had wanted to keep him overnight for observation, betting on a concussion, but after they'd stitched his split eyebrow, set his broken nose, and bandaged his cracked ribs, he declined further treatment and insisted on leaving the hospital. If he did have a concussion, I thought, that might work to our advantage.

Ruiz had gone home for the night, but Jen and I were still busy updating the paperwork.

"How do you think we should go at him?" I asked her.

"Marty'll take the interrogation."

"Maybe I should do it. After what went down, he might rattle."

She looked at me, and the corners of her mouth curled up. "Danny, get real."

"What?"

"You think just because Ruiz is gone any of us are going to let you get in the box with somebody you just beat the crap out of?"

"I'm guessing no?"

"Don't try to be cute." She turned her face back down to the report in front of her.

"Jen?"

She locked her eyes on mine. "You were going to kill him," she said. "You had him, and you were still going to do it."

"What are—"

"Don't." I tried to defend myself, but she wouldn't let me. "Just don't. You might be able to bullshit yourself, but not me." She flipped her file shut and took it with her as she left the room, stopping briefly at the door to turn and look at me, a weary sadness in her eyes.

Tropov's arms hung down at his sides, each hand cuffed separately to a leg of the Korean Conflict–era metal chair in which he sat. His left eye and nose were a swollen and misshapen mass of purple-black flesh. Dried blood caked his nostrils, and his bottom lip jutted to the right. With his black hair and the discolored skin of his face atop his narrow shoulders, he looked like a burnt match.

"What do you think?" Dave whispered.

"About what?" I asked.

"Tropov." Dave lifted his chin toward the two-way mirror.

"He's a piece of shit," I said.

Dave let out a satisfied grunt.

"But he's not our guy."

"What?" His eyes widened. He was actually surprised. "I think you're wrong on this one," he said quietly, regaining his confidence.

"I know you feel like you have a big stake in this, tracking down Tropov and all, but you shouldn't. A rookie uniform could have phoned that MO into ViCAP and done the follow up. It didn't take Joe Fucking Friday."

Dave blinked twice, turned away from me, and began throwing switches and pushing buttons on the recording equipment.

Jen stood against the wall of the interview room, arms crossed, staring at Tropov, and Marty sat across the table from him. Dave and I watched from behind the mirror. In addition to the video camera, which was mounted high in the corner of the room and would create the official record of the interrogation, we were also rolling an audiotape and a second video camera. It occurred to me that we were also doing an outstanding job of capturing the damage I'd managed to inflict on our only suspect. Dave tapped the glass lightly to let Marty know we were ready to go.

"It's 10:08 p.m. on November sixth. This is Detective Sergeant Marty Locklin of—"

Tropov let out a phlegmy, liquid chuckle and said, "Pleased to meet you." His voice was a low, throaty rumble, and he had a heavy accent. There was something odd about it, though, as if he were intentionally accentuating its foreignness. Marty shot him a look, and Tropov leaned back and tried to look smug, but the bruises got in his way.

Aware that the tape was rolling, Marty swallowed his irritation and went on with the identification. "Of the Long Beach Police Department Homicide Squad. Also present are Detective Second Grade Jennifer Tanaka and the suspect." Looking at Tropov, he went on. "State your name and address for the record."

"Yevgeny Vasilly Tropov," he said and then added the address at which we'd busted him.

"And you confirm that you've waived your right to legal counsel?"

"Yes."

Marty asked Tropov half a dozen general questions about his occupation and immigration status before he progressed to anything we actually cared about. "Where were you on the evening of November fourth?" He gave Tropov a moment to answer. "That was last Friday, two nights ago."

Tropov managed a swollen, lopsided grin.

"There it is," I whispered to Dave.

"What?"

"He's not our guy."

"What the hell are you talking about?" he said, traces of confusion sneaking into his voice. I wasn't sure if he'd missed Tropov's grin entirely or only its significance.

"Watch." I pointed back through the mirror.

"Well?" Marty asked.

"I was in Palm Springs." Tropov was sitting a bit straighter in his chair, and his eyes sparkled with arrogance.

"Can anyone else verify that?"

"Of course. I was at a social function celebrating the wedding anniversary of one of my many business associates. Not only can they verify it, but the staff of Melvyn's Restaurant will also support this."

"Yeah?"

"Oh yes. And you will see that my Visa card, which has not been reported as stolen or missing by myself, was used there. Also, you may see me making an ATM withdrawal on the video surveillance tape from the Bank of America." He tossed a broad smile at the camera. I noticed he was missing an incisor.

"Okay then," Marty said.

"This means I am free to go?"

Now it was Marty's turn to grin. "Oh no. It means we'll only be charging you with assault of an officer and attempted murder."

Tropov kept smiling.

"Maybe," Jen said, passing him on her way out of the room, "you'll want that lawyer after all."

When they closed the door, Tropov looked directly at the mirror and pointed his finger at us through the glass. He dropped his thumb and fired an imaginary bullet. I wanted to yank his spleen out through his nose.

Less than thirty minutes after the interview, Tropov had called his lawyer, and Ruiz had phoned in from home and told Marty we wouldn't be pressing charges against Tropov anytime soon.

Jen and I watched as Marty hung up the phone, took a deep breath through his nose, and told us the news. Dave was busy sulking and pretended to be deeply engrossed in the latest Long Beach public safety newsletter.

"Did he say why?" I asked.

"Only that he got the word from Baxter," Marty said, biting his lip and bouncing his huge fist lightly up and down on his desk. "Something about Tropov being knee-deep in some Organized Crime Detail shit."

"What?" Jen said. "He's a snitch?"

"Must be something like that," Marty said. "Why else would they kick him loose?"

"But what snitch has enough juice that someone would reach out to a deputy chief at home on Sunday night?" I asked.

Marty shook his head. "Somebody's yanking Baxter's chain too. That little dweeb would shit biscuits before he'd violate procedure."

"Tropov's got to be hooked into something big," Jen said. "Who, though?"

Marty was thinking out loud. "Mayor…DA…Chief? Who else has that kind of pull? City council, maybe?"

He looked at Jen and me as if we might be able to answer the question. I let it hang in the air unanswered for a moment before I spoke. "Doesn't matter, though," I said.

"Why?" Marty asked.

"Because," I said, "his alibi's gonna hold. Did you hear him?"

"So what?" Jen asked.

"So if his alibi holds," I said, "it means he didn't kill Beth, and he's not our problem."

"Danny," Marty said, "you just beat the shit out of a guy who has enough juice to wake up a deputy chief."

Jen finished his thought. "So like it or not, you made him our problem."

"Oh," I said. "I hadn't thought about it like that." At least she said *our* problem and not *your* problem.

"Well, it's about time you did," Jen said. She got up and left the room. As she walked away, she shook her head, and I thought I heard her mutter, "Jesus."

I looked at Marty and said, "Maybe next time she's tied to the railroad tracks I ought to just look the other way."

"You know what my old man used to say?" he asked, his eyes narrow.

"What?"

"When you're in a hole, stop digging." He got up and followed Jen out of the room. Dave just smiled into his newsletter.

TWELVE

Driving home, I listened to *Fresh Air* on KPCC. Terry Gross was interviewing an author about his new book, which traced the history of the first English translation of the Bible. A guy named Tyndale spent years and years cranking out great stuff like, "Blessed are the meek, for they shall inherit the earth." Then Henry VIII, because his pissing match with the pope hadn't yet reached full force, stuck with the Catholic hard-liners, who stood fast against letting the masses read the word of God in their own language, and let Tyndale be executed for heresy. Less than a decade later, Henry commissioned someone else to finish the work.

I stopped at Ralph's to do a bit of late-night grocery shopping, but found myself just pushing an empty cart up and down the aisles, unable to focus my attention on anything other than the memory of Tropov's shit-eating grin. In the magazine section, I tried to distract myself by reading a long-term test report on a Honda Odyssey in *Motor Trend* and then an article in *Outside* about the top-ten backpacking regions in the United States. Briefly, I thought about packing up a shiny new minivan with tents, sleeping bags, and backpacks and getting reacquainted with the glory of nature. Then I remembered the last time I'd been camping with Megan and how I had come home bug-bitten and exhausted, and I thought better of it.

I spent another fifteen minutes wheeling the cart back and forth indecisively and then eventually made it to the checkout with a box of Wild Berry Pop-Tarts, two packages of Stouffer's French Bread Pizza, a half gallon of orange juice, and two bottles of Grey Goose.

As I slid the bags into the passenger footwell of my Camry, my hand brushed the top of one of the vodka bottles, and I imagined myself cracking the cap and taking a long pull from the bottle. I turned the key in the ignition instead.

At home, though, I didn't think twice. I dropped my shoulder rig and leather briefcase on the table and carried the paper bags into the kitchen. I put the groceries, such as they were, on the counter and turned on the light, squinting at the bright Caribbean yellows and reds.

On my way to the fridge, I punched the button on the answering machine. As I opened the freezer, Geoffrey Hatcher's voice assaulted me with its unabashed politeness. "Daniel, give me a call if you would. I'll soon need to go with tomorrow's story, either with or without your input. I'd hate to put my foot in my mouth. I'll be up late, so call anytime. Thanks very much."

I put the two new bottles of Grey Goose in the freezer and took out the old one. I took a swallow straight from the bottle before pouring what was left into a glass and cutting it with No Pulp Tropicana. I drank as I dialed the phone.

"Hello?"

"Hi, Geoff."

"Daniel." He sounded bright and sunny, like he'd just set out on a fine morning's constitutional. "How are you?"

"I'm hanging in there."

"Funny, you don't sound much like it."

"Thanks," I said. "How *do* I sound?"

"Exhausted."

"And how do I usually sound?"

"Exhausted." He chuckled a bit on the other end of the line.

"Well then."

His voice softened and quieted. "I don't suppose you have anything new to share on the Williams murder, do you?"

"I wish I did. We're not any closer."

"I heard something about a ViCAP match?"

"No luck," I said, "not our guy. And he was the only thing resembling a lead we've come up with so far."

"Anything you'd rather not read in the paper tomorrow?"

"Well, it would be nice if this wasn't connected to the whole school-violence thing."

"But it is school violence, isn't it?"

"You know what I'm talking about, Geoff. This wasn't some alienated teenager tired of getting his ass kicked. We're looking at something else."

He was quiet for a moment. "Just what is it that you are looking at?"

"Off the record?"

"Of course."

"At this point, nobody wants to admit it, but there might not be any connection at all between the victim and the killer."

"And no apparent motive?"

"No." He paused, and I imagined I could hear him thinking. It was actually just the refrigerator humming on the other side of the room.

"Does that mean what I think it means?"

"I hope not," I said.

The graphic designer who'd lived in the duplex before me hadn't given up on the bold painting after the kitchen was finished. He and his wife had a daughter, and he'd decorated the second bedroom for her. The left wall, which faces east, had been painted a dark indigo, almost black, with pinpricks of yellow to simulate stars. In the center of the wall was a smiling crescent moon, over which jumped a cartoon cow. On the ceiling, the dark colors blended slowly into the lightening blue of a morning sky. Directly opposite the moon was a grinning, orange, noon sun, decked out with Ray-Bans and a zinc-oxide nose. Megan would have loved it—all those smiles. I was thinking of her when I signed the lease.

I use the room as an office. Actually, it's more just a place to keep the computer that I use once or twice a week to play Minesweeper or solitaire or stare at the walls. Sometimes, though, when I bring work home, I'll slide the keyboard out of the way and use the desk. Earlier that day, I'd put in a request with the Property Detail for copies of the student papers that Beth had been grading when she was murdered. I wasn't sure what I expected to find, but I thought they might help me get a bit closer to her state of mind at the time of her death. I took the copies out of my bag and spread them across the desk. Out of the original batch of thirty-two, four had been too damaged to copy, and of the twenty-eight remaining, Beth had commented on just more than half. I divided the fifteen marked papers into piles based on the grade. The A pile had four papers in it. I started my reading there.

It didn't take me long to realize that the students were writing essays about *Hamlet*, and I remembered the last time I attempted to read the play as a student at Long Beach State. I recalled the professor droning on about Freud and Oedipus and unresolved paternal issues. I remember spending a good amount of time with the Cliffs Notes version, but I'm not sure I ever actually finished reading the play.

The four students with A grades obviously had finished, though. The first paper was written by a girl named Elisa Santos who examined in detail the vast amounts of shit that Ophelia had to put up with and the reasons why it wasn't so surprising that she went nuts and drowned herself. The second, by the mono-named Lakeesha, wondered why everybody thought it was such a bad thing that Gertrude married Claudius so soon—a woman has to take care of herself, and it was lot harder to do so in those days. Susan Butler broke with the budding feminists and argued that Hamlet wasn't really crazy at all—just smart as hell for "getting everybody all wrapped around his fingers like that."

It was the fourth paper, though, that really got me. Someone named Jorge Hernandez had concluded his essay with this paragraph:

So I could totally sympathize with Hamlet and how he had that heavy-duty kind of angst because I know what that's like because of when my brother Hector got shot and died all I wanted to do was bust somebody's head just like Hamlet. It's like when he's talking to Rosencrantz and <u>Guildenstein</u> and he says that thing about he could feel like some kind of a king if it wasn't for his bad dreams. I still dream about Hector, too.

I looked away from the paper and turned to face the wall. The jumping cow had a silly-ass grin on her face that stretched from one side of her black-and-white-spotted bovine head to the other. She didn't look like the kind of cow who'd experienced much angst at all in her life. No last-minute reprieves from the slaughterhouse for her—no, just a happy-go-lucky free-range picnic all the way. She didn't fit in too well with the likes of Jorge and Hamlet. They knew angst.

In the closet was a box of books that had belonged to Megan. They were some of her favorites, which she'd kept in the small bookcase in our bedroom in the old house. I'd meant to go through them before I moved, but I always managed to put it off. Finally, I just gave up and lugged them and the dozen or so other boxes of her things to the new place with me. The books ranged from one of the first Oprah books to some that went all the way back to her days as a sociology major. I dug through them and found what I was looking for, a thick volume near the bottom of the box—*The Complete Works of William Shakespeare*. I opened the book, first to the table of contents and then to page 784 to find *The Tragedy of Hamlet, Prince of Denmark*.

Sitting cross-legged on the floor, turning the pages, I scanned the lines looking for the names of Rosencrantz and Guildenstern. (The listing of dramatis personae had corrected Jorge's spelling mistake and enlightened me as to why Beth had underlined the name on his paper.) Half an hour later, I discovered the line to which he'd been referring in act two, scene two: "I could be bounded in a nutshell and count myself a king of infinite space, were it not that I have bad dreams."

After I'd gone over the line a dozen or so times, I thumbed back to the beginning and read the play from beginning to end.

Repacking Megan's things, I came across her black leather-bound address book. The embossed cover had been smoothed by years of use. Seeing her handwriting inside filled me with a bone-deep melancholy. The way she dotted her *i*'s with tiny circles, the way she made her *e*'s like the front half of an eight, all curves and no sharp angles, the way she slanted her letters off to the right—all seemed to me then somehow evocative of her enduring warmth. I wanted to know that sensation again, to let it wash over me like a healing balm, but all I could feel was the fading ache of memory. Megan had alphabetized all the entries by first name because, she once told me, that was how she liked to think of the people she knew. Last names, she'd said, were too formal. She didn't want to impose that distance between herself and her friends. So it was under B that I discovered, in my wife's softly flowing hand, the phone number, address, and birthday of Beth Williams.

I didn't sleep that night. Instead, I spent three hours lying awake, my eyes itching, staring at the ceiling above the bed, trying to imagine myself in Beth's classroom at the time of her murder, trying to piece together the story. I couldn't do it. I wasn't there yet. But I would be. I had to be. For Beth. For Megan.

THIRTEEN

The next morning, I stood in a shower that was as hot as I could stand and let the water wash down my head and back. I'm not sure how long I stayed in, but the water had gone from scalding to tepid by the time I twisted the clear plastic knobs to the off position. My skin was a bright pink, and my fingertips had begun to pucker. I wiped the condensation off the mirror and rubbed artificial-lemon-scented shaving gel on my cheeks. As the gel transformed itself into a thick, rich foam, I remembered I'd forgotten to buy fresh blade cartridges for my razor the night before. Fuck it, I told myself as I began to scrape my face clean, let's live on the edge.

I shut off the faucets and wrapped a towel around my waist. A sound like silverware scraping a plate came from the kitchen, and I froze, listening. The bathroom door was half-open, and I wondered if I could slip through it and make my way to the nightstand next to my bed, where my pistol sat in its holster. To do that, though, I'd have to pass the kitchen—unlikely, I thought, unless whoever made the noise was facing away from the door. I looked around for something I might use as a weapon. Nothing.

Another clink. Had someone broken in to wash my dishes? I slipped into the hallway and peeked around the door frame. Jen was looking out the window over the sink, the Mr. Coffee gurgling on the counter next to her. She saw my reflection in the glass and turned around.

"Morning," I said.

She saw the question in my eyes. "I got a little worried when you didn't answer, so I let myself in." Her voice rose at the end of the statement, making it sound like a question. Last summer, after locking myself out of the house twice in two months, I decided a spare set of keys was called for. I gave the set to her for safekeeping. She'd never used it before.

"It's okay," I said. We stood there, the coffeemaker producing the only noise in the room. I knew that of the many reasons for the awkwardness, there was at least one about which I could do something. "Let me put some clothes on," I said.

I expected a snappy comeback, but instead she just looked at me, something far away in her eyes, and nodded.

"I'll be right back."

By the time I'd changed into a T-shirt and a pair of sweats, Jen had poured two cups of coffee, added cream and sugar, and sat down at my small kitchen table. The corners of her mouth turned up slightly as I sat across from her, but the smile didn't take hold in her eyes. I'd rarely seen her drink coffee—usually only on the occasional stakeout or all-nighter.

"How you doing?" I asked.

"Didn't sleep well." There was more she wanted to say, but I could tell it wasn't going to come out. "About yesterday—"

"Me too," I said. "Me too."

She reached across the table and put her hand on top of mine. We sat there a long time.

After the task force meeting—during which we ate doughnuts, drank coffee, and read our appointment books to each other—Jen made a call from her desk while I sorted new entries for the files. When she hung up, she turned to me and said, "Want to take a ride?"

Near the coast, Pine Avenue is among the hottest sections of Long Beach, with chic new restaurants and hip nightspots opening monthly. The upwardly mobile vie for the brand new (but oh-so-limited) "loft style" apartments that are popping up in the old downtown buildings. Just head north a few miles, past Pacific Coast Highway, which takes a break from its shore-hugging route for a bleak inner-city detour, and you'll find yourself in some of the diciest territory south of Los Angeles's famed South-Central district. You'll be right in the heart of the LBC made famous by Dr. Dre and by Snoop Dogg, way before he dropped the diminutive "Doggy" from the middle of his name. This is where, in a tiny two-bedroom house that shared a half-acre lot with three identical structures, Rudy Nguyen and his family lived.

Jen parked at the curb, and we got out. Across the street two late teen boys stared at us, not even bothering to put out their blunt, as we walked up the driveway. A tarnished brass C was fastened with twisted wire onto the rusting, black-steel security screen.

Jen rapped on the door frame, causing a hollow metallic rattle. A moment later, the door opened, and a young man in low-slung jeans and an olive T-shirt said softly, but with conviction, "Keep it down, I got—" Rudy cut himself off when he saw Jen outside the screen. "Sensei," he said quietly.

"Hi, Rudy," she said.

"What's up? What are…what are you doing here?" He seemed to be trying to process that odd disconnect that occurs when completely unrelated spheres of your life come crashing together.

"You haven't been to class in a while," she said. "We've been worried about you." She gave him a guilt-inducing eyebrow raise, but he wasn't having any of it.

"I can't come no more."

"Can we step inside?" she asked.

"No, my moms is sleeping." He opened the dead bolt with a twist of his hand and stepped out onto the small concrete porch, pulling the door softly closed behind him.

"She working nights again?" Jen asked.

"No." He looked down at his Reeboks.

"What, then?"

"She had to quit her job."

"Why?"

"She got cancer."

Jen was silent.

"Her pancreas and liver," he said. "She got to have chemotherapy three times a week."

Jen said, "I'm sorry, Rudy."

"So I gotta work now, and I can't come to class no more."

"You have a job?"

"Yeah."

She gave him time to say more. He didn't.

"Who you working for, Rudy?"

"Some guys."

"Some guys?"

"Some guys my brother hooked me up with."

"I can help you find a job," she said. "A real one."

He wrestled with his reply. His respect for her was obvious, and he chose his words deliberately, as if being careful not to offend. "You know she don't got no papers, right? They didn't never give no amnesty to the Vietnamese, so we don't get no help with the doctor, okay?"

Jen nodded.

"No disrespect, Sensei, you gonna get me some job in Burger King or Wendy's? Maybe I'm real lucky and I be busing tables down at Shoreline Village? I appreciate it, I do." He looked her straight in the eye. "But I'm gonna take care of my sisters and pay for my mom's doctor on minimum wage and tips?"

It was Jen's turn to look at her shoes.

"I'm sorry," he said to her.

"Me too," she said. "Me too."

When we were back in the car, Jen waited a long time before starting the engine.

"Danny, you check out her e-mail yet?" asked Pat Glenn, squeezing a neon lime ball in his hand.

"No, why? You find something?"

"Maybe. You should check it. Messages going back a while to this Waxler guy."

"What kind of messages?"

"Pretty standard cyberdating stuff. All the usual, getting-to-know-you, toeing-the-water kind of shit. He gets a little weirded out at the end when she cuts him loose. Nothing that screams psycho killer or anything, though."

"Can I get into her account to have a look?"

"No need. I printed it all out for you." He handed me a manila folder with a dozen or so pages inside. "And that's her screen name on the first page, if you want to check it out."

"We didn't, by any chance, get that court order yet, did we?" I asked.

"No," he said, dropping the ball into a large plastic bowl filled with Happy Meal toys and turning back to his monitor. "Kincaid didn't want to roust a judge on the weekend for it. Says he'll have it today, though."

"Do me a favor? Call me as soon as it comes through, okay?"

"Why?"

"Jen and I are hitting Waxler at lunch today. Don't want to use anything from the e-mail until we're official."

Jen was at her desk when I came in. "Take a look at this," she said as I sat down across from her.

"What is it?"

"It's our best guess so far as to Beth's last three days."

I looked at the paper-clipped sheets she slid across the top of my desk. They contained a straightforward, chronological list, assembled primarily from phone, computer, and bank records, cross-referenced with witness statements and any other information that might help to track Beth's actions during the last seventy-two hours of her life. Nothing stood out as being unusual or out of place.

When I finished reading, I looked up at Jen. "What do you think?"

"I don't know. Lot of time online. Lot of e-mail. We ought to talk to Pat about that."

"He's already on it," I said, holding up the file folder he'd just given me. "These are all the messages back and forth between her and Waxler."

"We have a warrant?"

"No comment."

Jen raised her eyebrows. "Anyone talk to Kincaid yet?"

"According to Pat, he's working on it."

"Let me talk to him. Maybe I can hurry it up." She brushed the hair off her forehead as she picked up her phone and dialed his extension. I wanted to make a smart-ass comment, but I couldn't think of anything to say.

I sat at my desk, waiting for Jen to come back from Kincaid's office and reading through Beth and Daryl's correspondence. Apparently they met online in a chat room book club discussion of *The Poisonwood Bible* and continued their exchange through e-mail and instant messages, of which, unfortunately, we had no record. Still, though, Waxler seemed sincere in his praise of the book, and only after the second e-mail in the folder did he begin to expand the scope of their conversation by inquiring about things other than her views on the Kingsolver book in particular and other literary matters in general.

His first question was simple and direct: "In your profile you mention that you're an English teacher. What grade do you teach?" He was either very patient, or he really wasn't just looking for an easy score. After addressing a few points he had made about the novel, Beth answered his question simply and directly—"high school"—and closed the message with "talk to you later, Beth." Daryl kept it cool, though, and peppered each message with a personal inquiry or two, and after the third letter, Beth was doing the same.

Gradually, they shared more and more. Daryl talked about raising a son on his own, Beth about teaching high school. The exchange was tentative and delicate on both their parts. A person less cynical than myself might have found it endearing, even a bit sweet. In his seventh e-mail, Daryl included his phone number and asked her if she wanted to get together for a cup of coffee. She took longer than usual to respond, but after two days, she agreed. The next few notes were short and simple, "had a nice time, talk to you soon" kinds of things. But near the end of September, Beth dropped the hammer:

Subject: RE: :-)
Date: 09/30 11:17:37 PM Pacific Daylight Time
From: Lizbeth67
To: WaxOn

Daryl:

I'm sorry to tell you like this, but I won't be able to see you anymore. You are a very kind and sweet man, but I'm not able to give you what you need and deserve. We're in different places, and looking for different things. I wish you nothing but the best, and I hope you are able to understand.

Sincerely,
Beth

Daryl kept trying, though, with four unanswered e-mails, each just a bit more pleading and desperate than the one before, asking for another chance, some reconsideration, before he finally gave up around the third week of October—just less than two weeks before the murder.

What was going through his mind? He didn't seem angry in the messages, just hurt and a little pathetic. How desperate might he have become in those twelve days? We were going to have to dig. I made a note to request a warrant for Daryl's phone records to see how many telephone calls went along with those e-mails.

I thumbed through the pages one more time, scanning the text for something I might have missed the first time through. Looking at Waxler's final message, I saw something I didn't catch on my first reading. He wrote, "But if this is what you really want, then alright, I'll have to accept it, and we'll both just have to live with the consequences of your decision."

It was only when I took that line out of context, separating it from the compliment that preceded it ("Beth, you are an amazing woman") and the well-wishing closing ("Have a beautiful life") that I saw the implications of Waxler's words and the veiled threat they contained. The message might have been only an instance of some simple and understandable passive-aggressiveness—or it could have been something more. If Jen ever came back from Kincaid's office, I thought, we might be able to find out.

FOURTEEN

As we wound through the Palos Verdes hills, ten minutes from Waxler's house, I said to Jen, "Call him again."

"We just called," she said, slowing the Explorer to look both ways as we approached a reflective yellow caution sign that showed a stick-figure horse and rider crossing the road. The rider looked to me like a spoiled thirteen-year-old girl, but I may have been reading too much into it.

"Call him anyway," I said.

"He said he'd call as soon as he talked to the judge."

"What's taking him so damn long?" I looked at my watch. "He's had three hours."

"Why are you so uptight?"

"I'm uptight?"

She took her eyes off the road just long enough to shoot me a look of disbelief.

"I don't know," I said. "I just want to be able to front him with the e-mail if we need to. Shit, what else do we have?" I watched the trees blur outside the passenger window as we passed them by. She didn't call Kincaid again.

A silver Audi A8 and an iridescent yellow New Beetle were parked next to each other at the end of Waxler's driveway. When Jen pulled to a stop next to the VW, there was still enough driveway width for at least two cars on either end of the row. One of the three garage doors was open, revealing enough gym equipment to stock a small health club.

As Jen and I got out of the Explorer, I looked inside the garage and saw the likely owner of the Bug—a spiky-haired young man about D.J.'s age. Trying just a bit too hard to look cool, he wore a sleeveless T-shirt and knee-length shorts above his Converse Chuck Taylors. The barbed-wire tattoo encircling his wiry biceps stretched like a black rubber band as he spotted D.J., who was straining to bench-press an Olympic bar with a twenty-five-pound plate on each end. We stood on the driveway until he grunted out another rep or two and then put the bar in its cradles.

I leaned against the frame of the door and took a look around. The garage was large, even by Palos Verdes standards. Space for six cars, with spotless shelving, cabinetry, and workbenches running all around the perimeter. On the far end, behind the closed doors, were three more cars—a Range Rover, a Mercedes-Benz E-Class, and an Acura RSX. Wasn't hard to figure out whose was whose. In the far corner stood a large refrigerator, the glossy black panels on its doors reflecting the shrunken images of the cars.

The nearest third of the space, though, was devoted to the fitness equipment. A Trotter treadmill, a Life Fitness elliptical trainer, and a Concept2 rowing machine lined the wall on the left. Opposite them stood a full complement of Cybex strength-training equipment, including a seven-pulley machine; flat, incline, and decline benches; and full sets of both dumbbells and free weights. In the corner, on a chain attached to a rafter, hung a seventy-pound Everlast heavy bag. I don't know why, but I wanted to see Jen shove the two of them out of the way and show them how it's done. I knew for a fact that she could easily bench more than twice what D.J. was doing, without even using a spotter. I stopped and tried to remember the last time I'd bench-pressed anything at all. What had it been? Four years? Five?

"D.J.," Jen said as he sat up on the bench. "How's it going?"

As she stepped toward the two guys, their eyes widened. "Okay," D.J., said, grinning and trying not to be obvious about tightening the ropy muscles in his thin arms. "How about you, Detective?"

"Just fine. Who's your friend?" Jen asked. She nodded toward the other teenager. The kid quickly raised his gaze, probably hoping not to be caught ogling her hips. He didn't quite make it in time.

"Max," he said, extending his hand to Jen. "Max Porter."

Jen took his hand and looked up at him. "Nice to meet you." She gripped his hand and waited for him to let go first, then turned back to D.J. "Where's your dad?"

"He's inside. Living room, I think." D.J. sounded disappointed, like maybe he'd been hoping she'd want to hang out and talk shop for a while. "I think he's waiting for you. Just go through there and go down the hall to the left. You can't miss him."

I wasn't sure that either one of them had noticed me at all until D.J. gave me half a nod as I followed Jen through the door into the kitchen hallway. Behind us, the weights clanked as D.J. started another set. A few yards down the hall, Jen stopped and looked at the kitchen. It impressed her even more than it had me when I'd seen it on our last visit.

"Damn," she said, looking out over the Pacific.

"It's like the Food Network and HGTV all rolled into one."

"Must be nice." She shrugged off the view and continued down the hall. Thirty paces later, the tile walkway opened into an expansive living area with a large brick fireplace and ceilings that stretched upward through the second floor and all the way to the exposed roof beams twenty-five feet above our heads.

There were two men in the room, and even though we'd never met either of them, it wasn't hard to tell who was who. Daryl sat on a dark brown leather sofa that seemed tiny in the large room. Next to him on the sofa, reaching forward and placing a highball glass on a ceramic coaster on the marble-topped coffee table, sat a man in a charcoal three-button suit, complete with burgundy power tie and salt-and-pepper temples. The lawyer didn't seem small.

"Hello, Daryl," I said.

"Hi," he said. He was wearing light-colored khakis and an untucked white polo shirt with a dark red stripe across the chest. The outfit, together with his narrow shoulders and wide ass, reminded me of a bowling pin. His curly brown hair was a bit too long for the style in which he wore it. With one surprisingly deft motion, he pushed his glasses back up his nose and wiped the hair away from his eyes. He stood up and stuck out his hand. I took it.

"I'm Detective Beckett," I said, putting a little extra muscle into my grip, "and this is Detective Tanaka." She shook his hand too.

"This is my attorney," Daryl said, raising his shoulders. "I didn't expect him to come, but when I told him what was going on, he insisted."

"Detectives," the lawyer said. He leaned forward a bit but couldn't be bothered to stand up. "Trevor Wells. A pleasure," he added. With his dull, nasal monotone, he made sure we understood it was anything but.

Now, the very first thing I'd do if I knew I were about to be questioned in a murder investigation would be to lawyer up. I would not say a single word to anyone without the benefit of legal counsel. Not a peep. Most of my detective colleagues would agree with me on this. So it might seem surprisingly counterintuitive that the first thing we cops suspect when someone brings a lawyer to an interview is that the person must have something to hide. What, I wondered, did Daryl have to hide? Maybe just some of the standard-issue skeletons in the closet that always seem to swarm the wealthy. Maybe something else? But then again, most of the cops I know have a thing or two they wouldn't mind keeping under the covers themselves.

At any rate, the lawyer reduced the potential value of our interview to very little if we were lucky or to nothing if we weren't. Any question we really hoped to find an answer for would now, in all likelihood, not even be asked. There wouldn't be any strikes for us—not even a spare. But we gave it a shot anyway.

We all sat down, Daryl and Wells in the same positions on the sofa they'd been in before, and Jen and I in matching chairs across the coffee table from them. Jen flipped open her spiral-bound notebook, and I took a small tape recorder out of my pocket. "Do you have any objections to our recording this conversation?" I asked. I figured that since Wells would make sure we didn't stray from the straight and narrow, we might as well have the interview verbatim.

Daryl looked at his lawyer, who gave his head a single small shake to each side. "No," Daryl said. "I guess it's okay." I pushed the red record button and stated the date, time, and location and identified the parties present.

"All right," Jen said. "Mr. Waxler, how would you characterize your relationship with Elizabeth Williams?"

Daryl glanced at Wells, who gave him half a nod. "We were close." He squinted at the lawyer. "Friends," he said, "close friends."

Jen pushed a little harder. "Would you characterize your relationship with Ms. Williams as one of a romantic nature?"

"Well, it wasn't exactly—"

Wells cut him off. "No," he said. "Mr. Waxler and Ms. Williams were not sexually involved."

"Is that right, Daryl?" Jen asked.

When he nodded and said yes, his hair fell across his forehead. His hand was a little less certain this time as he wiped his fingertips back across his temple and tried to tuck the hair behind his ear.

"Did you want to be?" I asked.

Daryl looked surprised, but he was learning the game quickly. He let his legal counsel answer for him. "That question," Wells said, his voice resonant with feigned indignation, "is neither appropriate nor relevant."

With the possible exception of Daryl, everyone knew that the question actually was both relevant and appropriate, as the answer might lay the foundation of a motive for Daryl. We didn't push the point, though. Arguing with a lawyer is about as good an idea as feeding an alligator raw beef from your palm.

I was ready to give up, but Jen kept going. "Can you tell us your whereabouts on the evening of Friday, November fourth?"

"I was out..." Daryl paused and checked in with Wells, who took over and finished his sentence.

"Out of town," the lawyer said. "I know you're already well aware of the credit card records that indicate—"

"With all due respect, Trev," I said, "those records only indicate the whereabouts of Daryl's credit card, not the where-abouts of Daryl himself."

Wells's nostrils flared, and the corners of his mouth turned down. "Just what are you implying, Detective?" Apparently he didn't like being called Trev.

"I'm implying that I'd like an answer to the question we actually asked." I stared directly into Daryl's dull brown eyes. He held my gaze for a moment and then looked away, his face a bit paler than it had been.

"That's enough." Wells adjusted his tie and stood up, moving forward and slightly to his right so we'd have to look around him to see Daryl. "This interview is over." He stepped around the table and, with a sweep of his hand, showed us the hall by which we'd entered. "Shall I show you out?"

"I think we can remember the way," I said. "Thanks just the same."

Jen turned back to Daryl and said, "Thank you for your time, Mr. Waxler. I know this is very difficult for you."

When he looked up at her, he looked like he might cry. He opened his mouth as if he were about to speak, but changed his mind and just nodded. His hair fell into his eyes again, but this time, he left it alone.

In the garage, Max held the heavy bag for D.J., who was practicing a side kick. The faint odor of sweat hung in the air. They grinned at Jen and adjusted their posture as we came in. "Let's see another one of those," she said. D.J. focused his attention on the bag and gave it his best shot, which wasn't very impressive.

"Kick through the target. The follow-through will give you more power." Both boys looked confused.

"Imagine," she said, as they locked their eyes on her, "that you're really kicking a target six inches behind the target you want to strike." They both pretended to understand what she was saying.

"Like this," she said. "D.J., hold the bag for me, okay?" He rushed behind the bag and leaned into it with his shoulder.

"Ready?" Jen asked.

"Ready," he said.

Faster than their eyes could follow, she cocked her left knee toward her chest, leaned to her right, and shot her left foot into the bag like a piston. The sound of her foot impacting the bag was simultaneous with that of the air bursting out of D.J.'s abdomen. He took a step back and leaned his hands on his knees, trying to catch his breath.

"See what I mean?" Jen asked.

Max seemed as surprised as D.J., and they both just nodded and stared at her as she turned and walked back down the driveway. Neither of them paid me any attention at all as I followed her and tried not to laugh.

D.J. caught up with us about halfway to the car. He was still trying to catch his breath. "That," he said, "was really good."

"Thanks," Jen said. "Just takes lots and lots of practice."

"No, I mean it. My teacher," he paused to suck in another breath, "he can't even kick that hard."

"I'm sure he can. He's just going easy on you like he's supposed to. Now get back to work." She tried to smile, but I could see that it didn't come easy.

She was silent and gripping the steering wheel too tightly as we drove through the gate and started down the hill. "What's the matter?" I asked, assuming she was pissed at me for forcing Wells into a defensive position too soon. "Didn't like the way I handled the interview?"

"It's not that. That was fine."

I watched her drive in silence. "I thought I was supposed to be the brooding one" I said.

She was quiet for another mile.

"Come on," I said. "What is it? You think you were too tough on D.J.?"

"No. Not that, either. Not hard enough."

"I don't follow you."

"Five years ago. . ." she said, glancing over at me. "Five years ago, I would have bounced his skinny ass off the wall." As I tried to think of the right thing to say, I realized that I was making a habit out of not knowing how to respond to my partner.

"Well," Marty asked as we walked into the squad, "did he do it?"

"Oh yeah," I said, "he confessed, but then he changed his mind, tried to escape. We had to shoot him."

"Damn, I wish some of those high school punks we had to interview tried to escape. There were a few could have used a bullet."

It was pushing four o'clock when Ruiz opened his office door and called Dave, Marty, Jen, and me inside. Just as we'd squeezed four chairs into the room and arranged them in a tight circle around the lieutenant's desk, Pat Glenn slid in against the wall next to the door to join us.

"Maybe we ought to go up to the conference room," Jen said as she tried to inch her chair toward the window to make a bit more space. Someone in the room needed a shower, but I couldn't tell who.

"No," Ruiz said, "I want to know the score before we take it upstairs to the big table. We find out anything today? Marty?"

"Well, the interviews at the school didn't turn up much. Spent the morning with the other teachers. Most of them really liked her."

"Most?" I asked.

"Yeah. There were maybe half a dozen who were jealous, maybe held a little grudge, but other than that, she was popular. Nobody with a big enough bug up their ass to have a motive."

"The students?"

"Crazy about her. She was the one who all the girls wanted to be like and all the boys just wanted."

"Yeah," Dave said, "I even had one banger wanted me to tell him who the doer was so he could 'fuck up his shit.'"

"But nothing solid?" Ruiz asked.

"Not really." Marty shook his head. "We're doing background checks, and we've still got uniforms taking statements from students, but no, nothing. She was teacher-of-the-year material. They're broken up." He closed his eyes a moment and then opened them again. "Nobody there wanted her dead. They've even got a little makeshift shrine outside her classroom. Candles and pictures and notes. It's hitting them hard."

Ruiz nodded and turned his head. "Jen?"

"Waxler might be a little hinky. Lawyered up before we even got there," she said. Eight eyebrows went up simultaneously.

"Get anything out of him?" Marty asked.

"Not really," she said. "He's insecure, a little mousy. I can maybe see the whole unrequited-love angle. She rejects him, he gets desperate enough…"

"Danny?" Ruiz asked.

"Doesn't seem the type to get violent," I said, "but we really didn't have much of a chance to push his buttons and see what happened. I wouldn't rule anything out, though." I turned to Pat. "Did his alibi hold?"

"I checked it out with the hotel's records. He used a credit card to make the reservation, but paid cash for the room. The hotel manager said that he still would have had to show the card to check in, but he wouldn't need any other ID."

"So," Marty said, "anybody could have checked in under his name."

"Right." Pat nodded and tapped the edge of Ruiz's desk with his palm. "And they wouldn't even have been committing a crime because they wouldn't be claiming to be the owner of the card or making any fraudulent charges."

"Spurned lover with a weak alibi," Marty said. "You've got to look hard at that."

"I want to take another run at him," I said. "See if I can get around the lawyer."

"What about Tropov?" Dave asked.

"Unless we get something hard on Waxler, we don't close any doors," Ruiz said. Dave leaned back in his chair, with a satisfied look on his face.

"One other thing," Marty said. "All the local channels had people out there. It's going to be all over the news."

Ruiz grimaced. "I know. Don't worry about it. Just keep doing what you're doing and let the brass handle the vultures."

Marty, Jen, and I gathered around the twelve-inch TV in the coffee room. Each of the local news broadcasts led with the story. They had shots of the school campus, the candles glowing softly among the remembrances outside the classroom, students crying, students thinking, students talking, teachers doing the same—everything they always show when someone who is in any way associated with a school is murdered. I wondered if any of what we were watching was actually stock footage. It would certainly save the news directors time and energy.

On the screen, a serious-faced young Asian woman with a Latino name and a microphone asked everyone inane questions and then summed up the story with this: "Elizabeth Ann Williams. The latest casualty in the ever-escalating epidemic of school violence. Kandi, back to you."

Marty reached over and turned off the TV. "Well, at least they're predictable." He drained a Styrofoam coffee cup and tossed it across the room into the wastebasket.

"The big question," Jen said, "is whether this hurts us or helps us."

"Depends on who's watching," I said.

"Right." Marty got up, went over to the Mr. Coffee, and filled another cup.

"You just threw one of those away," Jen said.

"I know," he said. "I thought I was done. I make up for it in other ways."

"Yeah, right," she said. "How?"

"Well, you don't see me driving around in an SUV now, do you?"

Jen looked at me. "Don't you even think about laughing at that," she said. I turned my head and looked out the window so she wouldn't see my face.

It was too early to contemplate another sleepless night, so I drove downtown and parked a block up and over from the house in which we'd busted Tropov. I took a musty-smelling charcoal-colored zip-up hooded sweatshirt and a black baseball cap out of the trunk and put them on. There was a chill in the night air, but no wind, so it didn't feel as cold as it might have.

A pit bull snarled at me from a backyard and set off a chain reaction of barking dogs, which worked its way up the street and faded off into the distance. I walked around the corner and up the block on the side of the street opposite the house, thinking about how close I had come to killing the Russian. Would I have done it if Jen hadn't stopped me? I want to say no, that I would have composed myself, that I would have held it together, that I would have done the right thing. But Jen knows me. She read me better than I read myself.

If Tropov were still occupying the house, there was little evidence. No lights. No sound. No movement. No car in front. No signs of life. Only the weeds. They seemed taller than they had the last time I'd been there. Probably just my imagination, though. Dead weeds don't grow.

From the darkened front room of a house across the street and two doors up from Tropov's, someone watched me pass. The curtains moved as I walked by. The window was closed, and even if it had not been, there was very little wind. I wondered who might be inside. Cops? It was the perfect location for a stakeout. I was curious enough to turn right at the corner and right again into the alley behind the row of houses I'd just passed.

In the driveway behind the home in which I'd seen the curtain move, there sat a pale silver metallic Ford Crown Victoria. The bargain Maaco paint job didn't fool me, though, nor would it fool the average urban ten-year-old. Even if the black-steel wheels weren't enough of a tip-off, you didn't see many citizens tooling around in the big Fords, at least not in Long Beach. I lifted the lid off the garbage can and saw several days worth of fast-food bags and take-out coffee cups and very little else. They might as well have parked a black-and-white on the front lawn.

I turned around and went back the way I came. In front of the window with the moving curtain, I turned, flashed my best shit-eating grin, and gave a double-fisted thumbs-up to the cops watching from inside.

On the way home I made one more stop. I pulled my Camry up to the curb in front of Beth's driveway. I got out and walked slowly past the front house on the lot. When

I could see her front door, I stopped and studied the small house she had lived in.

Had Daryl ever seen it? Had he been here? I should have asked him before I pissed off his lawyer. I tried to imagine myself in his position—if that front door had been closed in my face, I wondered, would it make me angry? Daryl didn't seem the angry type, but I could see him desperate, and that can be even worse. How attached had he been? How much had it hurt him to hear her say she wasn't interested? Was that pain, that desperation, enough? It would have had to push him to the edge, even a bit over it, for him to go so far in the commission of the crime. Would he have been able to make it back? I pictured Daryl in Beth's classroom, kneeling over her body, brown hair hanging over his eyes, raising the blade again and again. It didn't work for me. The story just didn't play right.

I walked onto the porch and checked the crime scene tape. It had lost most of its adhesion, as if perhaps someone had pulled it loose and tried to replace it. I ran through the list of people who might have been inside since we'd last been here. Daryl? Tropov? The colonel?

"Hello, Detective," said a voice behind me.

I spun and saw Harlan Gibbs loping toward the porch. "Hope I didn't startle you."

"Me? Hell no, I'm tough as nails."

He was wearing old Levi's and an untucked blue-plaid shirt with snaps. The walnut grips of his revolver protruded from his waistband. He noticed me noticing it. "I saw you walking up the drive. Didn't recognize you from behind."

"You haven't seen anybody nosing around here, have you, Mr. Gibbs?"

"No, not since all the crime scene people and news people left on Saturday morning. Why?"

"Tape on the door's a bit loose. Wondered if you might have seen something."

"Nope, not a thing," he said. But he'd been watching. Didn't take him even five minutes to make me.

FIFTEEN

As the first swallow of vodka and orange juice slid down my throat, it felt like a warm patch of sunlight on a spring day. The next two went down the same way. After refilling the glass, I went into the living room and turned on the TV. I thumbed all the way through the channels twice before settling on an old episode of *This Old House* on TLC. Kevin and Norm were performing a cost-benefit analysis of natural oak kitchen cabinetry. Kevin wondered about the cost savings of veneers, but Norm, the voice of reason and experience, convinced him of the long-term efficacy of solid hardwood.

After the show ended, I flipped through my bootleg copy of the murder book, trying to find an angle I'd missed before. If it was there, I couldn't spot it.

I stared at the ceiling and thought about our suspects, such as they were. We had nothing hard on either Waxler or Tropov. We barely had anything soft. If their alibis came anywhere near holding up, we'd be right back where we began.

Even with an alibi, I couldn't get past Tropov's cockiness. The smirk on his face when Marty asked where he'd been at the time of the murder was too much. He knew he had nothing to worry about, but he knew he was connected, too. Maybe I dismissed him too quickly. We knew he was capable of the savagery. That was more than we could say for Waxler. Still, if you're going with the odds, spurned lover is a hell of a lot more likely than crazed Russian mobster.

I couldn't honestly say I liked either one of them, but what else did we have? Harlan Gibbs? Not likely. Until someone better came skipping along, we were stuck. But what worried me most was the pressure—high-profile case, media coverage, task force, ambitious police chief and DA. It wouldn't be long before the brass would be pressing for an arrest—and they wouldn't particularly care if it was the right one, as long as it stuck.

My head began to hurt. I took a hot shower, got dressed, and decided to walk the mile and a quarter to Second Street to meet Geoff Hatcher at the Shorehouse.

The walk made me about ten minutes late, but it helped clear the confusion out of my head. It didn't replace it with anything, though. It just left me with a vaguely pleasant emptiness.

The stretch of Second Street that runs through Belmont Shore is where most of the locals spend their leisure time. It's a one-stop eating and shopping area for the neighborhood's upper and upper-upper middle class. I walked past half a dozen university hang-out bars, Rubio's Fish Tacos, Banana Republic, Gaps of both the standard and baby variety, and Starbucks before stopping at a newspaper machine outside the Rite Aid to pick up a *Press-Telegram*. I went by a second Starbucks, part of a vicious, corporate, flanking maneuver in the ongoing coffeehouse turf war, with the big Satan, Starbucks, and the little Satan, Coffee Bean, wantonly slaughtering the neighborhood's independent mom-and-pop caffeine pushers. As I walked, I read the paper. The story about Beth had made the front page below the fold. A sentence in the first paragraph linked the crime to "the growing incidence of violence in our public schools."

When I walked into the Shorehouse Cafe, Hatcher was already waiting at a table by the window overlooking the street. "Daniel," he said, standing up. "How are you?"

"Fuck you." I slapped the paper down on the table. He flinched as if I'd thrown a glass of water in his face. "One simple request—was it too much for you?"

Hatcher couldn't seem to stop blinking. I sat down across the table from him. He took the newspaper in his hands and scanned the text until he found the article. "I didn't write it like that. It was an editorial deci—"

"That's your byline isn't it?"

"Yes, but—"

"Is it or isn't it?"

"It is."

We sat there in silence.

"Now what?" he said.

"Now you apologize, and I pretend like I'm not pissed off."

"I'm sorry."

"All right. What the hell were they thinking?"

"Everyone's making that connection. It's violence. It's in school. Of course it's related."

"Who's everyone, Geoff? Channel Two? Channel Seven? Nine? Four? Who? It wasn't in the *Times*, and I know damn well no one in the department or the mayor's office gave you that shit. I thought you had a little integrity. Why else would I be here? I might as well be sitting down with Connie Chung."

"Are you done yet?" he asked.

"Yeah, I guess I am."

"Would you like something to eat?"

I had a grilled turkey sandwich and spent half an hour telling him nothing. It wasn't hard, considering how much I actually knew.

The night was cool and clear, with an ocean breeze blowing lightly inland, and I felt a bit chilly until the walking began to warm me. As I ambled along Park Avenue, I looked in the large picture windows, common in the old houses in Belmont Heights, and wondered how long it would be until Christmas trees and other decorations began to appear. We were only a few weeks shy of Thanksgiving, and it wouldn't take long after that.

I used to think the bright holiday displays were nothing but an invitation, shouting, "Come and get it," to burglars— and from my days in uniform, I knew it was true. There would be dozens of calls in the weeks before Christmas reporting break-ins and the theft of gifts right out from under the trees standing so proudly in the windows. I wasn't ever able to understand how people could be so stupid.

The last few years, though, have been different. I've found myself walking up and down the streets, pausing in front of curtainless windows, staring. Sometimes I'll walk an extra mile to Naples Island and gaze, openmouthed, at the displays of Christmas trees, lights, and other decorations. Last year, I even stood alongside the canal as Santa floated past, perched in a thronelike chair on a platform suspended between the hulls of two outrigger canoes, and watched him wave to the families crowded on each bank.

But it's the houses in the Heights that have held me the most—the Douglas and Noble firs dominating the expanses of glass fronting the old bungalows, restored Craftsmans, and aspiring Victorians. What once seemed so sad to me now seems something else entirely. These people aren't naïve, as I'd once believed. There's a tender and defiant hopefulness in their displays that's almost strong enough to make me believe in…I don't what, exactly, but something.

SIXTEEN

The next morning was sunny and clear, with the clean and crisp air that only appeared in Southern California in the late fall and winter. Every now and again, I am glad I live in Long Beach.

I called Jen before I left home. "I've got to make a stop on the way in."

"Where?" she asked.

"I'm going to see Waxler."

"By yourself?"

"I have something I want to try that I think might open him up, but I'll need to front him by myself for it to work."

"You sure this is a good idea?"

"What other kind do I ever have?"

Waxler's initial interview hadn't been as productive as we'd hoped. There was more there, and I thought if I played my cards right, I might be able to tease it out of him.

His office was on the top floor of a fairly modest brick building in the Torrance Crossroads shopping/dining/entertainment center that he'd had a hand in developing. I left my car in the acres of parking lot between the twenty-screen AMC megaplex and Romano's Macaroni Grill.

Behind a large oak-veneered door flanked by three-foot-wide swaths of glass brick, a receptionist named Stacey told me that "Mr. Waxler is unavailable."

I showed her my badge and said, "I think he'll want to see me."

She adjusted her glasses, checked the face in the photo on my ID against my face, and when she was satisfied, picked up the phone and dialed Daryl's extension. "There's a Detective Beckett here to see you." She nodded and hung up. "He'll be right out," she said.

"Thank you, Stacey," I said. "You've been very helpful." I held her gaze until she lowered her eyes.

"Hello, Detective," Daryl said, only seconds later, stepping around a potted palm at the corner of the reception desk.

I nodded. "Mr. Waxler."

"Before you say anything else, I should tell you that Trevor told me I'm not to say anything at all to you or to anyone else from the police without having him present." Daryl did have a bit more of an air of authority about him in his tailored white shirt and tie, but his remark still came out sounding almost like a question.

"That's all right, Mr. Waxler," I said. "You don't need to say anything at all. But I would appreciate it if you'd listen for just a moment."

That confused him. He looked at Stacey, then back at me, then he nodded, more to himself, it seemed, than to anyone else. "Why don't you come back into my office?" he said to me, his voice wary.

I followed him down the short hallway, past a few office-drone cubicles, his-and-her restrooms, and a couple of small offices, and on into his own. This office was larger by far than any of the others, much better appointed, and obviously meant for the company's head cheese. I walked over to the sliding glass door that opened out onto a small balcony carved into the corner of the building. The view over the tops of the eucalyptus trees surrounding the building and beyond Torrance Municipal Airport was much better than I had expected. "That's a great view," I said, looking out at the cloudless blue sky pressing down on the coastal hills of Redondo Beach.

"One of the perks of the office," he said. "Sometimes I just go sit out there and look. You wouldn't believe the sunsets."

I nodded and smiled. "I'm not really here officially, Mr. Waxler. It's actually sort of personal." He didn't know what to say to that.

"What is it, Detective?"

"Call me Danny," I said, trying to toss a little of that Waxler sheepishness back at him. "I just...I felt that we might have given you the wrong impression the other day. As far as I'm concerned, you're not a suspect in this case."

That surprised him. "Maybe we should sit down," he said. He gestured for me to sit in the chair in front of his desk and then took a seat of his own behind it. Both were upholstered in cocoa brown leather.

"My partner and I disagreed about this," I said. "That's why I'm here by myself. You're a resource that I don't believe we can do without."

"Really?"

"Absolutely."

"Why do you think that?"

"Well, a few reasons, really. I've talked to some people who know you. Just about everyone you've ever met swears you don't have a violent bone in your body. And I'm a pretty good judge of character. I get a feeling about you, and I'm not often wrong."

"You're not?"

"No," I said. "I'm not. But there's something else, too."

"What's that?"

I looked down at my lap and rolled the hem of my coat between my fingers before speaking. "I lost my wife eighteen months ago."

He studied me for what seemed a long time and then picked up the phone. "Stacey," he said, "could you make us up a couple of mochas?" He paused, a look of concern suddenly on his face. "You like mochas, Danny?"

"I do, Daryl, thank you."

He wanted to talk—about his failings in life before losing his wife, about her long illness, about how he blamed himself for the difficulties that D.J. experienced during the ordeal, about how he struggled to reconnect with his distant and sullen son after the death. We spent almost an hour there in his office, and by the time we finished, Daryl probably thought we were pals. Later, I would wonder what was worse—that I had exploited Megan's memory in such a way, or that it had worked so well.

"You really did that? With him?" Jen asked. There was an odd tone in her voice that I couldn't quite get a handle on—something between chagrin and indignation. It made me wonder what she had sounded like as a teenager. "What did you tell him about her?" she asked.

"Nothing, really," I said. "Just that she died in a car accident less than two years ago."

"That's all?"

"Yes."

"Nothing else?"

"Well, only that I missed her and I know how hard it is to lose someone."

She nodded.

"What's the big deal?" I asked.

"You don't think it's a big deal to be bonding with a murder suspect over your dead wives?"

I thought about it a moment and then said, "You use what you have."

"And what did you uncover with your brilliant investigative technique?"

"I don't think he did it."

"Well," she said. "Imagine that."

It was nearly noon when Jen pressed the buzzer outside Rachel and Susan's loft. The sun shone directly overhead and filled the alley with glaring light. It looked better in the dark.

"Who's there?" Susan said through the tinny-sounding intercom speaker.

Jen pushed the button and spoke. "It's Detectives Tanaka and Beckett." She released the button and took a step back, waiting for Susan to buzz us in. After several buzz-free seconds, Jen looked at me. "What do you think?"

"Maybe they're hightailing it down the fire escape."

"Maybe," Jen said. She reached for the button to ring again.

"Are you still outside?" Susan asked.

"Yeah," Jen answered.

"Shit. Hang on. The buzzer's fucked up again."

Twenty seconds later, we saw Susan through the dirty glass. She wore baggy, paint-stained jeans and a white T-shirt. The lines in her face looked more pronounced than they had the week before. Maybe it was the brightness of the sunlight. "Hi," she said, pushing the door open for us.

We nodded our hellos. "How's Rachel?" Jen asked.

"She's taking it hard. But she'll make it. She's stronger than she seems."

"She is?" Jen asked as we followed her upstairs.

"After everything she's been through, she'd have to be."

Jen looked over her shoulder at me. I shook my head. I didn't know what Susan was talking about either. She assumed we knew something about Rachel's past. We didn't.

Susan stopped on the landing above Jen and me and turned to face us, realizing she'd given us a new piece of information. We pretended we didn't notice. She took a long pause and then looked from Jen to me and back to Jen again. Opening the door, she said, "Come in."

Rachel's blond hair was pulled back and looked a shade or two darker than it had the last time we'd seen her. She sat on one of the two sofas facing each other on either side of a coffee table near the tall windows, with her legs curled beneath her. She wore a navy Long Beach State sweatshirt and khaki shorts. The sportiness of the outfit clashed with the dark circles under her eyes and the worn expression on her face. Susan sat next to her and motioned Jen and me toward the other sofa.

"Hi, Rachel," Jen said.

"Hello." She tried for a smile but didn't quite make it. "How are you?" she asked, obviously more out of habit than interest.

"We're fine, thanks," I said. Neither Jen nor I returned the question. It doesn't take long, working homicide, to discover that most people suffering from grief can't answer that question without telling a lie that trivializes their loss. Rachel uncurled one of her legs and pulled her knee into her chest.

"I'm sorry we have to do this now," Jen said, "but we need to ask you a few more questions about Beth." Jen looked into Rachel's eyes. "And about your family."

"It's okay," Rachel said, her voice barely bridging the distance across the coffee table.

"Have you thought of anything that might be relevant to the investigation?" Jen asked.

"No, not really," Rachel replied.

"Anyone Beth might have been involved with?"

"She hasn't been involved with anyone lately. Well, except for Daryl, I guess."

"You guess?" Jen asked.

"Well, she was never *involved* involved, I mean." Rachel tugged at her bottom lip with an incisor.

"You mean they never slept together?"

She nodded and looked down at the stack of magazines on the table.

"Does it make you uncomfortable to talk about this?" I asked.

She nodded again. "A little."

"How well do you know Daryl?"

"Oh," Rachel said, "I never met him. But Beth talked a lot about him."

"What did she say?" I asked.

"Well, she usually talked about how nice he was and how he was so kind and thoughtful."

"Anything else?"

"She felt bad about breaking up with him because she said he was such a sweet guy."

"Then why did she break up with him?" Jen asked.

"Because, she said, even though he was nice, they just didn't connect, you know?"

"No chemistry?" I said.

"Yes, no chemistry."

"Nice, but kind of dull?" Jen offered.

"Uh-huh, exactly." Rachel nodded. "You know how that is."

"Yeah." Jen looked at me. "I do."

The corners of Rachel's eyes crinkled, and she let go of her knee and wrapped her hands in the hem of her sweatshirt.

"And Daryl's the only guy she's been involved with lately?" I asked.

"Yeah. For a long time."

"Did she date much?"

"Hardly at all."

"How long had it been, before Daryl, since she'd gone out with anyone?"

"A long time."

"A year?" I said.

"Maybe two?" she said.

Jen took over. "When was the last time she was really serious about someone?"

"A long time. Seven or eight years."

"That is a long time," Jen said. "Do you remember his name?"

"Kirby. Roger Kirby. But everybody called him by his last name."

I recognized the name. In my mind's eye, I began connecting the dots, but then Jen unknowingly dropped the bomb. "Why is it, do you think, that she had such a hard time connecting with guys?"

The traces of comfort Rachel had found vanished as quickly as they'd appeared. She looked at Susan and hugged her knee to her chest again.

"She had some problems with guys. Issues," Rachel said, her eyes on the *Entertainment Weekly* on the top of the stack on the coffee table. Julia Roberts's head grinned back up at her. "She didn't trust men too easy."

"Do you have any idea why?" Jen asked quietly, inching herself forward.

"Uh..." Rachel looked at Susan.

Susan said, "No particular reason." She focused her attention on Jen, speaking directly to her. "You know how it is. So hard to meet anyone interesting. And if you do manage to find someone who can hold your attention, they turn out to be an asshole." She exhaled hard through her nose. "I'm glad I'm not out there anymore," she said, winking at Rachel. Rachel looked embarrassed. I couldn't tell if it was what Susan said or why she said it that was making her uncomfortable.

Jen looked at Rachel. "It must be a relief, I guess." Rachel nodded, and in her expression, I saw the reason for her discomfort—she didn't realize that Jen and I knew the nature of her relationship with Susan. She was either embarrassed that she was a lesbian or embarrassed to be with Susan. I was putting my money on the first, but I didn't rule anything out. Maybe her parents didn't know, and having them around made her insecure. Maybe they knew and didn't approve. Maybe she didn't approve herself. Too many maybes.

We let the silence sit awhile. Rachel adjusted herself on the sofa, sat for a moment, and then adjusted herself again. Susan spoke first.

"What will happen with Beth's body?"

"Hasn't anyone called you?" I asked.

"No."

I looked at Rachel. She shook her head and sunk deeper into the cushions.

"They should have. Rachel, you're listed as the next of kin, aren't you?"

"I don't know," she said. "Where would I be listed?"

"Well, you're the emergency contact person and the beneficiary of her school life insurance policy, right?"

"There was an insurance policy?" Rachel asked. The idea seemed troubling to her, as if there were something more palpable in the promise of bureaucratic paperwork than in the disposition of the body.

"Yes, there was," I said. I didn't want to lay anything on Paula or her office, but Rachel should have been notified. "Have you talked to your parents today?"

"No," Susan said, cutting off Rachel before she could answer.

"The coroner's office may have contacted them," I explained.

"But Rachel is the one to make the arrangements, right?"

"Technically, yes," I said, wondering about the animosity toward Beth and Rachel's parents that seemed to be oozing out of Susan. "But the colonel's been calling the office like clockwork. They may have assumed he was the responsible party."

Rachel leaned forward. "But they wouldn't let them take her, would they?"

"Is there some reason that would be a problem?" Jen asked.

"No," Rachel said, "um...I guess not."

Susan continued for her. "We just don't agree with them about the final arrangements. I'm sure we can work it out."

Jen locked her eyes on Rachel. "Is there something you're not telling us about your parents?"

Rachel shrunk back into her chair and looked at Susan. "No," she said. Her voice sounded small and far away. There obviously was something. I didn't think we should push too hard to find it out yet because we might risk the rapport we'd managed to build with Rachel. It wasn't much, but it was something. I kept my mouth closed, though, and let Jen deal the play.

Jen said, "We'll check with the coroner's office and make sure we get it straightened out, okay?"

Rachel tried to smile again and came a bit closer this time. "Thanks."

Jen and I stood up. "If you think of anything else, or if there's anything we can do to help, give us a call," I said to Rachel. Then Susan gave us a polite nod and showed us to the door.

In the alley on the way back to the car, Jen said, "So why do they hate the parents so much? Suppose it's a homophobia thing?"

"Don't know," I said distractedly.

She obviously expected something more in the way of an answer. "What do you know?"

"I know Roger Kirby."

SEVENTEEN

I've often wondered just how many people have managed to capture the happiest moment of their life on film. It seems that most would wish for this, the ability to experience again the instant of their greatest joy—to recapture and revisit those sensations, to relive that moment, to bask again in that warm glow of contentment. Not a bad thing to hope for, really. Not bad at all.

Unless things have changed.

And things change. They always change.

There's a photo of Megan and me in our wedding album. It's not one of the pictures that we spent two hours posing for before the ceremony, working our way through every possible combination of family members and members of the wedding party. It's not one of the five-by-sevens taken during the ceremony. It's not even one of those taken by a random guest with the disposable camera we left on each table, next to the centerpiece.

No, this particular photo is an eight-by-ten glossy taken by a crime scene photographer named Mikey who just happened to have half a roll of black-and-white film in his camera that he wanted to use up before his next call. I moved the picture to the front page of the album so it's always the first one I see when I flip open the cover. I don't often turn the page. I wonder if I would remember the moment so clearly without that photo. I like to think I would, but who knows?

It's after midnight, and most of the guests have gone. Megan wants one more slow dance before we let the DJ pack up. He plays "If I Should Fall Behind," and we hold each other and just sway back and forth. We're beat, my collar is open, and my jacket has long since been hung off the back of a chair somewhere. She's let down her hair and abandoned her high heels for bare feet. Halfway through the song, she stops moving, takes a small step back, her hands on my hips, mine on her shoulders, and looks up at me. The expression on her face is the most beautiful thing I've ever seen. I feel as if her eyes are somehow reaching out and pulling me into them, and in that moment, in that single instant, I see myself through her eyes. Never before have I felt such unconditional love. I don't even notice the flash go off.

I forgot all about Mikey's extra pictures until my first day back at work after the honeymoon, when the watch commander handed me a manila envelope with my name written on it in black Magic Marker. I tore it open and found a dozen photos with a note that said, "Danny, hope you guys enjoy these, Mikey."

This photo was the bottom photograph in the stack, the final shot before he'd run out of film. It went from last in the stack to first in the book.

As I tried to turn past it to find the picture I was looking for, Jen said, "Wait," and reached out her hand toward the album.

"What?" I said.

"I want to see that." She was sitting next to me on the couch in my living room.

I let her take the book out of my hands. She turned the page back and looked at Megan and me. I was busy being tough, so I just stared out the front window at her Explorer, which was parked outside at the curb. It really needed a wash.

"That's a beautiful picture," she said.

"I know." I was trying to discern whether the line across her fender was a scratch or just a smudge.

She touched my knee and said, "Show me the one you were thinking of."

I took the album back and began flipping through the plastic-covered pages. The photo I was looking for was near the back, with the other photos that guests had snapped with the centerpiece cameras. Megan was sitting at a table next to Roger Kirby. He was a friend of hers from college. His left arm was wrapped around the shoulders of Elizabeth Anne Williams.

EIGHTEEN

"I haven't seen him since Megan's funeral," I told Jen.

"How well did you know him?" she asked as she centered the steering wheel and accelerated into the traffic on Seventh Street.

"Not too well. Megan and I had these distinct groups of friends. There were the ones who were friends of both of us, and then she had her friends, and I had mine."

"And yours were cops, right?"

I nodded.

"We know how well they play with others."

"Exactly. Mine and hers didn't mix too well. Kirby was one of hers. I don't know that much about him. He was a sociology major with her, and then he got some kind of a consulting job for an insurance company in Irvine."

"Should we run him?" she asked.

"Why not?" I called Pat on my cell and asked him to get us everything he could on Kirby.

"I'll get right on it," he said.

"Anything new?" I asked him.

"Nothing spectacular. I've been checking out the shipping manifests from Cutting Edge. They moved almost two thousand kukri knives in the last year."

"That seems like a lot."

"It is, but we can narrow it down a bit. They have a couple of different models. And almost half the sales were direct to customers through the catalog or the Web site. I'm scanning the lists right now."

"What about the other half?"

"Not bad," he said. "Only about a quarter went to retail stores. The rest went out through other online and direct marketers."

"That's good." Finally, I thought, something positive.

"Yeah. I'll keep you posted."

"And get back to me with anything you can find on Kirby."

"Will do," he said and hung up.

I turned to Jen. "We might have caught a break on the weapon. Looks like Pat's going to be able to trace most of the buyers. The knife company does most of its business through direct catalog and Internet sales."

"Credit card records?"

"Yeah."

She didn't say anything.

"What?" I asked.

"If you were going to kill somebody, would you buy the murder weapon with your American Express?"

Kirby had a sixth-floor corner office in a shiny steel-and-glass building half a mile south of the 405. His secretary showed us in, and we sat in leather chairs facing an oversized, satin-finished cherry wood desk that was perfectly coordinated with the carpet, paint, and other furniture—even the door matched. "He'll be right with you," the woman said. "Would you like coffee or tea?"

"No," Jen said, answering for both of us.

The building was located on what was still the outlying edge of the Irvine Company's master-plan sprawl, so rolling, grass-covered hills filled the views from the windows that covered two walls of the room. I wondered how long the view would last before the landscape was filled with beige-stucco shopping centers and red-tile-roofed gated communities. Not long, I thought. I gave it two years before the first developments began popping up in the visible landscape.

Gazing out at the floor-to-ceiling panorama, I began to wonder how thick the glass was and how much force it might withstand before shattering. Maybe I'd seen too many movies, but there was something about a large window that just made me want to throw someone through it. I imagined propelling Tropov through the glass and watching him tumble in a cascade of glittering broken shards sixty feet to the pavement below.

"How thick do you think that glass is?" Jen asked.

I laughed.

"What?" she asked.

The door opened, and Roger Kirby came in. "Danny," he said, "long time no see." He was trimmer and more angular than I remembered him. He wore a finely tailored dark gray suit over a white-collared blue shirt and polka-dotted tie. His hand extended from his side as if it were an autonomous entity and gave me a hearty shake. I noticed he was much more delicate with Jen's hand when I introduced her. His gaze stayed on her a bit longer than it should have. "Can I get you anything? Coffee? Bottled water?" he asked.

"No, we're fine," I said.

"How long has it been?" he asked me.

"Megan's funeral."

"That long?"

"Uh-huh."

"Well, you look good," he said, staring into my bloodshot, dark-circled eyes and beginning the long walk around the desk. He must lie to people often, I thought. He's good at it.

"So do you," I said, wondering if I sounded as sincere as he did. The insurance business must have agreed with him. He looked as happy as a pig in shit. "This is quite an office."

He spun his chair around, sat down, leaned forward, and folded his hands in front of himself. "I manage," he said.

"Really," I said. "It looks like you've done well for yourself."

"Well, you know how it is," he said. "Survive a merger or two and a few rounds of layoffs, and they've got nothing to do with you except middle management." Jen and I both nodded as if we understood.

"In a way," he continued, "I wouldn't have made it this far without Megan."

"How do you mean?" I asked, my interest piqued.

"She encouraged me to go to graduate school. And that helped out," he said. "I wouldn't have been this successful without that."

I remembered a conversation with Megan in which she said she might be interested in going back to school for a master's degree. An MSW, I think she called it. Trying to be encouraging, I'd told her to go for it. I'd been close to making detective then, so the money wouldn't be a problem. Of course, I didn't realize until much later that money had nothing to do with it, that it was about something else entirely. She never brought it up again.

"She thought about graduate school herself," I said, remembering. Jen raised an eyebrow at me, in case I hadn't realized I was drifting. "Didn't realize you got an office like this with a master's in social work, though."

"Oh," Kirby said, "I changed disciplines for my graduate work. I went for an MBA. The sociology background gave me a good feel for urban demographics. Never figured out what to do with it until B-school." He leaned back in his chair and shot me a grin. When I didn't return it, he added, "Seemed like the thing to do at the time."

I took a long look around the office and said, "It still does." We all grinned at each other as if we'd lucked into a prime tee-off time at the country club. I wanted to tell him how disappointed Megan would have been, how she would have accused him of selling out, of shilling for elitist corporate interests, of conspiring to reap personal benefit from the exploitation of the poor. I wanted to, but I didn't. Instead I tried to act impressed and genuinely happy for his good fortune. "Really, Roger, this is impressive," I said.

He folded his hands again and said, so sincerely that I almost believed him, "Thank you."

"Unfortunately, though, we didn't come to see your office."

He leaned forward, now serious. "I didn't guess you had."

"Do you know why we're here?" Jen asked.

"I've got an idea," he said.

We waited for him to continue.

"It's about Beth, isn't it?"

I nodded and let him sit in the silence. As we watched him, I counted thousands in my head. He didn't fidget or twitch or look up or shift his position or any of the other things guilty people were said to do. In truth, though, the only people who ever really exhibited those behaviors were those who truly felt guilty. Whoever had murdered Beth was far beyond feeling any emotion so outwardly directed as guilt. Kirby was cool, if nothing else. I had to give him that. I made it to sixteen thousand before he spoke.

"I can't believe she's gone," he said, his voice thick with sincerity, but as the old joke goes, once you can fake that, you've got it made. "She was really a special woman."

"I know," I said.

Jen looked at me, realizing even before I did that my awareness had floated away and that I'd been thinking of Megan. Kirby didn't pick up on it.

"How long had it been since you'd seen Beth?" she asked him.

"Almost two years."

"But it was longer since you'd been involved?"

"Yes. Quite a bit longer. More than five years since we'd been serious. But we stayed friendly."

"How friendly?" Jen asked.

"What do you mean?" Kirby asked. He tilted his head to the right as if he didn't understand.

"Did you stay intimately involved?"

"No." He looked down at his desk and then back up at Jen. "Once Beth decided something like that, that was pretty much it. It took her a long time to make up her mind, but once she did, it stayed made up."

"Breaking up was her decision, then?" she asked.

"Yeah." The corners of his eyes fell, and his forehead wrinkled at the memory. "I thought she was the one, you know?" We nodded at him and let him go on.

"It took her a long time to trust me. After we'd been together for a little more than two years, I asked her to move in with me. I still remember the look on her face. She was surprised. I couldn't believe she hadn't expected it." Kirby's expression changed as he thought of her, his face softening, his posture relaxing. He looked more familiar to me, as if I'd only recognized him before but was now able to place him. "So we did it. And we were happy. At least I was. With Beth, though, there was always something you couldn't see, just below the surface, that she never quite let out. I guess I thought it was kind of mysterious or enigmatic or something." The edge of his mouth turned up, and he inhaled through his nose. "I should have let it go, you know?"

"Let what go?" I asked.

"The mystery, the unknown," he said. "I just couldn't, though. The longer I was with her, the more convinced I was that there was something she was holding back. Some secret she wouldn't...couldn't tell me. Of course," his voice dropped as he finished his sentence, "there was."

I leaned forward, and he saw the question in my face.

"Jesus," he said, "you don't know about her father, do you?"

NINETEEN

Jen and I didn't talk on the way down. We just looked at each other's dull reflection on the brushed stainless finish of the inside of the elevator door. A pleasant-toned chime sounded, telling us we'd reached the first floor, the doors slid open, and bright sunlight, reflecting off the polished marble walls of the lobby, spilled into the elevator. I squinted into the brightness and followed Jen past the concierge's desk, through the glass doors, and out into the open.

Just outside she stopped, put her hands on her hips, and breathed in deeply through her nose. "You okay?" I asked.

She nodded and took a few steps toward the fountain in front of the building. It shot a circle of pulsating water jets a dozen feet into the air, where they dissolved into large drops and fell back into the center of the gold-leaf-bottomed pool. She sat on the fountain's polished granite edge and rested her elbows on her knees. The air smelled of chlorine.

I sat next to her, knowing enough not to say anything. When my cell phone rang, I didn't answer it. Just to our left was a brass plaque that identified the name of the sculptor commissioned to make this particular work, *Water Feature: Rain in*

D Minor, Number 4. Eleven people walked past us. Most were men in suits, and their faces held expressions of mild surprise and disapproval to see us there. Apparently, they didn't like people sitting on the artwork. They looked away, though, as soon as they caught my eyes. My face must have told them all they needed to know.

Jen looked at me and said, "He's telling the truth, isn't he?"

"Yeah. I think he is."

"And so was she when she told him."

"Yeah. I think she was."

"Fuck."

"Yeah."

"Honestly," I said to Ruiz several hours later, "I'm not sure what it means to us. Maybe nothing at all. But it's big."

"And it was confirmed by the sister?"

I nodded.

"What should we do with it?" Jen asked.

"I don't know," Ruiz said. "How is it connected to the investigation? Does it go to motive?" I could see him considering the variables that this new information added to the equation. "What do you want to do?" he asked her.

Jen had been waiting for that. "I want to front him with it. See what he does."

"The colonel's been itching for action," I said. "Let's give him some."

"We bust him for the murder, I can get him to cop to the rest," Jen said.

"This could blow up in our faces," Ruiz said, as much to himself as to us. "I don't know."

"What's the worst that could happen?" I asked.

He just shook his head. "Bring him in for questioning. No charges yet."

Colonel and Mrs. Williams had moved from the downtown Long Beach Marriott to its smaller and cheaper cousin, the Marriott Residence Inn on Willow, just off the San Diego Freeway. In exchange for the loss of the hotel's first-class service and accommodations, they'd received a full, but tiny, kitchen, a one-hundred-dollar-a-night savings on the rate, and a touch of artificial homeyness. The complex itself was designed to increase that feeling, resembling nothing so much as a suburban LA apartment development. Clusters of four to six rooms were piled together, next to and on top of each other, and separated by concrete walkways and ornamental shrubs in a roughly formed rectangle around a courtyard and pool.

At the front desk, the clerk highlighted the route to the Williamses' room on a photocopied map and told us to walk past the jacuzzi and turn left at the second BBQ. A few seconds after we knocked on the door, a shadow covered the peephole briefly. We heard the dead bolt slide, and the door swung wide.

The colonel, dressed in chinos and a snug navy blue polo shirt, stood back and motioned us into the room. "Good evening, Detectives. Please make yourselves comfortable." The room was little more than a typical hotel room, about the size of a spacious studio apartment with an L-shaped floor plan and furnished with a king-sized bed, a small sofa and chair, and a dining table that doubled as a work area for the business traveler on the go. Mrs. Williams sat at the table, a newspaper open in front of her, and looked distractedly in our direction.

Jen took a step past the colonel into the room, but I stayed between him and the door. He turned his shoulders indecisively, not sure whether to look at Jen or at me, and said, "Have you found out something?"

"Yes, we have," Jen said.

As he turned to face her, she curled her right hand into a fist, shifted her stance to the balls of her feet, and centered her weight over her hips. She was going to hit him. On more than one occasion, I'd seen her break bones with her fists. I wanted to see her do it now. I wanted to hear the liquid crack and see the blood pour down the colonel's face—but her fist relaxed, and she let her breath out slowly.

"What is it?" he asked.

Earlier, after we'd left Kirby's office, on the way to see Ruiz, we made a stop on Broadway, a block east of Pine Avenue. As we walked past the Blue Cafe, a recording of a song that sounded like Muddy Waters's "Who Do You Trust" reverberated above the empty patios and across the promenade. The song faded when we turned the corner into the alley and buzzed Rachel Williams's apartment.

"Hello?" Her voice sounded far away. I wasn't sure whether it was her or the tinny speaker or a combination of the two that gave the sound its airy, distant quality. But it didn't matter. By that point, nothing would have eased the leaden feeling deep in my gut caused by anticipation of the conversation that Jen and I were about to have with Beth's little sister. At that moment, I was able to understand, if not forgive, their mother.

"Hi, Rachel," Jen said into the intercom. "It's Detective Tanaka. I'm sorry, but we need to speak with you again."

"Oh, okay."

The buzzer worked this time. We went in and walked up. The door was open when we reached the upper landing. "Hi," she said to us. I knew then that the speaker had nothing to do with the remoteness in her voice. It was almost as if she were somewhere else. She may very well have been. "Come in," she said, opening the door wide. "Susan's not here." That particular piece of news would have been welcome in any of our previous meetings with her, but now it was something of a disappointment. "You can sit down if you want." We walked across the loft and sat on the same couch we'd sat on during our last visit. Rachel curled up across from us, her feet tucked beneath her.

"I'm afraid we're going to have to talk about something very unpleasant," I said.

Her face wilted, and I thought she might begin to cry.

Jen took over. "Rachel," she said, her voice warm and tender, "we need you to tell us about your father."

She did cry then. Two tears rolled down her left cheek, but her expression took on a solidity we'd not seen there before.

"What about him?" she asked.

"I think you know," Jen said, her voice a whisper.

"Where should I start?"

For what I assume are much the same reasons why convicts brutalize child molesters in hideous ways behind prison walls, cops, no matter what their experience, never seem to develop defense mechanisms and coping strategies when it comes to crimes against children. I've never heard a homicide detective make a joke over the body of a dead child, although I once watched as Marty and another detective, the thirty-year vet whose slot I filled in for the detail, did a five-minute comedy routine crouched beside the corpse of a priest. ("Did you hear the one about the altar boy who ran away from home? He didn't like the way he was being reared!") I couldn't sleep that night, but now when I remember the scene, I smile. Sacredness, I suppose, is in the eye of the beholder. What intrigues me, though, is that it has always seemed to me that the less we hold sacred, the more fiercely we protect it.

It had started so unexpectedly and built so gradually that neither Elizabeth nor Rachel, four years later, could pinpoint the origin. "We'd been at Vandenberg for years," Rachel said. "It was the longest I'd ever been in one place. Four years at the same school. That was something for us then." She was quiet, lost in the memory. "Beth and me, I mean. We were always moving. A new school every year. So we really liked Vandenberg, you know? It felt like home."

We waited for her to go on. When she didn't, Jen said, "What was it that happened?"

"We didn't realize it then, but Beth figured it out later. She was always the smart one." Rachel's forehead crinkled, and she pulled her knee into her chest. "And the pretty one, too. I used to be so jealous of her." She was beginning to drift, but we let her go. We both wanted to ask just what Beth had figured out, but we didn't. She needed to find her own way.

"She was so popular. Partly just because we'd been there so long, longer than almost everybody else, and we knew everything about the school. But really it was her, you know? Not just because she was pretty, but because of who she was. She was smart and funny. And kind. All the boys just loved her. Everybody did. Everybody. I guess that was kind of the problem."

We let her sit a while. When it seemed as though she was ready to continue, I said, "A minute ago, you said Beth figured something out. What was it that she figured out?"

"It was about our father," she said. The sad fondness that had been in her voice just a few seconds earlier slipped away, and she looked like she'd eaten something that was beginning to sour her stomach. "He was supposed to be a general, you know."

"I didn't know that," I said.

"Yeah, second in his class at the Air Force Academy, knew all the right people. All that."

"But?" Jen asked.

"When he got to Vandenberg," Rachel said, "he just kind of topped out. See, that's what Beth realized later. He'd had a promotion every year or so and moved right up. When he made major and we moved to California, he just stopped moving up. And that's like a bad thing in the military. You have to keep the momentum up or you stall. Kind of like a plane." I saw a flash of something in her eyes, surprise, I thought, at her ability to make that connection. "So he had to think of something else to keep moving up the ladder. Major just wasn't good enough. And he did, he figured out a way." She let go of her leg and put both of her feet on the floor.

"How did he do it, Rachel?" Jen asked.

"I only found out about this later, when Beth told me the whole story. But you know how I said everybody loved her, right? Everybody did. Especially General McCabe. Our father used to bring him home a lot. He'd eat dinner with us, have barbecues, go to the beach. He'd bring us presents all the time. We had to call him Uncle Mac. He wore this cologne—I don't know what it was, but he always wore too much of it. Beth and I used to make fun of him. Called him McWank.

"But then, one day, around the same time our father finally made colonel, Beth just stopped. She changed. She got quiet. She stopped talking to people at school. She just kind of turned herself off. It was kind of funny, see, because I'd always wanted to be just like her, and all of a sudden, she was just like me." Rachel paused, and as she rubbed her fingers across her cheek, a realization swept over her. "No, that's not right. It wasn't funny. It was sad. And I never knew why she changed like that. Not until later. I asked her over and over again what had happened, because I knew something had. Something must have. But she wouldn't talk about it. She wouldn't tell me. Not until later."

"Later," Jen said softly, nodding.

"After she left for college. She couldn't wait to go. She even finished high school a semester early so she could go sooner. She was accepted all over, with scholarships and everything."

"She escaped," I said.

"Then, after she left, Uncle Mac started coming around again. And he got even weirder. He started hanging around me more and more. And my father started to leave us alone more and more. He'd make excuses, like going to the store for wine or something, and he'd take Mom with him. And then Uncle Mac started touching me. I knew it was wrong, but I didn't know what to do. Somehow I knew not to tell my parents. I called Beth."

"What happened then?" Jen asked.

"I remember it was a Wednesday morning. Beth was home that afternoon. She drove all the way up from school. Got there before Dad did. And before Mom, too—she had a job in the PX then. But Beth just came in the door and grabbed me and held me and said she should never have left me there. She just kept saying she was sorry. Over and over and over.

"When Dad came home, as soon as he came through the door, Beth just stood up and got right in his face. I'd never seen her like that. So strong. I couldn't believe it. And she said to him, 'It stops now.' He pretended not to know what she was talking about. She slapped him. Hard. He was so shocked. I don't think anybody had spoken up to him in years. *We* never had."

Rachel's eyes had dried, and her voice, in its growing strength, seemed to lead her deeper into the memory. "She said it again to him, 'It stops now.' 'You don't give me orders, young lady,' he said. 'Yes,' she said, 'I do.' She stared into his face and said it just like that. I thought he was going to have a stroke or something, the way he just stood there and trembled. 'Do you understand me?' she asked him.

"He didn't say anything. I didn't think he could, the way the veins in his neck were bulging out. I never saw him so angry. See, he never got mad because he never had to. But he was so…I don't know, it almost seemed like he was on fire. She asked him again. 'Do you understand me?' He still didn't move.

"'Here's how it's going to be,' she said, 'McCabe never comes into this house again. He never sees her again. Anywhere. At the school, on the base, at the store, anywhere. Ever. If she ever has to look at his face again, ever, I talk. To everyone who'll listen. Do you understand me?' He still didn't move. He looked like a statue. 'And you,' she said to him, 'you piece of shit, you leave and you don't come back until Rachel's out of the house. I don't care what you do, where you go, what you tell people, you just go.' He moved then. Just a little. He tilted his head to the side, just a little bit, but it seemed like so much. 'I know what you're thinking,' she said, 'but don't think it. It doesn't matter if I can prove anything. If I just make the charges, you're finished. Think about it. You know it's true. Look at me. Look in my eyes.' He did. 'You know I'll do it,' she said.

"That was the first time in my life I ever saw him look scared. But he did what she said. She sat with me on the couch while he went upstairs and packed his bags. She didn't budge an inch. And he did exactly what she told him to. He didn't say a word. While we sat there, I figured it out—what had happened to her. What he'd done. What he had let be done. He used her to make colonel, and he was going to use me to make general. But she turned it around on him. She wouldn't let him. She took control. I wouldn't have believed that could happen. That she could do that, be that strong.

"And now," Rachel said, the sadness edging back into her voice, "she's gone."

The colonel's eyes lost their focus and something let go in his posture as he read our faces. As his understanding of what we'd learned began to take root, he seemed to contract in upon himself like a dying star, collapsing into blackness. Part of me wanted him to keep going, to shrivel into nothing, to disappear completely—but only a small part of me. Mostly, I wanted to make him scream, to cry out in pain and anguish. I wanted to hurt him.

"Turn around," I said. I gave him about a second to comply, and when he wasn't quick enough, I shoved him into the wall so hard that bottles clinked in the minifridge. I spun him around and pressed his face into the ugly, oatmeal-colored wallpaper.

As I twisted his arms behind him and tightened the cuffs on his wrists, I let Jen speak. "Mr. Williams," she said, "you're wanted for questioning regarding the murder of Elizabeth Williams. You'll need to come with us."

I pulled him away from the wall and steered him out of the room. I imagined him falling down the stairs, his face scraping across the steel-edged treads, the weight and momentum of his body driving his head into the landing and snapping his neck with an audible crack—but he didn't fall, and even though the thought occurred to me, I didn't push him.

Forty-five minutes later, the colonel was handcuffed to a steel chair, which was itself chained to a D ring that was inset in the bare concrete floor of the interview room. Marty, Dave, Ruiz, Pat, Jen, and I were huddled behind the two-way mirror in the darkened observation room, staring at him.

"Well," Marty said, "at least it looks like somebody yanked the stick out of his ass."

The colonel slouched forward in the chair, which was not uncommon, as the two front legs were shorter than those on the back, causing anyone sitting in the chair to either slide forward or slouch in order to adjust for the slant. The colonel, though, was reacting to more than just the angle of the interrogation chair. He looked as though he'd been left in the sun too long, left to wither and rot.

We fidgeted in silence, crossing arms, rattling keys in pockets, tapping feet, scratching necks, all the while eyeballing the fresh specimen on the other side of the glass.

"What do we do with him?" Dave asked.

"Let him stew," Jen said. "He's not ready yet."

We watched him. One by one, detectives trickled out of the room until only Jen and I were left.

"Not yet," she said.

"Let's keep him overnight."

"Think Ruiz'll go for that?"

"Probably not," I said. "So let's take him downstairs and process him into the holding tank before we ask."

I expected her to at least acknowledge the end run around the lieutenant's authority, even if she didn't argue against it, but all she did was nod and say, "Okay."

By the time we'd finished checking the colonel in for the night and made our way back upstairs, Ruiz had gone home. "When he found out where you were," Marty said, "he was pretty pissed. Slammed his door and everything."

I said, "But he didn't stop us, did he?"

He answered by tossing an empty Styrofoam coffee cup across the room into a wastebasket. "Two points," he said.

Jen and I didn't speak much on the drive back to my house. The revelations about Beth and her father were considerable in their implications. The trouble was that we had no idea just what those implications were. The question foremost on our minds, of course, was whether these events provided the colonel with a motive to murder his daughter. Maybe she'd threatened to go public. That might do it. After pimping one of your daughters and attempting the same with the second, was killing one of them so long a leap? But why would Beth speak out now after so many years of silence?

When Jen stopped her Explorer to drop me off in front of my apartment, she said, "I could use a drink."

We sat in the living room and finished off two bottles of Sam Adams Winter Lager that had been on the bottom shelf of the refrigerator for the last few weeks. I turned on the TV, and we pretended to be interested in a show on the History

Channel, something about WWII and the "greatest genera-
tion," just brimming with the warm glow of nostalgia. Nothing like sepia-toned reminiscences to beef up the powers of de-
nial. Apparently only foreigners did bad things in the 1940s.
The program never got around to the racially segregated bat-
talions, internment camps, or Fat Man and Little Boy.

Jen swallowed the last of her beer. "Got any more?"

"Nope," I said. "Those were the last."

"I'll have a screwdriver, then."

I was surprised that she knew I had all the ingredients. It
had never occurred to me that someone else might be aware of
my proclivity for Grey Goose and Minute Maid. I tossed the
empty beer bottles in the trash in the kitchen and wondered
how she knew. It wouldn't take much. A glance in the freezer
and fridge would have done it. Maybe it was just a lucky guess.
Still. I filled two glasses and went back into the living room.

Jen had turned the volume down on the TV, but the same
program was still airing. In newsreel footage and black-and-
white stills, American bombers flew silently over Eastern
Europe, dropping their payloads. Jews were gassed. Dresden
burned.

"You think he killed her?" Jen asked.

"Honestly? After the way he imploded today, I don't see it.
But he's as good as anybody else we've got."

"Could be the reason he's been hanging around." She
sipped her drink. "See what we know, if we suspect him. Typical patterns of guilt."

"Yeah, unless he's just trying to figure out if we know about
the alternate career trajectory that got him promoted. He had
to figure it would come out, right? Maybe that's the guilt he's
dragging around." I noticed that my glass held about a third

as much liquid as Jen's. I reached forward and put the glass down on the coffee table.

"Maybe." She let her head flop back and looked at the ceiling. "Shit. Three suspects and we can't even make a decent circumstantial case against any one of them."

"It could be it's not any of them," I said. "Actually, if I had to make a bet right now…" I didn't finish the sentence.

"All I know," Jen said, "is that we still don't fucking know." She drained her glass in a long pull and handed it to me. "Barkeep, another round." I think she was shooting for whimsical, but she missed the mark by a wide margin.

"You sure?" I asked.

She nodded. We kept drinking.

Two hours and three glasses later, she fell asleep on the couch and started to snore. That was the first time I had seen her sleep. I wished I had a video camera—or at least a tape recorder to get the sounds. "Hey," I said softly, patting her knee. I said it again a bit louder and patted a bit harder, and she still didn't wake up. "Jen!" I said, with what I felt surely was enough volume and force to wake her. She stirred a bit, rubbed her nose, and made an odd grunting sound before settling down again. She wasn't going to budge. I thought about leaving her on the couch to sleep it off, but the couch left quite a bit to be desired in the comfort department. I tried to rouse her one more time and still had no luck. Her breathing settled into a slow, deep rhythm. I slipped one hand between the back of the sofa and her shoulder blades and the other under her knees and lifted her.

I was surprised by how light she felt in my arms. For a reason I couldn't articulate, I felt a pang of fear ripple through my chest. She seemed so small, so vulnerable, so different from her waking self that, as I carried her down the hallway toward my bedroom, more than once I stopped and adjusted her position in my arms to avoid even the possibility of an unexpected bump or scrape.

As soon as I laid her down on the bed, she shifted her position, rolling onto her side. I took off her shoes and pulled the comforter up over her. Kneeling by the side of the bed, I studied her face, her closed eyes, her parted lips, her mussed hair, and tried to reconcile this new image of my partner with the many already dancing around my head. Her ability to astonish me seemed, at that moment, infinite.

TWENTY

I turned on the CD player in the living room and set the volume low. *Mule Variations* was next up in the changer, and I sat down and leaned back into the couch. I didn't think I'd be able to sleep before midnight, but after a few minutes I kicked off my shoes, put up my feet, and rested my head on the armrest. I thought of Jen in the bedroom. No one other than Megan and myself had ever slept in that bed. I found it difficult not to attach any significance to that fact. I tried not to think about it. But there it was.

The last thing I heard before closing my eyes was the broken glass tenderness of Tom Waits's voice as he sang "Georgia Lee."

I slept a solid six and a half hours, the best I'd done in a long time, and I thought that perhaps I should switch to the couch on a permanent basis. Even then, though, I knew it wasn't really the couch that had made the difference. I'd had a dream, but its details eluded me every time I came close to capturing them in my memory. A woman had been there, but I wasn't sure who it was. Each time I almost glimpsed her face in my mind's eye, she slipped away again, as if turning away and disappearing.

As I stood in the bedroom doorway and watched, Jen rolled from her back to her side and tucked her arm beneath her head. My stomach tingling, I felt like a child who couldn't help but do something he knew he shouldn't—say, rifling through his parents' closet in mid-December, finding the Christmas bounty, and not being able to tear himself away.

When Jen opened her eyes a few minutes later, I was still watching. She opened and closed them a few more times, trying to reconcile the unfamiliar surroundings with her recollection of the night before. As her awareness fell into synch with her memories, she lifted her head and saw me leaning a shoulder against the doorjamb.

"Morning," I said, attempting an upbeat inflection.

"Hi," she said, pressing her palms to her cheeks and rubbing her eyes with her fingertips. After a jaw-straining yawn and a feline stretch, she began to rub her tongue around the inside of her mouth and then pouted at the taste. Her voice resonating somewhere deep in her chest, she said, "Ewwwww."

While she showered, I tried to remember the last time I cleaned the bathroom. I rummaged through the kitchen cabinets looking for something "breakfasty" that I wouldn't be embarrassed to offer her. Behind cans of Stagg Steakhouse Chili and Chef Boyardee Ravioli, I found an old box of Twinings Irish Breakfast Tea. Sniffing one of the bags, I decided it would do, although I wasn't convinced I'd even be able to tell the difference between fresh and stale tea with my sense of smell. I rinsed out the kettle, filled it with water, and put it on the stove. It began to whistle just before Jen came out of the bathroom, freshly showered, wearing yesterday's clothes.

"I've got some tea," I said.

"Thanks." Her eyes didn't seem to be quite open yet. "Anything to eat?"

"I'm thinking either Egg Heaven or The Potholder. If we stay here, it's either marshmallow Fruit Loops or Wild Magic Burst Pop-Tarts."

"You're intentionally trying to make me puke, right?"

"Not intentionally, no." I poured a cup of hot water over a tea bag in a ceramic Smith & Wesson mug. A sales rep had dropped off several cases of the mugs last year when he was trying to persuade the LBPD to change its standard sidearm. We didn't buy the guns, but now half the cops in the department had matching sets of coffee mugs.

"I'd forgotten what it feels like to have a hangover," she said.

I hadn't, so I dunked the tea bag up and down in the cup, hoping the subject would change of its own accord. "Here you go," I said, sliding the cup across the counter. "I've got some orange juice too. I'll get you a glass."

"Thanks."

After we downed our tea and juice, I suggested breakfast.

"I'm not sure that's a good idea," she said.

"Trust me, you'll want to eat."

The sadness in her eyes as she looked into my face caught me by surprise.

The Potholder is a breakfast-only restaurant on Broadway that, in order to accommodate even the most liberal definitions of the most important meal of the day, closes its doors in midafternoon. I indulged myself with an overflowing plate of French toast, scrambled eggs, and sausage. Jen had a fruit plate and an order of one of the kitchen's specialties—super spuds.

"Do you want some of these hash browns?" she asked after she'd spooned half of the uneaten mound of potatoes from one side of the plate to the other and back again.

"Sure," I said.

She hadn't spoken much since we left my apartment. At first I attributed her silence to her hangover, but as we ate, I began to suspect that there was something more on her mind.

"You all right?" I asked.

"You mean other than feeling like I'm going to vomit until my head explodes?"

"Yeah," I said, "other than that."

"I'm fine."

"What if I said I don't believe you?"

"I'd say it's a very sad thing when the trust scampers out of a partnership."

"Then I won't say that."

"Probably for the best."

The number of attendees at each task force meeting was dwindling, as was the actual size of the force itself. The deputy chief hadn't put in an appearance in more than a week, and one by one, the other detectives and uniforms assigned to the investigation were returning to their normal duties and case rotations.

"Is this everybody?" Marty asked. Around the table with him were the lieutenant, Dave, Pat, Kincaid, Jen, and myself.

"Yeah," Ruiz said.

"And then there were seven," I said, referring to the ever-decreasing size of our meetings. No one got the Christie reference. That, or no one wanted to encourage me.

"Unless we put in a request for assistance," Ruiz said, "the rest of the crew will be returning to regular assignments."

"Why?" Jen asked.

"Because it's been days since we made *Eyewitness News*." Ruiz rubbed his temples. "What have we got?"

Jen asked, "The colonel?"

One of the advantages, I thought, to our new, sleeker, leaner task force—if there were any at all—was that everyone in the room already knew the major developments of the case, saving us the monotony of regurgitating the story over and over again. Jen could ask her two-word question, and everyone knew who and what she was talking about.

"He's right where you left him," Ruiz said. "We didn't talk about holding him."

"No," I said. "We didn't."

Judging by Ruiz's expression, I was well beyond his glibness threshold. He glared at me and asked, "What are you going do with him?"

"How about we tattoo 'short eyes' on his forehead and toss him in with the general population at county?"

His lip quivered, and I knew I'd gone too far.

"Honestly," Jen said, "we can't figure out what to charge him with. We don't have jurisdiction on the sexual abuse, and we've got nothing to use to charge him on the murder." She looked at Kincaid. "Any ideas?"

"Do we just want to hold him, or do we want something we can make a case with?" Kincaid asked.

"I want to see him burn," Jen said.

"We can book him on a withholding charge," Kincaid said, "and hope it sticks long enough to figure out just who does have jurisdiction. It's a long shot, though. We'd have to convince whoever winds up prosecuting that they have a case—and one that's worth pursuing. Then we'd have to arrange extradition. I doubt we'd manage that. Not if his lawyer's even halfway decent. Give it a go, though, if you want." He smiled at Jen. The glare of his bleached teeth made me want to squint.

"Is it worth it?" Ruiz asked no one in particular.

"Yes," Jen said. "We take it as far as we can. I'm not going to have a hand in kicking that fuck loose."

Ruiz thought a moment and then nodded. "We're sure he's not our guy on the murder?"

"Sure?" she asked. "No. We're not sure. We've got serious doubts. But sure? No."

"What about a suspicion charge?" Ruiz asked Kincaid.

"Again, depends on the lawyer. It's another option, though. Definitely."

"He hasn't lawyered up yet," I said. "Maybe he won't."

Kincaid considered that. "If he doesn't, we can keep him under the key a while. Eventually, we'll have to get him a public defender, though. And the longer we dick him around, the more likely it is a judge'll cut him loose when we get to court. We need to think about how we want to play it."

"Bottom line, though," Ruiz said, "we're still looking for a killer."

Jen and I nodded. I added a "yep" for emphasis.

Ruiz turned the page of his notepad. "Dave has something for us," Ruiz said.

We all looked at Dave expectantly. "Something on Tropov." Dave must have heard me sigh because he fixed his eyes on mine as he continued. "Possible motive. The guy Tropov works for, name's Anton Samuels. Changed it from some three-foot-long Russian name with no vowels. Anyway, this guy, he's supposed to be some former KGB honcho, right? And he's got a history in Seattle, too. Just like Tropov. Turns out Anton has a kid in high school. And back up north, some of this kid's teachers filed a police report saying they felt intimidated by Anton and his goons whenever junior's report cards didn't measure up. Now, guess where the kid went to school last year."

"Warren," Ruiz said. It didn't sound like a guess.

"And he was in Beth's class?" I asked.

"And guess what grade she gave him."

"I have a better idea, Dave," I said. "Why don't you just tell us?"

"She gave him an F. He had to go to summer school to graduate."

"And that made him so bitter and resentful he had his old man whack out his English teacher," I said. "Not sure I buy that."

Ruiz eyeballed me again. "I don't remember you bringing a better motive to the table. You might want to think about shutting your mouth." I took his advice.

"What are we supposed to do with that, though?" Marty asked. "Wasn't the official word from the brass to lay off Tropov?"

"It was," Ruiz said. "But we're not going to. Keep digging. Just find something solid and let me worry about the deputy chief." He looked around the room. "What else?"

No one spoke.

"Pat," he said. "Anything on those knife sales?"

"Nothing that looks promising on the direct online sales," Pat answered. "But I'm looking at the company's shipping manifests. A few dozen units went to LA and Orange County stores. I'm working my way through their sales records. Maybe we'll get lucky."

"Think our boy was dumb enough to buy the murder weapon with plastic?" Marty said to no one in particular.

"Keep working on it." Ruiz thought a moment. "Jen, anything new on Waxler?"

She shook her head. I stared at him, but he pretended not to notice. "What else?" he said again. "Anyone?" There was a long, awkward pause while we all shuffled our feet under the table, looked down at our notepads, fidgeted with our pens, and above all, avoided Ruiz's eyes. I had a sudden impulse to pass a note to Jen telling her to meet me behind the gym after study hall, but I fought it off.

When I got back to my desk, the message light on my phone was blinking. The colonel had been rushed to the emergency room.

TWENTY-ONE

"How the fuck did he hang himself?" I yelled at the poor schlub of a city jailer unlucky enough to have answered the phone. "Didn't you take his belt and laces?"

"Um...yeah, we did."

"Then what did he hang himself with?"

"Uh...his underwear?"

"Are you asking me?"

"No," he said. He was new and not used to dealing with pissed-off detectives. The fact that I'd forgotten his name probably wasn't helping. "He used his underwear," he repeated.

"How does someone hang himself with underwear?"

"Well, from what I understand, he was up on the top bunk, okay? And he took one leg hole and wrapped it around the bed frame, okay? Oh, and these are briefs, not boxers. You know, tighty whities? So he takes the rest of them and pulls them through the loop around the frame so they're tied off like a lanyard or something, and then he squeezes his head through the other leg hole and just rolls right off the bunk."

"Shit," I said.

"Yeah, the other guys, the sergeant and everybody, they were real impressed."

"They don't get out much do they?"

"Huh?"

"He was alive when they took him away?"

"Barely, they said."

"Thanks, you've been a big help."

"Sure thing, Detective Beckett," he said, his eagerness raising the pitch of his voice. "Anytime."

I wished I could remember his name.

"What did the hospital say?" Ruiz asked. Jen, Marty, Dave, and I were huddled around the lieutenant's desk.

"The prognosis isn't good," Jen said. "He's in a coma, and there's major brain damage from lack of oxygen. Even if he wakes up, he's probably going to be vegetable stew."

"So what's that mean for us?" Marty asked.

"Nothing," I said. "He isn't our doer."

Dave folded his arms across his chest. "You sound sure of yourself."

"I am," I said, turning to face him.

"And your dicks are exactly the same size," Jen said. "Can we move on?"

"What's Baxter going to say about this?" Marty asked.

Ruiz said, "I think we all know the answer to that, don't we?"

Two hours later, Deputy Chief Baxter called a press conference, ostensibly to announce that the case was closed and that Elizabeth Williams's father had murdered her, and then, just as the intrepid task force began to piece the puzzle together, had taken his own life out of either remorse or the fear of spending the rest of his days behind bars.

"He wants us to stand behind him while he makes the announcement," Ruiz said, his voice a low, rumbling grunt.

"What did you tell him?" Jen said.

"Not what I wanted to," he said. "I told him we'd be there." Everyone grumbled.

"Is this case really closed?" I asked.

"Officially," Ruiz said, obviously upset at being forced to toe the party line. "Yes, it is."

To avoid saying something we'd all be sure to regret, I stormed out of the office. I didn't really have anywhere to go, so after marching up and down the hall several times, I went into the bathroom, washed my hands and face, realized I had to take a leak, took one, washed my hands again, and wandered back to my desk.

I hadn't been gone more than fifteen minutes, but Ruiz's office was empty, and no one was in the squad room. The deputy chief had timed the press conference to coincide with the local late-morning newscasts, just far enough past eleven to avoid conflicts with the headlines and, most likely, assuring that the news directors wouldn't have anything more titillating to broadcast.

After turning on the small TV and tuning it to KCAL, I sat down with a fresh cup of coffee and a slightly stale apple fritter and waited. That was a bad idea.

Before they even cut away to the live feed, I'd dialed Geoff Hatcher's number. The phone was still ringing as the liaison officer on the screen introduced Baxter. The deputy chief took the podium and called the task force up to stand behind him. Guess he must have never heard that old coach's axiom, "There's no *I* in *team*."

"Hello?" Geoff said in my ear.

"Hey, Geoff," I said. "So how pissed are you?"

"Daniel?"

"Yeah."

"It's not really a good time. I'm driving like a madman to get to your news conference. It seems very unlikely I'm going to make it." Although a bit of traffic noise filtered through his cell phone, there was no indication of any tension in his voice. He might just as well have been sitting in an overstuffed easy chair sipping brandy from a snifter.

"Not a problem," I said.

"It's not? I was led to believe that Deputy Chief Baxter would be making a significant announcement. And by the way, I am still quite pissed."

"Well, get ready to be unpissed. In fact, in a few minutes I think you're going be in love with me all over again."

I spent three minutes giving him a brief rundown of everything we knew about Tropov, Waxler, and the colonel.

"So he wasn't even a suspect?" Geoff asked.

"Not seriously, no."

"Well."

"I need to run. But I'll call you later with more. In the meantime, start digging. And do me a favor, will you?"

"What?" he asked.

"I want you to use Tropov's name."

"Are you quite—"

"Yes." As I hung up the phone, Baxter was on the TV, praising the diligence of the task force. The camera panned the team. Marty, Dave, and Jen looked merely uncomfortable. The lieutenant looked like he was about to explode. I knew he'd maintain through the press conference, though. But if he heard about what I'd just done, the shrapnel would fly. Oh yeah.

Before everyone came back, I decided to go get lunch. I walked across Broadway to a Mexican place that, despite the fact that not a single sign in the restaurant was written in English, was constantly filled with white cops sucking down tacos and tamales and marveling at how "authentic" the food was. I ordered my usual carne asada burrito and wondered what everyone back in the squad was doing. I knew they'd be angry that I flaked out on the conference. Too bad. There was no way I was going to stand up for Baxter and even pretend to support him in closing the case. Not when I knew that Beth's killer was still walking and talking. And I did know that. I kept muttering it to myself under my breath. I wanted a reckoning. And I didn't care what it cost.

Ruiz didn't waste any time. As soon I walked back into the squad, he yelled, "Beckett!" Jen looked at me the way an embarrassed mother watches her child caught in an inappropriate act.

I stood in front of the desk in Ruiz's office and crossed my arms over my chest. "Hey, Boss," I said. I made a point of speaking so softly that no one outside would be able to hear. I knew without turning my head that at least six eyes were locked on us.

He leaned back in his chair, trying to hold his anger in check. "Danny, you're crossing lines here that can't be uncrossed."

"I'm sorry, Lieutenant. I really am. But I can't let this one go. Not like this. I don't believe the colonel killed Beth. I'm still working it."

"No, you're not. Marty and Dave are going to stay on it. I told Baxter they'd be 'tying up loose ends,' and he seemed all right with that."

"That's bullshit, and you know it. There are a lot more than loose ends here. But we're getting close. I'm almost there." I looked in his eyes. If there was any forgiveness in them, I couldn't see it.

"Look," he said, leaning forward, running a finger between his collar and his neck. "I understand what you're going through. You're connected to this. Nobody's trying to edge you out. We'll keep you in the loop. You've put a lot into this. We won't forget."

"You think I'm worried about who gets the collar?"

"Sit down, Danny."

"Look, you just—"

"Sit down," he said, his voice almost a whisper, "or I'll come over there and sit you down." I sat.

"You feel bad about Baxter exploiting this," Ruiz said. "So do I. As far as the media is concerned, this case is closed. We know different, though, don't we, Danny?"

I didn't answer.

"We do. You know what hurts me, though? What really hurts me? You believed I'd let him bury this. Hang it on the old man and forget all about it. You actually believed that, didn't you?"

I told him the truth. "Yes."

"That's why I put Dave and Marty on it. I brownnosed Baxter and let him put on his show because I knew that if I did, then we'd still be able to work the case, as long as we did it quietly. No more task force. No more politics getting in our way. Did you think of that?"

"No."

"The reason I'm putting Marty and Dave on it is because they've been able to maintain their perspective. You haven't."

"Give it to me and Jen."

"No."

"Please," I said, lowering my head. There would be no turning back now. "I need this."

He leaned back in his chair, watched me, and then picked up a pencil and began rolling it between his fingers. "You sure you can handle it?"

"Yes."

"You know, if you drop the ball on this one, you're going to hurt Jen too."

"I understand."

He watched me to make sure I did. "Only if everyone's okay with it."

I turned around and looked at them through the window Marty and Dave both shrugged their shoulders. I looked at Jen. She nodded.

"All right," he said. "Don't screw up."

Too late for that, I thought.

Jen and I went to the hospital to check on the colonel. On the way up Long Beach Boulevard, she asked me, "You okay?"

"Sure," I said. "I'm fine."

After a long silence, she said, "I know you're having a hard time with this one."

"What makes you think that?"

"You're coming unglued, Danny. We're all worried about you."

"I'm fine," I said again, trying as much to convince myself as her. "It's just..." My voice trailed off, and I let the silence hang in the air.

She cut off a UPS van and pulled over to the curb. "I know," she said, turning in her seat to face me. "It keeps you thinking about Megan." I was taken aback that she found this fact so obvious. "But I have to say this—it's not about her, Danny. It's not. And no matter how many cases you crack, no matter how many Tropovs you beat the shit out of, no matter how many skells you take down, it's not going to change what happened."

I just kept looking out the passenger window, not wanting to acknowledge the fact that she knew me so much better than I knew myself.

At the hospital, we learned nothing new. I watched the colonel for a while. He was reclined in the hospital bed, intubated, a respirator doing his breathing for him. He looked gaunt and haggard, a thousand years old. I'd be lying if I said I didn't feel some small measure of satisfaction in his complete loss of dignity and in knowing how humiliated he'd be if he were able to understand his situation. I hoped that somewhere deep inside his withered carcass, some part of him did understand, some part of him felt his degradation and shrank from it.

Maybe his wife had felt the same emotions I was feeling. She'd stayed only long enough to see that he was stabilized, and then she went back to the hotel. No one had seen or heard from her since. She didn't even leave a number to call with any news.

"I hope he wakes up," Jen said to me in a soft voice. "He doesn't deserve to get off this easy."

"No," I said. "He doesn't. But how many of us get what we deserve?"

TWENTY-TWO

"What's this shit about the case being closed?" Pat asked as I walked into his office.

"Exactly that," I said. "Shit."

"But the task force is over, right?"

"Yeah. As far as the brass is concerned, we're done. Jen and I are just mopping up."

"Until you figure out who really killed her," he said. "Then Baxter's gonna be eating a big-ass plate of crow."

"Yeah. Assuming we do manage to figure it out."

"You'll manage." He spun half a rotation on his ergonomic chair and dug through a pile of papers on his desk. "Speaking of which," he said, "I have a list of all the Cutting Edge sales invoices for LA and Orange counties, going back a year. I found seventy-eight direct sales of the kukri we're looking for. Another fifty-odd units to retail outlets. I'm running backgrounds on all the buyers we can track."

"Don't suppose Tropov or Waxler bought one, did they?" I asked.

"Not directly from the company, but maybe from one of the stores. I'm going to start making the rounds this afternoon. Maybe we'll get lucky."

"Uh, Pat," I said, "you know you're not technically on the case anymore, right?"

"Who'll know the difference? You think anybody upstairs has the slightest idea what I do down here?"

I didn't have an answer for him. "Tell you what," I said. "Why don't we split up that list? We'll get through them faster that way."

"Sure. How should we divide them?"

"Geographically."

"Okay," he said, working his keyboard. "We'll split them at the county line." He punched a few more keys. "Hang on," he said as the printer behind him hummed to life. He handed me a sheet of paper that listed dozens of sporting goods, gun, surplus, and specialty stores sorted into two groups: twenty-six locations in LA County and another twenty-nine in Orange. "You guys want to go north or south?"

"You live in Huntington, right?"

"Yep."

"Why don't Jen and I take LA? Keep you closer to home."

"Sure thing."

"Thanks, Pat," I said.

"No sweat." He opened his desk drawer and took out a long, thin, red and yellow cellophane package. "You want some turkey jerky?"

"So," I said, looking up from the list to look at Jen behind the wheel of her Explorer. We were still parked outside the station. "If you were Tropov or Waxler, where would you go to buy a big-ass knife?"

"We triangulate with the address closest to both of them and work outward in concentric circles," she said. She unfolded the LA map that the Thomas Brothers had graciously pasted inside the cover of their once-popular street guide. Online services like MapQuest and in-car navigation systems were eroding the book's market, but for our needs, the good old fashioned paper version beat the new technology hands down.

Jen slipped a stubby pencil out of a slot on the sun visor and began drawing on the map. "Okay," she said, making an X on Rancho Palos Verdes and another on the edge of Long Beach Harbor. "The midpoint's here—San Pedro." She made another mark. "Where do we start?"

"Let's see," I said, running my finger down the list of addresses. "There's Union Surplus in Pedro and Quartermaster and Turner's Outdoorsman in Long Beach." We decided to hit them in reverse order, starting at the closest point and working east to west and, if necessary, north. Turned out it was necessary.

We came up empty at the first three places, and we weren't holding out much hope for number four on the list, J&J Paintball and Martial Arts Supply. The store was in an old converted warehouse that was snuggled in the crook of the interchange between the Harbor and San Diego freeways in Carson. The merchandise, along with the clientele, fell somewhere between the full-bore fantasy of Jackie Chan movies and first-person shooter games and the all-too-visceral reality of Glock and Beretta 9s and 40s.

Inside, a mulleted twentysomething clerk almost choked on his Subway sandwich when Jen leaned against the counter, let her coat slip open to show off her weapon, and said, "Do you think you might be able to help me?"

He still had a mouthful of bread and meat, so he nodded and mumbled "uh-huh" into her chest. She'd undone an extra button on her silk blouse while she was walking from the car to the front door. The day's experience dealing with knife-selling clerks hadn't been lost on her.

While Jen was busy engaging him in the interview, I let my eyes wander up and down the aisles, which were filled with martial arts uniforms, pads, dummies, and weapons. On the far side of the large store was a glass case. The wall behind it held rack after rack of paintball guns and accessories. In the far corner, a multicolored rainbow of paintball bursts covered two sheets of plywood that had been mounted on the wall as a makeshift firing range.

"I'm investigating a murder," Jen said, flashing her shield. She introduced herself and went on. "What's your name?"

"Bill."

"Bill, I need to know about a knife."

"What…" His voice came out at a higher pitch than he'd expected, so he cleared his throat before he continued, but it didn't seem to help. "What kind of knife?"

"Oh, what is it?" she asked casually, pretending to consult her notes. "A kukri. Made by a company called Cutting Edge."

"Oh yeah," Bill said. "We have those. Right over here." He walked three yards down the long glass counter, inside of which, on three mirrored shelves, was arranged the largest display of cutlery I'd ever seen—folding hunters, Swiss Armys, butterflies, stilettos, daggers, KA-BARs, bayonets, tantos, bowies, and just about everything else imaginable. At the far end of the display, easily recognizable, were half a dozen variations of the blade in question. Three of the six kukris were obviously cheap, low-quality numbers, the polished gleam of their blades and hardware not quite covering up the tool marks and the rough fit of the dull wood handles. In contrast, the satin-finished brass and stainless steel of the Cutting Edge models seemed almost to warrant the exponentially higher prices.

"The Cutting Edge ones are the best," he said. "Nolo contendere."

Even though half a dozen came to mind, I didn't make a wisecrack. As far as I could tell, he still hadn't even noticed I was there. Just in case, I thought it wise not to give up the element of surprise.

The clerk took the knife out of the case and handed it, handle first, to Jen. "The other ones," he continued, "are pretty much just import crap, if you don't mind my saying so."

"You seem to know a lot about this stuff," Jen said, holding the big knife in her hand, managing to sound genuinely impressed.

"Well, I've been here almost two years now."

"So you're pretty much an expert?" Jen asked.

"I wouldn't go quite that far," he said.

"How far would you go?" she asked.

I looked down into the case and pretended to study a folding Spyderco clip point.

"Uh, pretty far I guess." His voice cracked and rose another octave halfway through the sentence, reminding me of those classic "Is it live, or is it Memorex?" commercials of my youth. I wondered if he'd be able to shatter a wineglass with his falsetto too.

"I need you to do something for me," Jen said.

"Yeah, of course. Anything. Sure——" He would have gone on, perhaps indefinitely, but Jen stopped him.

"Take a look at these pictures," she said, pulling three five-by-sevens out of her bag. She put them down on the counter, and the clerk looked down at the faces of Waxler, Tropov, and the colonel. "Does any one of these men look familiar?" she asked.

He studied the photos, one at time, giving each several seconds of his full attention. "You're looking for someone who bought a Cutting Edge kukri?"

"Yes," Jen said, "we are."

"Honestly," he said, "I don't think any one of these guys has ever come in here."

"You sound pretty sure," Jen said.

"Well, I couldn't say I'm positive, of course. But I'm here most of the time that the store is open, and I think I would remember if they did."

"Why?"

"Most of our customers fall into a certain demographic." There was a newfound authority in his voice, a confidence that hadn't been there before, and it dropped down into a lower register. "Primarily, the guys who come in here are young, mostly teenagers. It's the paintball and martial arts crowd, playing with the fantasy. They usually outgrow it before they hit twenty-five. So it's rare we get anybody as old as any of those guys. Maybe once in a while somebody's buying something for their kid, but that doesn't happen too often. Kind of spoils the fun if your mom has to buy your ninja equipment for you, you know?"

Jen laughed, and her laugh sounded genuine. Inexplicably, I felt good for him. Maybe I couldn't help rooting for the underdog.

"But these three guys, I really don't think so."

She questioned him for another five minutes about sales records. Turned out we probably wouldn't need a court order for the records because Bill really wanted to help out and "do his part," and he was pretty sure the store's owner would too. I doubted that, but I didn't say anything. We left with Bill's assurance that he'd have the sales records ready for us in a day or two.

South of the San Diego Freeway in Carson, just across the interstate from the landing field of the Goodyear Blimp, is the Dominguez Golf Course. For as long as I can remember, they've had a piece of statuary so impressive that it's been featured in at least two books on Southern California roadside kitsch.

It's a twenty-foot-tall fiberglass golfer, who stands, smiling, putter in hand, to greet the southbound motorist with glad tidings and an unspoken reminder about the wholesome goodness of golf. A few years ago, in an inexplicable fit of political correctness, the owners of the course gave the golfer a paint job to make him more closely resemble the predominantly African-American residents of the surrounding community. Unfortunately, the resulting figure resembled nothing so much as the world's largest lawn jockey. After numerous complaints from the local citizenry, the statue underwent another race change and became white again. Out of a habit rooted deeply in my childhood, I waved at him as we passed.

"Think we'll get anywhere with this?" Jen asked.

"No, but what else do we have?"

At a quarter past six, we decided to hang it up for the day. We'd covered most of the stores on the list and come up with nothing of any apparent usefulness. We stopped for dinner at the Belmont Brewing Company, a beachfront restaurant with its own line of brewed beers and ales.

The sun had set, and a chilly winter wind blew along the coast, but still we chose to sit on the patio. With its six-foot Plexiglas walls and the space heaters, it was downright cozy. I had a pale ale and a jerk chicken pizza. Jen surprised me by ordering both a lager and a platter of fish and chips. I worried that I was becoming a bad influence. She laughed when I told her that.

"Danny," she said, brushing a dark strand of hair behind her ear, "if my biggest vice is fish and chips, I think I'm in pretty good shape."

"But you know what they say about cod."

"No, what do they say?"

"It's a gateway fish."

"Yeah?"

"Uh-huh. Next thing you know, it's chicken fingers, and then you're only a hair's breadth away from mozzarella sticks."

She laughed again. That was the happiest I'd felt in days.

It was after eight when I finished the day's paperwork, made copies, three-hole-punched the handful of pages, and inserted them into the back of the three-ring binder that held the record of our investigation. More than a hundred pages in, and we still didn't know the story. Not the whole story, anyway. We were missing the most important part.

I was about to pack it in for the evening when the phone rang. "Homicide," I said. "Beckett speaking."

"Danny?" The voice was familiar, but I couldn't quite place it. "This is Brad Hynes. Down in Gang Enforcement."

"Hey, Brad." I tried to place him. There was a Brian on the squad too, and they were both big guys with dark hair and mustaches. Actually, now that I thought about it, that description fit about eighty percent of the squad. "What can I do for you?" I asked.

"Jen Tanaka's not still around is she?"

"Nope. She called it a night. I was about to do the same. Something I can help you with?"

"Not sure. Maybe. Got a kid down here, Rudy Nguyen, one of her cards in his wallet."

"What'd he do?"

"Nothing, really. We're holding him on suspicion. Found him driving a car registered to Milo Tran."

"Should I know him?"

"He's high up in one of the Westminster Viet crews. We've got an APB out on him. That's how we picked up the kid."

"You sweat him so far?"

"Not too much. We wanted to give Tanaka a heads-up before we go at him hard."

"You think he can help you?" I asked.

"I doubt he's got much to give up. If he did, Tran wouldn't have had the kid toolin' around in his Lexus."

"So you kick him loose, you're not really going to lose anything?"

"Nah. We've impounded the car. Anything we get's gonna come from that. We'll just book him, hold him overnight, then kick him tomorrow. Shake him up a little bit. Unless Tanaka wants to reach out."

"You know what? I'm sure she would," I said. "She's got some family stuff going on right now, though. Do me a favor, would you? Ride him hard awhile, see if you can shake him up a bit. I'll come down and take him off your hands in about an hour."

"You got it. See you then."

I knew I should call Jen, but I didn't.

Outside in the parking lot, Rudy slumped in the passenger seat of my Camry. When I had picked him up from the interview room in Gang Enforcement, I could tell he'd been crying, so I had gone easy on him, asking only if he remembered me. He nodded, so I thanked Brad for the heads-up and led Rudy by the elbow out to my car.

"You gonna tell Sensei Jen?" Rudy looked all of about ten years old as he spoke.

"What do you think?"

"I don't know," he said, his eyes staring down at the floor between his feet. "That's how come I asked."

"You've got bigger things to worry about."

"What do you mean?"

"You know why they were busting your ass back there, right?"

He didn't say anything. I went on. "Milo Tran's into some bad shit, Rudy. You don't know the half of it. You think you do, but you're wrong. Driving around in his car makes you an accessory after the fact." This was the first lie I told him. "That's a felony."

"It is?"

"Yeah, it is. You ready for your first strike?"

"I'm still a minor."

"That doesn't float anymore, Rudy. Not with felonies, and not with gangbangers. They're cracking down. These days just about every gang felon over sixteen's getting tried as an adult."

That was lie number two. I wanted to scare him, but I was also trying to see how deep he was in. The more of my shtick he bought, the cleaner he was.

"You shittin' me?" he said.

"Would Sensei Jen shit you?"

"No."

"Well, I'm her partner, so I won't shit you either."

He eyeballed me, like a carpenter taking measurements. Then I saw it in his eyes. He believed me.

"Besides," I said, "if I did, she'd kick my ass."

He smiled. It was the first time I'd seen him do that.

"You know I'm doing you a solid here, right?"

He nodded.

"I'm gonna need some payback on this."

Another nod.

"I know this won't be easy," I said, "but whatever you have to do, you go to class. I don't care what it is, if it's for your mom, for your brother, even for Milo Tran. Whatever you do, you go to class. That's how you square this with me."

He looked at me again. I couldn't read him this time. "Okay," he said, finally. I turned the key in the ignition.

Across the street from Beth's house, the blue luminescence of a TV screen glowed in the darkness behind the windows that looked in on Harlan Gibbs's living room, but I didn't turn my head in that direction as I got out of my Camry and walked to Beth's front door. The crime scene tape was gone, and before long, another tenant would move in. What would they know about the woman who'd lived there? What would they ask? What would they even want to know?

I didn't bring the key, so I just sat down on the porch with my elbows on my knees and stared at the oil stains on the concrete in front of the one-car garage.

"Hello, Detective," Harlan Gibbs said, limping up the driveway.

"Mr. Gibbs," I said, nodding toward his leg. "Are you all right?"

"Hip acts up every once in a while."

"Pull up a brick," I said.

He sat down next to me on the porch. "I saw the story on the news." He looked up at the sky, took a toothpick from his pocket, and worked it in between his incisors. "Father did it, did he?"

"That's the story."

"And you're just sitting here reflecting on a job well done," he said. Then he was quiet a moment. "How's it feel?"

"Like shit."

"I'll bet."

"You must know the feeling. Thirty plus on the job."

"I surely do." There was no awkwardness in the long silence that followed.

"Have any idea who really did it?" he asked.

"No more than the last time we talked."

"Any possibility it really was the old man?"

"A small one."

"But doubtful?"

"Yes."

"What are you going to do now?"

I looked at the lines spiderwebbing across his eroded profile. "Can I ask you something personal?"

"First time I ever heard a detective ask that question." He let out a snort that seemed to come from somewhere deep down in his rib cage. "Go right ahead."

"You had feelings for Elizabeth, didn't you?"

He scratched the crown of his head as he answered. "Probably make me sound like a dirty old man, but yes sir, I did."

"For what it's worth, I don't believe it makes you sound that way at all."

"She had a quality about her that—" He cut himself off midsentence and swallowed hard. "She understood that there's darkness in the world, but she managed to keep herself...in the light." He turned away from me and brought a hand to his face. "I don't mean to say I ever..."

I put my hand on his arm, thinking his description of Beth would have been as apt for Megan. "I know you didn't."

He nodded, sat quietly a moment, and then said, "Don't get old, son. You only wind up one of two ways—bitter asshole or sentimental fool. And the hell of it is, you never even get to choose."

TWENTY-THREE

The next morning, just after dawn began to glow in the eastern sky, I went outside in my shorts and T-shirt to retrieve the *Press-Telegram,* the cold concrete biting at the soles of my bare feet. Geoff's story, it turned out, was worthy of neither my initial enthusiasm nor the trepidation I'd felt when Ruiz changed his mind and reassigned Jen and me to the mop-up instead of Marty and Dave.

The story rated only about two column inches on the bottom corner of page six, in a sidebar to the continued-from-page-one story about the colonel's suicide. Having no solution at all to the case must not have been sensational enough, I guessed. But a military hero who pimped his daughter more than twenty years ago and finally killed her to shut her up scaled off the chart. It didn't matter whether or not it was true.

I don't know how I would have felt if I'd known the case would be making headlines again only a week later.

"How's it going?" Marty asked me as I walked into the squad room. He was the only one there, but the day's first pot of coffee was already more than half-gone. He'd turned the

TV on too, but had kept the volume low. On the small screen, Matt Lauer was interviewing an African-American hip-hop singer who'd recently started showing up in movies. I couldn't remember her name.

"Been at it a while?" I asked Marty, filling a cup for myself.

"Only about an hour or so. Caught a case yesterday afternoon." He shuffled a stack of papers on his desk. "Self-inflicted GSW. Just want to make sure it all adds up before we put it to bed."

I looked at my watch. It was five past seven. "Things still dicey at home?"

"Dicey? No. I wouldn't say that. Everything's settled. I'm apartment hunting after work tonight."

"I'm sorry to hear that."

"Me too. You come up with anything on those knives yesterday?"

"Nothing. Going to finish them up today, though."

"You got to do the legwork. You never know where you'll catch a break," he said.

My cell phone rang. I looked down at the caller ID display and saw Jen's number. "No," I said. "You never do."

"You should have called me," Jen said, her voice even. I couldn't tell how upset she was. I think that was her intent.

"I know," I said. "The gang guys wanted to know right then." I exaggerated a bit, though I wasn't sure if it was for her benefit or mine. "They were going to book him on suspicion of some crap or other, so I had to make a judgment call. I thought it was better to err on the side of keeping his jacket clean."

"I suppose it was."

"What would you have done?"

"I don't know," she said. "I want to say I would have let him learn his own lessons. But I probably would have caved."

I wondered about that. That's why I didn't call her the night before, even though I knew I should have. I was afraid she wouldn't reach out and that she'd regret it later. Either way, it would eat at her. "So I did the right thing?" I asked.

"I suppose."

"At least he'll be in class."

"That's good," she said. "But you should have called."

We spent most of the day running down kukri buyers, but still had no luck. Pat hit the same stone walls that Jen and I did. At half past three, he was in his office squeezing a racquetball in one hand and punching the keyboard with the other. Even with one hand, he was still typing faster than I'd ever been able to manage with two.

"No luck, huh?" he asked.

"Nope," I said. "Got a couple of shops say they'll provide credit card records, but I'm not holding my breath."

"Same here. One hard ass said we'd need a court order or a subpoena, though. Should I talk to Kincaid?"

"Can't. Case is closed, remember?"

"Well, that's fucked." He bounced the ball off his monitor screen and faced me. "Now what?"

"I wish I knew," I said.

I sat in my car, parked behind a new Starbucks, and watched people walking back and forth in the messy, palm-treed sprawl of the parking lot. My eyes kept drifting back to the ginormous AMC 20 sign that dominated my field of vision. The new George Clooney movie had just opened, and it was easier to think about that than to watch Daryl Waxler's empty Range Rover. I'd come to stake him out, to follow him around for a while. Maybe even to have another chat with him. Anything to get a fresh read. We were running low on suspects.

But I kept remembering that day in his office. He didn't seem like a killer—just a sad, scared man. I remember the look on his face when he talked about his wife's battle with breast cancer, about losing her, about the rough ride he'd gone through with D.J. afterward, and about the shock and pain of Beth's killing. Of course, he could have been lying. It wouldn't be the first time I wanted to believe an honest-sounding story coming from an apparently kindhearted suspect. But if he were the murderer, then he was one of the best I'd come across. Maybe he was a criminal mastermind after all. Or maybe just another smooth-talking sociopath.

"Fuck this," I whispered to myself as I twisted the key in the ignition. Hanging a left into the thickening southbound traffic on PCH, I turned on the radio. The tail end of *All Things Considered* came on, but I couldn't bear to listen to another story about violence in the Middle East, so I hit the CD button. Johnny Cash sang "Bird on a Wire," his baritone voice so rich and intense, so deeply connected to the melancholy longing of the song, that it was hard to believe Leonard Cohen had beaten him to it.

I had an updated copy of the murder book with me, a ten-by-thirteen manila envelope loaded with dozens of crime scene photos tucked into the cover of the binder. I planned to spend the evening going back to the beginning. Again. On the way home, I stopped for a cup of coffee at yet another Starbucks on Pacific Coast Highway.

The patio outside was filled with high school students who were ignoring the open textbooks on the metal tables in front of them to talk on cell phones and smoke cigarettes.

I ordered a venti-sized mocha. There was a seat open in the corner by the front window, so I could sit with my back to the wall and a view of the door. Ray Charles covered "Ring of Fire" on the sound system. I smiled at the coincidence. The man at the next table saw my expression and nodded at me as I took my chair. I made the mistake of nodding back.

"How are you?" he asked.

I mumbled a noncommittal reply and flipped the binder open. "Taking some work home, are you?"

I didn't answer him, but some deep-rooted resistance to simple and straightforward rudeness compelled me to acknowledge his question with another nod.

"What kind of work do you do?" he asked. I looked at him. He was a pleasant-enough looking little guy, fortyish, thinning at the hairline and thickening at the waist. His smile was so big it had the effect of making the rest of his face appear too small for his head.

"I'm a cop."

"Really?" He seemed impressed.

"Yeah."

"Wow. That's terrific. You guys do terrific work. And people don't appreciate it nearly as much as they should."

"Thanks," I said and turned my head back down to the report in the open book, hoping to ease my way out of the conversation. It didn't work.

"No, really," he said. "It's quite a thing to be able to live a life of service."

I felt the weight of my automatic hanging under my arm. I thought about unholstering it, but I couldn't decide whether I wanted to use it on him or on myself.

"Are you a religious man?" he asked.

"I take it you are."

"Yes sir, I most certainly am."

"Can I ask you something?" My curiosity seemed to please him.

"Certainly."

"They say when you're born again, you have a personal relationship with Christ. Is that right?" As I spoke, I slid the manila envelope out of the murder book and undid the metal clasp.

"Yes, that's true," he said.

"Really?"

He nodded.

"Would you do something for me?"

"What?"

"Next time you talk to him," I said, pulling the sheaf of photos out and fanning them across his table like a magician performing a favorite card trick, "ask him what kind of vicious fucking deity lets something like this happen."

His eyes went from the pictures of Beth's butchered body to me and back again. As the weight of what he was seeing took hold, a great sadness filled his eyes, he stifled a gag, and something solid caught in his throat, making his Adam's apple rise. I wondered if he was swallowing his own vomit. After his third breath, he looked me directly in the eyes and said, "The world can be a cruel place."

"Yes," I said, "it can."

I stared at him and left the pictures on the table until he got up and left. As I watched him waddle through the door, I was glad that he hadn't said anything about God's will or "His special plan" or Divine Providence because, in all honesty, I didn't feel like breaking his jaw anymore.

Jen and I spent the next three days running criminal background checks on the names of any kukri buyers we could get our hands on from the local retailers. When we'd run out of names, we came up with four possibles, but we eliminated all of them with another half an hour or so of digging.

"Now what?" Jen asked me.

"I'd really like to get in Waxler's face. Tail him for a couple days. Let him know we're watching. See if we can rattle him."

"You know we can't. Not as long as the deputy chief considers the case closed."

"I know," I said. "Shit. We can't even fuck with Tropov without tipping off the brass."

"So where does that leave us?"

"The school. How many times have you been over all the interview reports?"

"Only once," she said.

"Same here."

"Let's go through them again."

"Maybe do some reinterviews," I added.

"How many are there total?"

I didn't need to look at my notes. "Two hundred seven."

She looked up at the clock. It was a quarter to four.

"First thing tomorrow?" I asked.

She shook her head. "Pizza or Chinese?"

"I hope you're happy, Beckett." I stood in front of a urinal in the fifth-floor men's room, and since I had nearly finished the business that brought me there, I was, at the very least, relieved.

"Actually," I said, looking over my shoulder at Efram Kennedy from the Organized Crime Detail, "I am rather content. Happy might be stretching it a bit." It was the first time I'd seen him since he disappeared from the task force after the first meeting. I shook, zipped, and flushed, hoping he'd be willing to leave it at that.

Of course, he wasn't. The running joke about his unit among the other detectives was that the detail's acronym—OCD—was no coincidence. As if in an effort to be true to the label, Kennedy was wiry and twitchy, with a nervous energy that always made me irritable whenever I found myself in the same room with him. I didn't like him the same way I don't like Chihuahuas. He said, "Tropov's gone, you know."

"Well," I said, washing my hands, "I'm sure you'll miss him. I know how close you two were."

He blinked hard at me. Three times. My bet was that he didn't know whether to follow up with his intended attack or to respond to my insinuation. He went with option one. "Somebody planted an article in the *Press-Telegram*."

"Now who would do a thing like that?"

"You know what the Russians do when somebody gets attention like that? Do you?" He waited for me to answer. I reached past him for a paper towel instead.

"They kill them," he said. He stuck his chin out as if to emphasize his point. "That's right. They kill them." He crossed his arms and shot beams of superciliousness at me out of his tiny eyeballs.

"What was your case again?" I asked. "Some kind of check-kiting thing?"

"Money laundering."

"Oh, well." I nodded. "Money laundering. That's some big time stuff, there. Boy. You know what Tropov did to that woman in Seattle, don't you?"

This time I waited for him. He kept his mouth puckered shut, so I went on, moving closer to him as I spoke. "The way he chopped her up? Cut out her womb, just to teach her husband a lesson? You know about that, right? Because I can show you the pictures. I've got them right back in the squad. You want to see them? You want to?"

"I know what he did."

"You do? Good. Then you'll understand why I'm not too broken up over the fact that you didn't get to lock him up in Chino for fifteen months on that class-three felony bullshit. Maybe, and I like to think this is true, maybe we're all just a little bit better off with that piece of shit scraping the bottom of the harbor."

He seemed to find something of great interest in his shoes.

"Are we done here, or should I do like they used to do in junior high and stick your head in the toilet and give it a good flush?"

Sometimes nothing goes down quite so easy as a great big juicy chunk of righteous indignation.

Back in the squad, sitting across the desk from Jen, I was peeling a cold, leftover, pepperoni-and-sausage slice from a large Papa John's pizza when the call came in.

TWENTY-FOUR

Jen picked up the phone. "Homicide," she said, "this is Tanaka." The chair squeaked and her shoulders tensed as she sat up and leaned over the yellow writing pad on the desk. She began scribbling notes with a tooth-scarred pencil, tapping on the desk to get my attention.

I stopped chewing.

Jen spoke into the phone in monosyllables. "When? Where? Who's there?" She nodded, scrawled a few lines, and hung up.

"What?" I asked.

She was on her feet and holstering her pistol before I finished swallowing. "The case isn't closed anymore."

Jen drove. Ruiz and Marty were already en route to the scene, a residence in the Bixby Knolls area. She pulled into the northbound traffic on the 710 Freeway. In front of us, the brake lights on a tractor-trailer flashed, and my grip tightened on the passenger grab handle. Jen slowed.

"Could you give us a little more space there?" I gestured toward the truck ahead of us.

She cocked her head. It was the first time I had ever made a comment on her driving. That's why she was always the one behind the wheel. I had a much higher tolerance for her driving habits than she had for mine.

"What are you—" She stopped herself before she finished the thought. I assumed she remembered then how Megan had died. We rode in silence for a few minutes.

What I said then surprised me as much as it confused Jen. "Megan was pregnant."

Without looking, I could feel Jen fighting the urge to look at me, to keep her eyes on the highway. I stared straight ahead at the back end of the semitruck. Red block letters on the bottom edge of the passenger side swing-out door read, "Drivers Wanted! Great Pay! Great Benefits! Call 1-888-U-DRIVE-2."

I wasn't sorry I'd said what I had, but I didn't particularly want to continue, either. The air in the Explorer, though, felt thicker, and Jen felt farther away. I knew I couldn't let that one hang any longer. "That's why she was on her way out of town. She was going to her mother's. She didn't know what she wanted to do…thought that maybe she should…" I sucked air in through my nose. "That maybe she should do something about it. I didn't even know."

Jen said something I couldn't quite hear. Two syllables.

"That's how far I'd let her slip away. She wasn't even sure if she still wanted to have my child. She had to leave to figure that out."

"That's not your fault, Danny."

"Yes, it is."

She didn't argue. She just merged onto the Atlantic Avenue off-ramp. I hadn't even noticed the transition to the

San Diego Freeway. I was trying to see my reflection in the passenger window when I felt her hand on my knee. "Are you up for this?" she asked.

The ghostly outline of my head moved up and down on the glass, my face a transparent blur, and I was grateful that neither of us could see the tears welling in the corners of my eyes.

Bixby Knolls is the best-kept secret of Long Beach's old money crowd. It's a neighborhood of multimillion-dollar homes that surround an exclusive country club in the northwest corner of the city, an area not much more than a bullet's flight from the city of Compton and the parts of the LBC that have given birth to the hardest of the West Coast rappers. Beyond the locals, few knew about the Knolls—and all the rich folks who lived there liked it that way.

The murder victim we were rolling on had been found in a home on the border of Bixby Knolls and California Heights, one of the neighborhoods that insulated it from the rest of the world. The dividing line between the two communities is a fuzzy one, occurring somewhere between the thought that "someday, if things went well and you had a few lucky breaks and you married someone with an income a bit better than yours you just might live someplace like this" and "Jesus Christ, that place must cost more than my entire family will make if we all live to be a hundred fucking years old." Mary Ellen Robbins lived just south of that line.

Her house was a well-kept four-bedroom on a three-quarter-acre lot with an impressively sized pool and an equally impressive landscaped backyard that made room for a variety of ornamental flora, a bit of outdoor statuary, and even some homegrown tomatoes and strawberries. It was all, of course, very elegant and chic. The only thing that detracted from the suburban-posh scene was the wide swath of Mary Ellen's blood, splattered on the inside of the wide, glass expanse of the sliding patio door. Each time the crime scene photographer's flash went off, the blood gleamed a bright, translucent purple-pink and then faded to opaque crimson. There was something vaguely psychedelic about the effect.

Inside, the room itself was done up in off-whites and neutrals, and the lead crime scene tech was all wound up about how much data he was going to be able to get from the splatter patterns. Other than him and the photographer, the only person in the room was Ruiz, who stood in a far corner and looked down at the body, his hands in his pockets. Mary Ellen had been alone for a while, and she'd ripened—from the thickness of the earthy odor seeping out onto the patio, I guessed somewhere in the neighborhood of fifteen hours.

Marty stood outside with Jen and me. "Well," he said, peering through the glass at the body, "I guess it's safe to assume the case is open again." There was no irony in his voice, only a deep weariness that oozed out of him and made me want to rest my eyes, just for a minute. But Marty kept his own eyes open and glued on Mary Ellen's body.

Even from outside, it was clear that this murder was the work of the same perpetrator who had killed Beth. Mary Ellen lay on her back, eyes open, her face turned toward the motionless white ceiling fan, her abdomen a bloody pulp of hack-and-slash wounds. The purple-black puddle of her blood had soaked into the tufts of the white Berber carpet, coagulating to a dull sheen. The stump of her handless left arm pointed to a whitewashed bookcase built into the back wall.

Ruiz walked around the perimeter of the room and came out onto the patio. He nodded at Jen and me and then turned to Marty. "Where's your partner?"

"Went straight to the squad," Marty said. "Who found her?"

"Neighbor's dog was going nuts," the lieutenant said. "Neighbor came outside, looked over the wall, saw the open patio door, and when she couldn't get ahold of the vic, she phoned it in."

"The door was open?" I asked.

Ruiz nodded.

"How do we play it?" Jen asked.

He didn't answer for a moment. When he finally spoke, he sounded as if he'd been up for days, his voice like a rasp on wood. "Marty, I want you to get to work on the neighborhood." He tilted his head toward a huddle of uniforms on the other side of the pool. "Take Stan and a couple of the others with you."

"How long has she been down?" Marty asked.

"More than twelve, less than twenty-four," Ruiz answered. "They're working on the lividity. She's lost so much blood, it's hard to say."

Marty nodded.

"Jen, Danny, get on the victimology. Find me a connection," Ruiz said. "I don't want another scene like this."

In the kitchen, Jen and I found Mary Ellen's embossed, saddle-brown leather purse on the counter. I slipped my hands into a pair of latex gloves and opened the flap.

Jen said, "That looks like a Kate Spade."

"Huh?"

"The purse. It's a Kate Spade."

"What does that mean?"

"She's a designer. A handbag designer."

"Expensive?"

"Yeah."

"Well," I said, "I guess it matches everything else."

Jen looked around the kitchen as I pulled a wallet out of the handbag. "Why did it take so long to find her?" she asked.

"It wasn't that long."

"Look around, Danny. She had money. She lived pretty well. She's dead maybe eighteen hours before someone notices?"

"Let's figure it out."

She nodded. "I'm going to take a look around."

"Okay," I said. "I'll catch up with you in a minute."

I snapped the wallet's flap open and found her driver's license. I hit a speed-dial number on my cell phone and cradled the phone between my shoulder and ear as I flipped through the wallet. Platinum MasterCard. Visa. American Express. Several photos of an older teenage boy. In two of them, he wore a Stanford University sweatshirt.

"Pat Glenn. Computer Crimes."

"Hey, Pat. Hear the news yet?"

"Danny? No. What news?"

"Case is open again. You in?"

"What do you need?"

"We got another vic. Her name is Mary Ellen Robbins." I gave Pat her DOB and social.

"Give me half an hour or so, and I'll have something for you to work with."

"Thanks, Pat."

"No sweat."

I was still sorting through the business, video rental, and membership cards in the wallet when I heard Jen calling me from the other room. Her voice was far louder than it needed to be. "Danny!" she yelled again as I hurried down a hallway toward the sound of her voice.

In what looked like a former bedroom that had been converted into a home office, Jen stood behind a large glass-topped desk, her back to the wide window that overlooked the quiet, tree-lined street. She was about to yell again as I came through the door.

"What is it?" I asked. "Are you okay?"

"Oh yeah." She spun a leather-covered address book around and slid it across the desk toward me. "Bottom right-hand side."

Finding the connection was easier than we had anticipated. The last entry on the page was the telephone number and home address of Daryl Waxler.

TWENTY-FIVE

The squad and a handful of uniforms huddled on the concrete by the edge of the pool in the backyard. There was no breeze, and the pungent chemical smell of the overchlorinated water hung in the air. At least it was better than the odor in the house. Stan and his rookie partner stood at the edge of our loose circle. "Greg," I said, only half-sure I had the right name. "How you doing?"

"Fine," he said, the beginnings of a new mustache shadowing his lip.

Ruiz held up the evidence bag with Mary Ellen's phone book inside. "Okay. Now we've got probable cause for a search. Even an arrest. But before we move, I want to know everything about her connection to Waxler. We need to make this case before anybody else knows about it. Clear?"

Jen and I nodded.

Marty asked, "Still want us on the same jobs?"

"Yeah. Let's keep it simple."

"How about a picture of Waxler to show around?"

"Jen?" Ruiz asked.

"Have one back at the squad," she said. "How many copies?"

"If we want to keep it quiet," I said, "the fewer the better."

The lieutenant nodded. "Good point. Just one for Marty and one for Stan."

"Got it," she said.

"What kind of car does he drive?" Marty asked.

"A black Range Rover or a silver Mercedes E-Class sedan," I said, thumbing through my notebook to find the license plate numbers. When I found them, I copied them on a blank page, tore out the page, and handed it to Marty.

"You have his shoe size too?" he asked.

"Ten wide," I said.

"You serious?"

"Educated guess."

Jen made copies of Waxler's picture while I went upstairs to talk to Pat. "I was just going to call you," he said as I walked into his darkened office.

"You were?"

"Yeah. Big news."

"I got some too," I said.

"Let me guess Mary Ellen Robbins knows Daryl Waxler?"

"Son of a bitch," I said. "How'd you find that out?"

"Cell phone records. You?"

"She's got him listed in her address book."

"Small world, I suppose."

"No," I said, "not that small."

"Well, then, this must be evidence." He handed me a manila file folder.

"It is. Waxler's our boy," I said. I flipped open the folder. Inside were half a dozen pages of information about Mary

Ellen. Pat had found the basics—birth, marriage, divorce, tax information, and the like—in about a quarter of the time it would have taken me. "But we need to figure out his connection to her before we go at him. Come up with anything on that yet?"

"Not yet," he said, his face glowing white in the glare of the monitor, "but give me an hour or two. If there's a paper trail, I'll find it." I didn't doubt he would.

Mary Ellen's ex-husband, Seth, lived in Manhattan Beach. Technically, her son would be the next of kin, but we decided to notify her ex because the son was in Palo Alto, a freshman at Stanford. A face-to-face notification is usually better for the family than a long-distance phone call—that, and we wanted to needle him for information on her connection to Waxler.

"Should we call him first?" Jen asked. "Hate to drive all the way out there if he's not home."

"Don't want to tip him off," I said.

"No problem." She picked up the phone on her desk and dialed a number that she read from her notebook. Someone answered on the other end. "Bob?" she asked. The person on the other end said something. "Oh, I'm sorry. Is Bob there?... Well, who are *you?* Oh, okay, sorry about that." She hung up. "He's home."

"Good enough for me."

Seth Robbins lived in a brand-spanking-new, trilevel, steel-and-stucco home on Ninth and Highland, less than half a mile from the beach. The building itself, with its wide expanses of glass and the multiple balconies that undoubtedly provided spectacular sunset views, looked as though it might be auditioning for a centerfold spread in *Architectural Digest*. Compared to that place, his ex-wife's house might as well have had a rusting washing machine and a '72 Impala propped up on concrete blocks on the lawn. Halfway up the white flagstone walkway to the front door, Jen said, "Well, I guess we know who got custody of the money."

After we badged him through the crack in the door and told him we needed a few minutes of his time, Robbins let us inside. He was wearing a pair of drawstring shorts and a baggy, green, pigment-dyed T-shirt. He looked too old and too paunchy to have a name like Seth.

"What is it that I can do for you?" he asked. We stood in his foyer—an atrium, really—and his voice echoed softly in the thirty feet of empty space between our heads and the skylight above. He made no move to invite us any farther into the house.

I started. "Do you know a man named Daryl Waxler?"

"Yes," he said. Like most men in his income bracket, he knew enough to remain as taciturn as possible when dealing with government representatives.

"How do you know him?" I asked.

"He's a former business associate."

"And what kind of business are you in?"

"Consulting."

"And you've *consulted* with Daryl Waxler?"

"In a manner of speaking."

"Could you elaborate on that?"

"With my former employer, I was involved more directly in real estate development. We worked on several projects together."

"Did you have a personal relationship with him?" I asked.

"I'm not sure what you're implying."

"I'm not implying anything. I'm asking you a question. Was your relationship with him social or strictly business?"

"My former wife and I had dinner on several occasions with him and his late wife."

"Would you say you were friends?"

"We were."

"Past tense?"

"Yes," he said.

"So you no longer consider him a friend?"

"No."

"Why?"

Robbins paused. He didn't want to answer. He looked at me, at Jen, and at me again. "Shortly after my wife and I were divorced, she began dating him."

"And that upset you?"

"Yes."

"That's interesting," Jen said. "In the divorce papers you signed, she gave her reason for leaving you as infidelity. You cheated on her."

He was quiet and shifted his weight back and forth between his feet, probably wishing we were all sitting down. Because no question was asked, he didn't offer an answer.

"You're not denying that?" she asked.

"No."

"But you got upset when Waxler and your wife started dating?"

"Yes."

"Interesting."

He couldn't keep a solid grip on his tongue, though. "Have you ever been in love, Detective?" he asked. He stood a little taller than Jen.

She nodded. I tried to catch her eye, but she kept her gaze drilling into Robbins. "Yeah," she said, "have you?" Game, set, match.

"Look," he said, his hand working the keys in his pocket, "I'm not sure what it is you're trying to do, but if you'll just get to the point, I'll tell you whatever you want to know."

"Good," I said. "We're trying to figure out who killed your ex-wife."

His mouth opened and he reached out his hand as if to take hold of something for balance, but in the expansive emptiness of the foyer, there was nothing close enough.

"Think we were too hard on him?" Jen asked. We were eastbound on Rosecrans Avenue, heading back toward the San Diego Freeway. We'd just passed the new studio complex that was hard at work putting the South Bay on the entertainment industry's radar screen. From what I'd heard, the only noticeable effect its opening had had—aside from employing a handful of security guards and maintenance people who could barely afford the bus ride in to work from their homes in Inglewood and South LA—was to raise the prices in the swanky restaurants across the street from merely overinflated to completely absurd.

I thought about Jen's question. "No," I said, "and who cares if we were? He can go up to his rooftop garden, sit on a chaise lounge, and sip a martini while the sun sets into the Pacific and a twenty-two-year-old rubs his face in her breast implants. That ought to make him feel better."

"There's always that," she said.

"And besides," I said, "we've finally got a case."

It was after midnight when Ruiz sent us home. We had more than enough for full search warrants on Waxler's house and office—and enough probable cause for an arrest even if the searches came up dry. The lieutenant had talked to Paula about the autopsy, and she'd agreed to rush it through, moving Mary Ellen to the head of the line first thing in the morning. Ruiz's plan was to gather as much evidence as we could to link Waxler to the two murders and then move hard on him. None of us disagreed. If all went as planned, we would be arresting Daryl sometime before dinner tomorrow.

For me, this meant another night of counting the ridges and points in the acoustic ceiling above my bed. I'd finished off a bottle of Grey Goose with my second vodka and orange juice. I'd stopped there, I told myself, because I didn't have another cold bottle, and only people who drink too much do things like drink warm vodka.

As I looked at the ceiling, though, I couldn't stop thinking about what I'd said to Jen in the car on the way to the murder scene. I hadn't meant to tell her about Megan. I hadn't meant to tell anyone at all. Only three people knew that Megan had been pregnant—the medical examiner who had performed her autopsy, her mother, and me. And I only knew because I'd used LBPD connections to get my hands on an unauthorized copy of the ME's report on her death. That was that, I thought, no secrets left.

I wondered if there was any irony there. The last real fight that Megan and I ever had was shortly after I'd first partnered with Jen. It had been about secrets. We had celebrated Megan's birthday a few days before. I'd enlisted Jen's help to pick out a present, and Megan was concerned about the details of our life that I might have shared in the process. She was angry about all of the secrets, she said—or, more accurately, she yelled. Because I didn't know what she was talking about, I yelled back. Of course, I was too dim to realize until much later that she wasn't hurt by the secrets I might be telling, but rather by those I might be keeping.

Later, when sleep finally came, I dreamt of Daryl Waxler crossing the classroom toward Beth, with a kukri raised above his head.

TWENTY-SIX

By ten thirty the next morning, we had the makings of a solid case against Waxler. Two victims, same MO, and he'd been romantically linked to both of them. It was too much to be only a coincidence. We just needed something concrete to make the case, and we were confident we'd get it from the autopsy, the search, or the interrogation. With any luck, we'd get it from all three.

"Hey, Boss," Marty said as Ruiz made his way from the coffee room to his office.

"Yeah?"

"Anything?"

"Nothing new. Paula's going to brief us as soon as she's through. Kincaid's got the search and arrest warrants." He took a sip of too-hot coffee and grimaced at the pain on his tongue. "Just keep going on the background."

Last night's canvas of Mary Ellen's California Heights neighborhood had yielded nothing, and neither had Marty's recanvassing this morning. Dave put his current project, a jelly-filled croissant, down on a folded paper towel on his desk and asked, "Are we moving on Waxler as soon as we hear from Paula?"

"Maybe," Ruiz said. "We might wait until quitting time. I want to take him down at home."

"We should wait," I said. Taking him at work meant splitting the squad in order to exercise both warrants at the same time. Otherwise, someone might be able to tamper with evidence in the house between the time of Waxler's arrest and the time the search began. Mostly, though, I knew I couldn't be in two places at once and couldn't bear the thought of missing either the bust or the search.

"Probably for the best," Marty said. "Keep the squad together. Won't need as much outside backup. Fewer cooks."

Ruiz agreed. We all looked into the center of the room, waiting for someone to add something to the conversation. No one did.

We were beginning to entertain thoughts of lunch when Paula called to tell us that she was on her way to court in Long Beach and would stop by on her way with the results of Mary Ellen's autopsy. The crime scene technicians had found several fibers that we might be able to use to ID a perpetrator. The hope was that Paula would be able to add to that body of evidence, ideally with a bit of Daryl Waxler's DNA. On the phone she'd told Ruiz she was ten minutes away. It seemed longer.

Jen was at her desk, one of Pat Glenn's enormous sample kukri knives in her small hand. Every now and again, she'd toss it, spinning into the air, and then catch it by the handle. She didn't seem to be thinking about it. I did. I couldn't stop imagining two or three severed fingers bouncing in splashes of blood on her desk calendar. After what seemed like a very long time, she stopped throwing the kukri and began twirling it in her hand, like a uniform spinning his nightstick in a Joseph Wambaugh movie.

Marty spoke for the rest of us. "Uh, Master Po?"

She turned her head and looked at him.

"You mind putting that thing down? You're making us nervous."

"Sure," Jen said. She didn't put the knife down, though. She just held it in front of her stomach and looked down at the fluorescent light shining on the brushed stainless steel blade.

"Hey," Dave said, his eyes bright with inspiration, "bet you can't throw that thing and stick it in the boss's door."

She looked at him, eyebrows raised. "How much?"

He leaned over onto one butt cheek and extracted his wallet from his hip pocket. Flipping it open, he ran his finger between the bills, his lips moving with the count. "Sixty bucks," he said.

Jen held up the knife, aimed the point at Ruiz's door, sighted down the top of its curved blade, tested its heft with two bends of her wrist, and then looked back at Dave. Just as she was about to speak, Paula Henderson came in with the lieutenant on her heels.

"Nothing momentous," Paula said, stopping in the middle of the room between the islands formed by our clustered desks. "But a few interesting findings." She took off her glasses and let them hang from the chain around her neck. The file folder in her hands held copies of her report for each of us. She spoke as she handed them out. It felt like the first day of class. "Most important," she said, "it was the same murder weapon—no doubt about that. And the findings are consistent with a single perpetrator too."

We nodded in unison. Just as we had expected.

"We also found a few fibers that might prove useful and a single hair," she added.

"What color?" Jen asked.

"Brown."

Jen looked at me. "Any DNA?" I asked.

"Not sure yet," Paula said. "We're trying to salvage some from a bit of root that was still attached to the shaft. Even money we'll get it."

"So he wasn't as careful this time around," Marty said.

"I don't know if I'd say that, exactly," Paula replied. "But here's where it gets interesting. This time, there were fewer wounds. The first victim had too many wounds to count, remember? Not this time around. He cut her abdomen sixty-two times. Maybe half, two-thirds as many as with the first victim." She gave us a minute to let that sink in. Thrill killers virtually never decrease the severity of their attacks. The opposite is nearly a universal truth—the violence escalates.

"Could he have been interrupted?" I asked.

"Doubtful," Paula said. "He had plenty of time after the abdomen to sever the wrist. That was postmortem by several minutes at least. And he had some difficulty there."

She reached out to take the kukri that was still in Jen's hand. "May I?" she asked. Jen took the dull edge of the blade in her palm and passed the knife, handle first, to Paula. "See the downward curve in the belly here?" She pointed to the hollow inside the curve of the cutting edge. "Well, the point caught on the floor before hacking all the way through."

She held her wrist up alongside the curve so we could visualize how the blade's progress would be impeded in an attempt to chop through something on a flat surface. "Didn't even make it through the bone, actually. Gave it three tries before he realized the problem. Then he picked up her arm and sawed the hand off."

"Prints?" Marty asked.

"No. A powder residue. Hypoallergenic latex gloves," she answered.

"We can match the hair, though," Jen said. "We don't need prints."

"Even without DNA, I can give you a hair match with reasonable certainty," Paula said.

"What about the 'interesting' findings?" Dave asked.

"She already told us," I said.

"She did?" Dave raised his hands off his lap. "Funny, I don't remember going to the bathroom. How'd I miss that part?"

I tried not to let any of the anger percolating in my stomach come out in my voice, but I'm not sure I succeeded. "Well, Detective, if you'd been paying attention, you would have noticed that the crime Paula has just described was committed in a more methodical manner than the first. The perpetrator was calmer, less excited."

"Yeah?" Dave said, the retort skirting the edge of his capacity for convincing rebuttal.

"Yeah," I said.

"And what's so interesting about that?"

"Predators, thrill killers, serials—they don't work that way. They get more excited as they go along. Not less. He didn't get off on it as much this time."

Paula said, "Danny's right. Even though we got a few bits of evidence, it appears the perpetrator was far more careful with this victim than with the first."

"He had privacy this time around," Dave said.

"That's true." Paula held up the copy of the report. She decided to make a break for it rather than get pulled into the disagreement. "I think you'll find everything else you need in here," she said. "Give me a call if you have any questions. I've got to get to court."

Ruiz stood up and put out his hand. She shook it. "Thanks for coming by, Paula."

We all nodded and mumbled our own thank-yous. As Paula walked out of the squad room, we turned to the lieutenant, waiting to hear our next play. If he had told me to buttonhook behind the old Ford on the hike and then go long to the stop sign and look for the pass, I would have. Instead, he just said, "I'll call Kincaid," went into his office, and closed the door.

Jen and I were parked in an unmarked Crown Vic outside Waxler's office, two rows away from his black Range Rover, waiting for him to come out, get in, and drive home. By my watch, we'd been there almost long enough to have popped into the AMC megaplex across the parking lot to catch a movie when he finally ambled between the flanking palm trees in the lobby atrium and out through the glass doors that fronted the building. He was dressed in the latest business casual—khakis and a long-sleeve black polo shirt, just baggy enough to make you wonder where the fabric ended and the bulging flesh began. He had a tweedy sport coat slung over one shoulder and carried a brown-leather briefcase in his other hand. He spent a confused moment at his car door, the briefcase on the hood, juggling the coat from left to right as he patted his pockets searching for the car keys.

The rest of the Homicide Detail, along with Kincaid, half a dozen uniforms, and the Crime Scene Unit, were waiting, conveniently out of sight, a block and a half from Waxler's Palos Verdes home. When Marty answered his cell phone, I told him we were on our way.

Someone had done his homework. Just after Waxler's Range Rover slid through the gated driveway entrance, a black-and-white swooped around the corner and screeched to a stop in the entryway, its bumper little more than an inch from the edge of the stone wall that fronted the property. When the gate began its automatic roll back to a closed and secure position, its leading edge caught on the steel-and-rubber push bar mounted on the cruiser's front end, leaving just enough room for the other vehicles, filled with cops and technicians, to squeeze through the remaining opening. Jen followed them up the driveway.

Waxler stood in the open garage and watched the police vehicles pile up in his driveway. One by one, each car came to a stop, its doors opened, and its occupants rose out. We held back as Ruiz, with a sheaf of court-approved documents in his hand, approached Waxler.

"Daryl Waxler?" Ruiz asked.

"Yes," Waxler replied, his voice soft, hinting at his growing certainty that more than a dozen cops appearing unannounced in your front yard cannot, by any possible imaginative stretch, be construed as a good sign.

Ruiz spoke in a clear, slow monotone. "We have a search warrant here, authorizing us to search the entirety of these premises for any evidence or potential evidence relating to the murders of Elizabeth Williams and Mary Ellen Robbins."

Waxler still looked confused. "Mary Ellen?" he said, his voice falling. "Her too?" His eyes wandered across the sea of strangers in his driveway, assembled to comb through his home and all of its contents with the hope of finding that one damning piece of evidence that would send him to Quentin to wait in line for a needle in the arm. His inability to recognize this new reality confronting him was completely understandable. For just a second, the befuddled confusion on his face almost made me feel sorry for him. Almost. For just a second.

Ruiz took hold of Waxler's elbow and led him out to the unmarked unit next to which stood Dave and Marty. "Mr. Waxler," the lieutenant said, "I'm going to need you to sit here in the backseat while we execute this warrant. Watch your head."

As the realization began to sink in, Waxler asked, "Can I call my attorney?"

"Oh, you're not under arrest," Ruiz said, knowing with absolute certainty that within an hour or two he very well would be.

"I'm...I'm free to go?"

"Of course," the lieutenant said.

Waxler looked at the interior of the rear doors. There were no handles. They opened only from the outside. He turned his face back to Ruiz, his expression signifying his understanding of just how "free to go" he really was.

I was running my gloved hands across the bottom of Daryl's underwear drawer when Marty stuck his head in the doorway. "Danny," he said, "you're going to want to take a look at this." I followed him down the long hall and through the granite-countered kitchen into the garage. A tech was photographing the interior of the refrigerator on the far wall. Another tech stood on the edge of the driveway under the raised garage door, recording the entire search process with a digital video camera.

"What's going on?" I said.

"We got something," Marty said.

Ruiz and Kincaid walked in from the yard, with Jen and Dave close on their heels. We all converged on the open refrigerator at the same time, turning our attention to Marty.

"What's up?" Kincaid asked him, brushing a few stray blond hairs from his forehead.

"I wanted to make sure everybody was here for this," Marty said. The photographer moved out of his way, and Marty stepped up to the door of the refrigerator, his reflection visible in the glossy black luster of its surface.

"Nothing much down here," he said, pulling open the lower door. Inside were six-packs of Coke and Mountain Dew, big bottles of Gatorade, and a few dozen twenty-four-ouncers of Aquafina. He closed the door. "Up on top's where it gets interesting."

The freezer was empty but for three items, each wrapped in white butcher paper and spaced evenly apart on the bottom shelf. We all moved in closer for a better look. The two on the left might have been steaks or chicken breasts, but the item farthest to the right was larger and oddly shaped, like a lopsided triangle with one of the points shaved off. There was something familiar about its shape and proportions.

Jen took a step forward, reached into the freezer, and ran her fingertips over the package. Even through her latex glove and the layers of heavy paper, she had no trouble identifying its contents. She said, "It's a kukri."

"The other two..." Marty said.

I nodded. "They're his trophies."

TWENTY-SEVEN

We watched as Ruiz looked down at Daryl Waxler, slumped in the backseat of the unmarked cruiser. "Mr. Waxler?"

"Yes," Daryl said, turning his face up and squinting into the sunlight.

"We're going to need you to come to the station to answer some questions."

Daryl's face became more pinched, and he nodded, the confusion and pain in his eyes deepening by the minute. Ruiz closed the car door.

We waited for the lieutenant to turn his attention back to us. When he did, he said, "Who wants to take him back to the squad?"

"I'll do it," I said.

Ruiz looked at Jen. She nodded. He faced me and said, "Look, I know I don't have to tell you this, but you don't talk to him. Clear? Not until we finish here and everybody gets back. We don't know what else we're going to find."

"Got it," I said.

"What about Waxler's son?" Jen asked.

"Well, maybe he'll show up before we're done. I'll be sure the uniforms keep an eye out."

After I'd gotten into the backseat next to Daryl, Jen slid in behind the wheel, started the car, backed into a three-point turn, and drove down the long driveway. Daryl watched through the side window until we passed through the gate, and then he turned his face forward and looked straight ahead. He seemed to whither as we put more and more distance between our car and his house.

At one point, as we sped south on the Harbor Freeway toward the Vincent Thomas Bridge, his eyes, still unfocused and bleary, grew moist and heavy. I waited for a tear to spill down his cheek. It never did. Instead, he closed his eyes for several seconds, as if he were willing himself not to cry. When he opened them again, he'd succeeded. They were dry. I wondered, my own eyes drilling into the side of his head, what he was thinking. I wondered if, perhaps, he was trying to conserve his tears. I wondered if he knew how much more he'd need them later.

We locked Daryl in the interview room and let him stew while we watched through the mirror of the observation room next door.

"Does he look smaller to you?" I asked Jen.

"What do you mean?"

"I don't know, just smaller."

"No. He looks exactly the same size as he always has."

"Okay."

"You think he's shrinking?"

"No, of course not. It's just, I don't know, he seems different."

"Different how?"

"Smaller."

"Is this some kind of 'Who's on First?' routine?"

"I don't know."

"Third base." That one got a smile out of me.

Daryl had been in the box close to two hours when the rest of the detail returned. "Anything?" Ruiz wanted to know.

"No," I said. "He hasn't said a word since we put him in there."

Kincaid asked, "You think he'll want a lawyer?"

"Probably," I said. "He wanted one back at his house. He's got a guy. Trevor—uh." I tried to remember the lawyer's last name. "Trevor somebody. Jen and I talked to him during the initial interview."

Kincaid looked through the glass at Daryl. "What do you think, Jen? How should we go at him?" Kincaid's teeth looked brighter in the darkness of the observation room. That was the first time I'd ever heard him ask a detective for advice. He was nothing if not persistent.

"Wait until Paula's gone over the evidence," Jen said. "If it's as good as it looks, let him lawyer up for the interview. At that point, it won't matter what he says, anyway."

"Exactly what I was thinking," Kincaid said. I didn't believe him.

Paula positively identified the two severed hands we'd found in Waxler's freezer as belonging to Beth and Mary Ellen. The tests on the kukri were inconclusive, but at the very least, the knife we found in the freezer was identical to the weapon used in both murders.

Daryl sat next to his attorney, Trevor Wells, on one side of the table in the interview room. Across from them sat Bob Kincaid, with Lieutenant Ruiz behind him, leaning against the cinder-block wall and ready to bust out the bad-cop attitude at a moment's notice.

"Where were you the night before last, Mr. Waxler?" Kincaid asked.

Daryl began to speak, but Wells took over. "He was at dinner at a restaurant in Redondo Beach. Zazou. Several witnesses can testify as to his presence there for several hours. He's a regular, and most of the staff know him by sight. We'll also be happy to provide credit card records that will confirm this."

Kincaid spent another three-quarters of an hour dancing and shuffling with Wells over his client's relationship with Mary Ellen Robbins and with her husband, trying—and failing—to convincingly draw a clear motive out of Daryl.

When Kincaid had pushed as far as Wells was going to let him, he dropped the bomb. "Mr. Waxler," Kincaid said, "you should think this over very carefully. You know what we found in the refrigerator in your garage." Daryl looked confused. A strand of brown hair fell across his forehead. Wells looked at his client and then at Kincaid.

"What are you talking about? What did you find?" Wells asked.

"Would you like to tell him what I'm talking about, Mr. Waxler?"

"I don't..." Daryl said. "I don't have any idea what you mean."

"Well, Mr. Wells, you should know that we found, in your client's refrigerator, not only the murder weapon, but severed hands taken as trophies from the body of each victim."

Wells was surprised, but a look of horror and pain filled Daryl's face, contorting it into an almost unrecognizable mask.

"We'll give you a minute," Kincaid said. He rose from the table, and Ruiz followed him out. Daryl wept.

"He's falling apart in there," Jen said. We were all gathered behind the mirror, watching Daryl and his lawyer whisper in each other's ears. We couldn't tell what they were saying, but it was clear that they were disagreeing about something significant. Wells would whisper and then Daryl would shake his head. When they seemed to have reached an understanding, if not an agreement, Kincaid and Ruiz went back into the room.

Kincaid took the same chair, Ruiz the same section of wall. Kincaid began. "Now that you've had a chance to talk about things, is there anything you'd like to tell us?"

Daryl spoke, his voice stronger and clearer than I'd ever heard it. He sounded fearless. "I did it," he said. "I killed them both."

When I saw the pain and sorrow in his eyes, I felt a tightness in my abdomen and I knew I finally understood. I pulled Jen out into the hallway and asked, "Do you know if anyone's still at Waxler's house?"

"No. Why? What's wrong?"

I took a deep breath before I spoke. "I think we arrested the wrong Daryl Waxler."

Jen shook her head. "What?"

"Think about it," I said. "Daryl Senior's got two alibis, no clear motive, and the killer instinct of a bowl of Jell-O. He's bawling like a little girl until he finds out about the evidence that we found in his home. Then he grows a spine in about two seconds. How does that make sense?"

She still wasn't biting.

"I'm just saying, maybe, all right? If Daryl knows he didn't do it, but cops to the charge as soon as he finds out we found a smoking gun in his house, what does that suggest?"

Jen saw it then, but she still resisted. "You're just speculating. That's not even probable cause."

"But what if I'm right?"

"We need to question him," she said.

"What do you suppose is in that sealed juvie file? And all those books? If he knows how to investigate a homicide—"

"Is anybody still at Waxler's house?" she asked.

"Let's find out."

TWENTY-EIGHT

"No," Marty said when we arrived. "The techs were wrapping up when we left."

"What about the kid?" I asked.

"He didn't show up. The boss left a business card on the kitchen counter."

"The lawyer tried to call him when he got here," Dave said. "Sounded like he just left a message."

"Why?" Marty asked me.

"I was just thinking," I said, "maybe we should have waited for him. Brought him in for questioning before he got a heads-up from the lawyer."

Marty clapped me on the shoulder. "Don't sweat it, Danny. We got a slam dunk here. You were right all along."

"Lieutenant?" I knocked once on Ruiz's open door. He looked up from the report on his desk.

"Yeah, Danny?"

"I was just thinking, maybe we should question the son before Wells has a chance to coach him."

"Good idea. Run it past Kincaid, and if he's okay with it, go grab up the kid."

"Thanks, Boss." As I turned, I gave Jen a thumbs-up.

She called Kincaid on her cell as we were on our way down to the garage. I listened as she gave him the same line I'd given Ruiz. "Thanks, Bob," she said and folded her phone and slipped it into her jacket pocket. "We're good."

I checked my watch as we started up the hill into Palos Verdes. It had been just under three hours since we'd last left Daryl's house. There were still faint purple-orange traces of the sunset hanging over the horizon.

"Money," I said.

"What?" Jen asked.

"The motive. He's twisted to begin with. Homicide fanboy, that whole pathology. Toss a little good old-fashioned greed into the mix. Then his mom dies." I thought about it. The story was starting to hold. "Makes him even angrier at his father, so he sets him up for the murder. Daryl Senior gets the needle or a lifetime's supply of prison. Even after the lawyers got through with him, there'd still be a shitload in the bank."

She thought a moment. "Except we screw it up. Close the case with the tail pinned on the wrong donkey."

"So he has to kill Mary Ellen," I said, "to set us straight."

"Jesus," Jen said. "That fits."

"I want to hit him hard. See how he holds up."

"Think he'll spook?"

"Don't have a clue. Only one way to find out."

It took four rings of the doorbell and two minutes for Daryl Waxler Jr. to answer the door. We were almost ready to give up and start peering in the windows when we saw his shadow behind the peephole. The door swung open slowly.

"Hi," he said.

"Hey, D.J.," Jen said, her voice warm and thick as honey. "You've heard about your father?"

He nodded.

"What took you so long to answer the door?"

"I was down in the game room, eating dinner." He wore a sleeveless T-shirt and gray shorts. His arms and shoulders looked pumped up, as if he'd been lifting weights.

We'd seen the game room for the first time earlier that day. The house was built on a slope, with the lower level carved out of the hillside, so what appeared from the front to be a relatively modest two-story was, in actuality, much larger. The game room was built in the former basement, and it filled nearly the entire lower level of the house. It was easily fifty feet long and half again as wide, with four thick concrete columns that were equidistant from the corners and supported the main floor.

The room held an enormous television, a horseshoe-shaped, leather-covered sectional sofa that had space enough for at least a dozen people, a full-sized bar right out of the neighborhood pub, billiard and air-hockey tables, and a large felt topped card table. On the far side of the room, ten yards of French door looked out over the pool and the hill that sloped away from the house.

"We need to ask you a few questions," Jen said.

"About my dad?"

"Yes."

"Mr. Wells called me," he said, the sadness heavy in his voice. I eyed him. If he was feigning the emotion, he was doing it well.

"Come in," he said.

"Thanks, D.J.," Jen said, flashing her teeth at him. I thought I saw his chest swell slightly, but it might just as easily have been my imagination.

"I wasn't sure what to do. So I ordered a pizza. You guys want some?" he asked, leading us through the kitchen. "I got a large, so there's plenty."

"Sure," Jen said.

We followed him downstairs and sat with him, facing the muted big-screen TV. I watched a nearly life-sized skateboarder rolling up and down the curved sides of a large half-pipe. Statistics I didn't understand scrolled across the bottom of the screen in six-inch-high letters. On a wide, glass-topped coffee table in front of D.J. was an open Domino's Pizza box with three-quarters of a Canadian-bacon-and-pineapple pizza still uneaten.

"What's going to happen to my dad?"

"It's a little too soon to know for sure," I said.

"You guys must have had probable cause to arrest him, right?"

Jen answered. "We really can't be too specific."

"No, I understand. Here's some paper towels," he said, pulling two sheets from a roll on the floor and sliding the pizza box toward Jen. She spread the sheets like a placemat on the glass, took a slice, and placed it down on the paper. "What did you need to know?" D.J. asked, taking a bite of pizza. Too much cheese slid off, and he tried to catch it between his fingers before it fell onto his chin.

"Okay," I said. "Just one question, really. Why are you trying to set your father up for the murders you committed?"

D.J.'s jaw tensed for a fraction of a second and then relaxed again. He finished chewing. He looked at me the way a poker player looks at someone who's just raised the bet a little too high. And I knew.

He hooked the glass top of the table with both hands as Jen and I went for our guns. The glass was in the air and falling toward us before we had finished our draws. D.J. sprung himself over the back of the couch and made a break for the French doors. We each put up a hand to catch the tabletop and shove it away. The glass shattered when its center caught the corner of the table's wooden frame.

"Don't let him get to a car," I said, hopping over the couch, pistol drawn, following him outside.

As we passed through the doors, there was a large deck overhead, extending fifteen feet off the back of the house. I heard footsteps above me. The stairs were on my right. I took them two at a time and made it to the top of the stone-and-tile deck just in time to hear one of the doors slam shut. I tried the knob, but he had locked it as he went through.

I took two steps back and threw a hard front kick at the wood next to the knob. The door cracked and splintered, but the lock held. One more kick, and the door exploded open. I took two quick peeks inside, one to each side of the door, and then went in. I didn't see him. I moved through the living room. He could have gone any of half a dozen ways. Into the kitchen. The dining room. The foyer. Three hallways.

I stood silently in the middle of the room and listened. The sound came from downstairs. Just a second or two of noise from the TV, then silence—as if he'd hit the wrong button on the remote, then quickly corrected himself.

He'd doubled back.

As I started down the stairs, the room was darker than it had been. The TV was turned off. So were the lights on the ceiling fans. Slowly, my Glock extended in front of me, I went down. The only light in the room was spilling in from the yard beyond the French doors.

Motionless at the bottom of the stairs, I listened, waiting for my eyes to adjust to the low light. When they had, I swept along the back wall of the room, moving slowly into the far corner, looking anywhere he might be able to hide. When I'd cleared the area behind the bar, I surveyed the room. Darkness and shadow.

If he was still here, he was quiet. And patient.

I worked my way around the perimeter of the room, breathing slowly through my nose. As I passed in front of the TV screen, the broken glass crunched beneath my feet. I'd given away my position.

I'd also made it halfway around the room. There weren't many places left for him to hide. I started across the room, my eyes on the air hockey table. Halfway there, in the periphery of my vision, I saw the flash of steel.

I turned toward him as he spun out from behind the concrete column, a kukri raised above his head. The knife in the freezer had been a decoy.

He charged me.

I raised my left hand into a defensive position and pulled the trigger of my pistol. By the time he had closed the distance between us, I'd gotten off six rounds point-blank into his chest, but his momentum carried him into me. I shoved him back, and he collapsed into a pile on the floor. I kept my gun leveled on his chest.

I heard Jen yelling from upstairs. I stood over D.J.'s convulsing body and tried to catch my breath. Then I noticed something odd. I was covered in blood. Too much to have been back splatter from D.J., even at such close range. Odd, I thought.

I looked down to see my feet in a puddle of blood. That's when I noticed my left wrist. I held it up. My hand was hanging from my forearm at an impossible angle, as if I had an extra joint in my wrist, allowing my thumb to fold flat against my arm.

Something was wrong.

I knew I shouldn't be able to see the bone protruding from my wrist. And I knew I shouldn't be able to count my own heartbeats in the thick flow of blood pulsing from the wound.

Something was wrong.

The lights came on then, and I heard Jen scream from somewhere far away. "Danny!"

Then I was sitting on the floor. I could feel the warmth of the blood soaking though my pants. Jen was there. She did something to my hand. "It's going to be okay," she said. She looked scared.

"I'm cold."

"I know," she said. "Help's on the way. Hang on, okay?"

"Okay."

She was crying. I couldn't remember if I'd ever seen her cry before.

"I'm cold."

"Hang on, Danny. For me."

I could feel the floor beneath my shoulders and her hand on the side of my face. A ceiling fan spun above her head. It looked like a halo.

TWENTY-NINE

When I woke up two days later in Long Beach Memorial, Jen was slumped in a chair next to my bed, holding my hand. I was confused, but somehow I knew everything was all right. It was late at night, but even the small, solitary lamp over my head seemed bright. My whole body ached, and a taste like dirty sand filled my mouth. It might have been minutes before I remembered what had happened. Then I felt a wave of fear rise through me like a chill. I tried to raise my left hand, but couldn't. There was a sharp pain behind my eyes as I raised my head off the pillow. I couldn't lift it far enough to get a look at my arm.

I let go of Jen's hand and pushed against the bed frame to raise myself up far enough to see that my left hand was still there—wrapped in yards of gauze, splinted in a metal cage, and in traction, but still there. I tried to wiggle the fingertips protruding from the bandages. They didn't move.

"You're going to be okay," Jen said.

I leaned back on the pillow and turned to face her. The light in her eyes convinced me that she was right.

"You'll need more surgery and a lot of physical therapy. But the doctors say ninety, ninety-five percent recovery. They were more worried about blood loss than anything."

I tried to say something, but the words dried up and disappeared in my throat. She poured me a glass of water, put a straw in it, and held the straw to my mouth. The cool liquid eased the soreness as I swallowed.

"Thank you," I said

"No sweat."

The next day, Ruiz, Marty, Dave, and Pat crowded into the room. Jen excused herself.

"You know," Marty said, "she's been here the whole time." When he saw the expression on my face, he repeated himself. "The whole time."

I nodded.

"We got the story from D.J.'s friend," Ruiz said. "Max Porter? D.J. had trouble keeping his mouth shut. Promised to cut his pal in on the action. We've got him in lockup as an accessory. He was just the sidekick, though. Junior was the real prize."

"Yeah?" I said.

"That sealed file of his? It's a fun read. He started out torturing neighborhood cats, then moved on up to assault and date rape. Had charges filed half a dozen times, but none ever made it to court. Wonder how that happened. No surprise he wound up where he did."

"The motive?" I asked.

"Multiple choice. Psychosis, money, revenge. And convenient timing. Daryl Senior had been riding D.J. about college, a career, productive citizenry, all that. Kid didn't like it. But he came up with a plan. Figured it was too risky to kill his old man with so much money on the line, but if dad were doing time waiting on a lethal injection, well, then, he'd have it made. He was right, too. When Waxler figured it out, he was going to ride the rap for the kid. Good thing somebody caught on."

"Was that a compliment?" I asked.

Ruiz ducked the question. "Now that we're shorthanded, we've had three new cases come in."

"You should bump Pat upstairs," I said.

Ruiz turned to face him. "That's not a bad idea. You interested in a temp transfer to Homicide?"

"Sure," Pat said, obviously pleased.

We talked about nothing in particular for another half hour or so until Jen came back with a small, blue plastic bag in her hand. Not long after that, everyone else said their good-byes and left.

"That's weird," I said.

"What?" she asked.

"Why are they in such a hurry to leave us alone?"

"I got you something."

She took a box out of her bag. I tilted my head to read the embossed Seiko logo on the side. She opened the box and slid the gold-and-stainless band off of its oval holder.

"Hey," I said as she held it up for me to see, "that's the same watch I was looking at."

"Figured you'd need a new one."

"Why?"

"The doctor didn't tell you?"

"Tell me what?"

"The reason the kukri didn't go all the way through your wrist. The blade caught on your watchband. They think it saved your hand."

"Thank you," I said. She leaned over and kissed my forehead.

We didn't say much to each other that night, but there was a stillness and something that felt like contentment in the quiet that we shared. I thought about Megan and about Beth and wondered what, if anything, I had put to rest. Had I found my reckoning?

More than anything else, though, I thought about Jen. Just before midnight, when I fell asleep, she was still there, next to me, her fingers soft against my palm.

I didn't dream.

ACKNOWLEDGEMENTS

A number of people offered invaluable assistance in the completion of *A King of Infinite Space*. My most sincere and heartfelt thanks to:

Eileen Klink, Tim Caron, Gerry Locklin, Elliot Fried, and all of my workshop colleagues, who gave me the confidence in the early stages to soldier on;

Moira Sullivan and Maria Carvainis, who saw the novel's potential and helped me realize it;

Sharon Dilts, who is the world's best proofreader (and no slouch in the mom department, either);

Paul Tayyar, LeeAnne Langton, David Aimerito, Chad Tsuyuki, and Dean Tsuyuki, who made it real;

The faculty and staff of the Department of English at California State University, Long Beach, who gave me unflagging and unlimited support;

And finally, my students, who would certainly call me on any of the myriad clichés with which I considered ending this sentence.

ABOUT THE AUTHOR

Tyler Dilts is a native of southern California and a graduate of the MFA program at California State University, Long Beach, where he now teaches. His writing has appeared in the *Los Angeles Times*, *The Chronicle of Higher Education*, *The Best American Mystery Stories*, and numerous other publications. *A King of Infinite Space* is his first novel. For more information and to contact him online, please visit www.tylerdilts.com.